Pan was founded in 1944 by Alan Bott, then owner of The Book Society. Over the next eight years he was joined by a consortium of four leading publishers – William Collins, Macmillan, Hodder & Stoughton and William Heinemann – and together they launched an imprint that is an international leader in popular paperback publishing to this day.

Pan's first mass-market paperback was *Ten Stories* by Rudyard Kipling. Published in 1947, and priced at one shilling and sixpence, it had a distinctive logo based on a design by artist and novelist Mervyn Peake. Paper was scarce in post-war Britain, but happily the Board of Trade agreed that Pan could print its books abroad and import them into Britain provided that they exported half the total number of books printed. The first batch of 250,000 books were dispatched from Paris to Pan's warehouse in Esher on an ex-Royal Navy launch named *Laloun*. The vessel's first mate, Gordon Young, was to become the first export manager for Pan.

Around fifty titles appeared in the first year, each with average print runs of 25,000 copies. Success came quickly, largely due to the choice of vibrant, descriptive

book covers that distinguished Pan books from the uniformity of Penguin paperbacks, which were the only real competitors at the time.

Pan's expertise lay in its ability to popularize its authors, and a combination of arresting design coupled with energetic marketing and sales helped turn the likes of Leslie Charteris, Eric Ambler, Nevil Shute, Ian Fleming and John Buchan into bestsellers. The first book to sell a million copies was *The Dam Busters* by Paul Brickhill, first published in 1951. Brickhill was among the first to receive a Golden Pan award, for sales of one million copies. His fellow prize winners in 1964 were Alan Sillitoe for *Saturday Night and Sunday Morning* and Ian Fleming, who won it seven times over. It was also given posthumously to Grace Metalious for *Peyton Place*.

In the Sixties and Seventies authors such as Dick Francis, Wilbur Smith and Jack Higgins joined the fold, and 1972 saw the founding of the ground-breaking literary paperback imprint, Picador. Then-Editorial Director Clarence Paget signed up the third novel by the relatively unknown John le Carré, and transformed the author's career. Pan also secured paperback rights in James Herriot's memoirs of a Yorkshire vet in 1973, and a year later fought off tough competition to publish *Jaws* by Peter Benchley. Inspector Morse made his first appearance in Colin Dexter's *Last Bus to Woodstock* in 1974.

By 1976 Pan had sold over 30 million copies of its books and was outperforming all its rivals. Over the ensuing decades they published some of the biggest names in popular fiction, such as Jackie Collins, Dick Francis, Martin Cruz Smith and Colin Forbes.

By the late Eighties, publishers had stopped buying and selling paperback licences and in 1987 Pan, now wholly owned by Macmillan, became its paperback imprint. This was a turbulent time of readjustment for Pan, but with characteristic energy and zeal Pan Macmillan soon established itself as one of the largest book publishers in the UK. By 2010, the advent of ebooks allowed the audience for popular fiction to grow dramatically, and Pan's bestselling authors, such as Peter James, Jeffrey Archer, Ken Follett and Kate Morton – not to mention bestselling saga writers Margaret Dickinson and Annie Murray – now reach an even wider readership.

Personally, my years working at Pan were incredibly exciting and a time of countless opportunities. The paperback market was exploding, and Pan was at the forefront. Sales were incredible – I remember selling close to a million copies of a Colin Dexter novella alone. I'm proud that today, Pan retains the same energy and vibrancy.

In the year that Pan celebrates its 70th anniversary its mission remains the same – to publish the best popular fiction and non-fiction for the widest audience.

David Macmillan

The Provincial Lady

E. M. DELAFIELD was born in Sussex in 1890. Her mother was also a well-known novelist, writing as Mrs Henry de la Pasture, and Delafield chose her pen name based on a suggestion by her sister Yoé. Delafield worked as a nurse in a Voluntary Aid Detachment following the outbreak of the First World War, and her first novel *Zella Sees Herself* was written during this time and published in 1917. *Diary of a Provincial Lady*, her most successful novel, inspired several sequels and is a tongue-in-cheek portrayal of Delafield herself, written after a request by the editor of *Time and Tide* for some 'light middles' in serial form. She died in 1943.

E. M. DELAFIELD

The Provincial Lady

PAN 70

This abridged edition first published 1951 by Pan Books Ltd.

This edition published 2017 by Pan Books
an imprint of Pan Macmillan
20 New Wharf Road, London N1 9RR
Associated companies throughout the world
www.panmacmillan.com

ISBN 978-1-5098-5845-3

1 3 5 7 9 8 6 4 2

A CIP catalogue record for this book is available from the British Library.

Typeset by Palimpsest Book Production Limited, Falkirk, Stirlingshire
Printed and bound by CPI Group (UK) Ltd, Croydon, CRO 4YY

Visit **www.panmacmillan.com** to read more about all our books
and to buy them. You will also find features, author interviews and
news of any author events, and you can sign up for e-newsletters
so that you're always first to hear about our new releases.

Contents

Foreword

Diary of a Provincial Lady, by the late E. M. Delafield, first appeared as a serial in 1930 in the weekly *Time and Tide*, and was afterwards published in book form. Its popularity was immediate and far-reaching; it was acclaimed by both critics and the reading public for its entertainment, its character-drawing—at which the author excelled—its humanity, and its complete understanding of the personal lives, with their troubles and their happiness, of everyday people.

The book not only brought pleasure to thousands—it brought comfort too; for many people who secretly thought that at times their wives or husbands were trying and their children and friends maddening, but who could not or would not admit it, found consolation and encouragement in the semi-humorous, always sympathetic, and crystal-clear-sighted attitude of the Provincial Lady, whose family life and friends, whose affections and problems, were inwardly so like theirs even if her external circumstances differed.

The success of this domestic chronicle was so great that the author soon produced a sequel, *The Provincial Lady Goes Further*, to be followed in time by *The Provincial Lady in America* and *The Provincial Lady in Wartime*. This quartet, covering the ten years from 1930 to 1940, was subsequently published as an omnibus by Messrs. Macmillan.

Readers will find in *The Provincial Lady* omnibus edition an admirable critical preface by Kate O'Brien, in which she gives her reasons for her conviction that "E. M. Delafield will be remembered and read when writers who may now be called 'better' than her are dusted in oblivion." The author has, she says, left behind "here in these forever-living pages of the Diaries the whole eternal everyday farce-comedy of ourselves and our friends with all our personal follies thick and bright upon us, as hers lie too upon the gentle heroine".

The present PAN edition contains a shortened version of the first two books—the original *Diary* and *The Provincial Lady Goes Further*. Considerable cuts have had to be made to meet the space requirements of such an edition—no easy task owing to the uniformly high standard of the books. I have had to omit certain complete episodes and shorten others; and have left out many references to contemporary books and persons which might be viewed as of topical rather than general interest to-day. I hope that these unavoidable curtailments have in no way taken from the character—or characters—of the *Diaries*.

A short and inexpensive edition will make this faithful picture of a certain section of pre-war life available to a new public; and a new generation will, it is hoped, be introduced to the work of a gay and discriminating writer, whose untimely death in 1943 was an immeasurable loss to her many readers.

"Life takes on entirely new aspect, owing to astonishing and unprecedented success of minute and unpretentious literary effort, incredibly written by myself." . . . This modest phrase, which opens *The*

Provincial Lady Goes Further, sums up the self-critical outlook of E. M. Delafield, most unassuming and unspoilt of authors, who was always generous in praising the work of others and enthusiastic over the successes of her friends. Her own triumphs delighted and surprised her in her lifetime. They continue to delight, but not to surprise, those who were privileged to know and to love her, and who realised her worth perhaps more clearly than she did herself.

LORNA LEWIS

Diary of a Provincial Lady

November 7th.—Plant the indoor bulbs. Just as I am in the middle of them, Lady Boxe calls. I say, untruthfully, how nice to see her, and beg her to sit down while I just finish the bulbs. Lady B. makes determined attempt to sit down in armchair where I have already placed two bulb-bowls and the bag of charcoal, is headed off just in time, and takes the sofa.

Do I know, she asks, how very late it is for indoor bulbs? September, really, or even October, is the time. Do I know that the only really reliable firm for hyacinths is Somebody of Haarlem? Cannot catch the name of the firm, which is Dutch, but reply Yes, I do know, but think it my duty to buy Empire products. Feel at the time, and still think, that this is an excellent reply. Unfortunately Vicky comes into the drawing-room later and says: "Oh, Mummie, are those the bulbs we got at Woolworth's?"

Lady B. stays to tea. (*Mem.*: Bread-and-butter too thick. Speak to Ethel.) She enquires after the children. Tell her that Robin—whom I refer to in a detached way as "the boy" so that she shan't think I am foolish about him—is getting on fairly well at school, and that Mademoiselle says Vicky is starting a cold.

Do I realise, says Lady B., that the Cold Habit is entirely unnecessary, and can be avoided by giving the child a nasal douche of salt-and-water every morning before breakfast? Think of several rather tart and witty rejoinders to this, but unfortunately not until Lady B.'s Bentley has taken her away.

Finish the bulbs and put them in the cellar. Feel that after all cellar is probably draughty, change my mind, and take them all up to the attic.

Cook says something is wrong with the range.

November 8th.—Robert has looked at the range and says nothing wrong whatever. Makes unoriginal suggestion about pulling out dampers. Cook very angry, and will probably give notice. Try to propitiate her by saying that we are going to Bournemouth for Robin's half-term, and that will give the household a rest. Cook replied austerely that they will take the opportunity to do some extra cleaning. Wish I could believe this was true.

Preparations for Bournemouth rather marred by discovering that Robert, in bringing down the suit-cases from the attic, has broken three of the bulb-bowls. Says he understood that I had put them in the cellar, and so wasn't expecting them.

November 11th.—*Bournemouth.* Find that history, as usual, repeats itself. Same hotel, same frenzied scurry round the school to find Robin, same collection of parents, most of them also staying at the hotel. Discover strong tendency to exchange with fellow-parents exactly the same remarks as last year, and the year before that. Speak of this to Robert, who returns no answer. Perhaps he is afraid of repeating himself? This suggests Query: Does Robert, perhaps, take in what I say even when he makes no reply?

Find Robin looking thin, and speak to Matron, who says brightly, Oh no, she thinks on the whole he's put *on* weight this term, and then begins to talk about the New Buildings. (Query: Why do all schools have to run up New Buildings about once in every six months?)

Take Robin out. He eats several meals, and a good many sweets. He produces a friend, and we take both to Corfe Castle. The boys climb, Robert smokes in silence, and I sit about on stones. Overhear a woman remark, as she gazes up at half a tower, that has withstood several centuries, that This looks *fragile*—which strikes me as a singular choice of adjective. Same woman, climbing over a block of solid masonry, points out that This has evidently fallen off somewhere.

Take the boys back to the hotel for dinner. Robin says, whilst the friend is out of hearing: "It's been nice for us, taking out Williams, hasn't it?" Hastily express appreciation of this privilege.

Robert takes the boys back after dinner, and I sit in hotel lounge with several other mothers and we all talk about our boys in tones of disparagement, and about one another's boys with great enthusiasm.

Robert comes up very late and says he must have dropped asleep over *The Times*. (Query: Why come to Bournemouth to do this?)

Postcard by the last post from Lady B. to ask if I have remembered that there is a Committee Meeting of the Women's Institute on the 14th. Should not dream of answering this.

November 12th.—Home yesterday and am struck, as so often before, by immense accumulation of domestic disasters that always await one after any absence. Trouble with kitchen range has resulted in no hot water, also Cook says the mutton has *gone*, and will I speak to the butcher, there being no excuse weather like this. Vicky's cold, unlike the mutton, hasn't gone. Mademoiselle says *Ah, cette petite! Elle ne sera peut-être pas longtemps pour ce bas monde, madame.* Hope that this is only her Latin way of dramatising the situation.

Robert reads *The Times* after dinner, and goes to sleep.

November 13th.—Interesting, but disconcerting, train of thought started by prolonged discussion with Vicky as to the existence or otherwise of a locality which she refers to throughout as H. E. L. Am determined to be a modern parent, and assure her that there is not, never has been, and never could be, such a place. Vicky maintains that there *is*, and refers me to the Bible. I become more modern than ever, and tell her that theories of eternal punishment were invented to frighten people. Vicky replies indignantly that they don't frighten her in the least, she *likes* to think about H. E. L. Feel that deadlock has been reached, and can only leave her to her singular method of enjoying herself.

(Query: Are modern children going to revolt against being modern, and if so, what form will reaction of modern parents take?)

Much worried by letter from the Bank to say that my account is overdrawn to the extent of Eight Pounds, four shillings, and fourpence. Cannot understand this, as was convinced that I still had credit balance of Two Pounds, seven shillings, and sixpence. Annoyed to find that my accounts, contents of cash-box, and counterfoils in cheque-book, do not tally. *(Mem.:* Find envelope on which I jotted down Bournemouth expenses, also little piece of paper, probably last leaf of grocer's book, with note about cash payment to sweep. This may clear things up.)

Take a look at bulb-bowls on returning suit-case to attic, and am inclined to think it looks as though the cat had been up here. If so, this will be the last straw. Shall tell Lady Boxe that I sent all my bulbs to a sick friend in a nursing-home.

November 14th. — Letter by second post from my dear old school-friend Cissie Crabbe, asking if she may come here for two nights or so on her way to Norwich.

Many years since we last met, writes Cissie, and she expects we have both *changed* a good deal. *P.S.* Do I remember the dear old *pond*, and the day of the Spanish Arrowroot? Can recall, after some thought, dear old pond, at bottom of Cissie's father's garden, but am completely baffled by Spanish Arrowroot. (Query: Could this be one of the Sherlock Holmes stories? Sounds like it.)

Reply that we shall be delighted to see her, and what a lot we shall have to talk about, after all these years! (This, I find on reflection, is not true, but cannot rewrite letter on that account.) Ignore Spanish Arrowroot altogether.

Robert, when I tell him about dear old school-friend's impending arrival, does not seem pleased. Asks what we are expected to *do* with her. I suggest showing her the garden, and remember too late that this is hardly the right time of the year. At any rate, I say, it will be nice to talk over old times—(which reminds me of the Spanish Arrowroot reference still unfathomed).

Speak to Ethel about the spare room, and am much annoyed to find that one blue candlestick has been broken, and the bedside rug has gone to the cleaners, and cannot be retrieved in time. Take away bedside rug from Robert's dressing-room, and put it in spare room instead, hoping he will not notice its absence.

November 15th.—Robert *does* notice absence of rug, and says he must have it back again. Return it to dressing-room and take small and inferior dyed mat from the night-nursery to put in spare room. Mademoiselle is hurt about this and says to Vicky, who repeats it to me, that in this country she finds herself treated like a worm.

November 17th.—Dear old school-friend Cissie Crabbe due by the three o'clock train. On telling Robert this, he says it is most inconvenient to meet her, owing to Vestry Meeting, but eventually agrees to abandon Vestry Meeting. Am touched. Unfortunately, just after he has started, telegram arrives to say that dear old school-friend has missed the connection and will not arrive until seven o'clock. This means putting off dinner till eight, which Cook won't like. Cannot send message to kitchen by Ethel, as it is her afternoon out, so am obliged to tell Cook myself. She is not pleased. Robert returns from station, not pleased either. Mademoiselle, quite inexplicably, says *Il ne manquait que ça!* (This comment wholly unjustifiable, as non-appearance of

Cissie Crabbe cannot concern her in any way. Have often thought that the French are tactless.)

Ethel returns, ten minutes late, and says Shall she light fire in spare room? I say No, it is not cold enough—but really mean that Cissie is no longer, in my opinion, deserving of luxuries. Subsequently feel this to be unworthy attitude, and light fire myself. It smokes.

Robert calls up to know What is that Smoke? I call down that It is Nothing. Robert comes up and opens the window and shuts the door and says It will Go all right Now. Do not like to point out that the open window will make the room cold.

Play Ludo with Vicky in drawing-room.

Robert reads *The Times* and goes to sleep, but wakes in time to make second expedition to the station. Thankful to say that this time he returns with Cissie Crabbe, who has put on weight, and says several times that she supposes we have both *changed* a good deal, which I consider unnecessary.

Take her upstairs—spare room like an ice-house, owing to open window, and fire still smoking, though less—She says room is delightful, and I leave her, begging her to ask for anything she wants—(*Mem.*: Tell Ethel she *must* answer spare-room bell if it rings—hope it won't.)

Ask Robert while dressing for dinner what he thinks of Cissie. He says he has not known her long enough to judge. Ask if he thinks her good-looking. He says he has not thought about it. Ask what they talked about on the way from the station. He says he does not remember.

November 19th.—Consult Cissie about the bulbs, which look very much as if the mice had been at them. She says: Unlimited Watering, and tells me about her own bulbs at Norwich. Am discouraged.

Administer Unlimited Water to the bulbs (some of which goes through the attic floor on to the landing below), and move half of them down to the cellar, as Cissie Crabbe says attic is airless.

Our Vicar's Wife calls this afternoon. Says she once knew someone who had relations living near Norwich, but cannot remember their name. Cissie Crabbe replies that very likely if we knew their name we might find she'd heard of them, or even *met* them. We agree that the world is a small place.

November 22nd.—Cissie Crabbe leaves. Begs me in the kindest way to stay with her in Norwich (where she has already told me that she lives in a bed-sitting-room with two cats, and cooks on a gas-ring). I say Yes, I should love to. We part effusively.

Spend entire morning writing letters I have had to leave unanswered during Cissie's visit.

Invitation from Lady Boxe to us to dine and meet distinguished literary friends staying with her, one of whom is the author of *Symphony in Three Sexes*. Hesitate to write back and say that I have never heard of *Symphony in Three Sexes*, so merely accept. Ask for *Symphony in Three Sexes* at the library, although doubtfully. Doubt more than justified by tone in which Mr. Jones replies that it is not in stock, and never has been.

Ask Robert whether he thinks I had better wear my

Blue or my Black-and-gold at Lady B.'s. He says that either will do. Ask if he can remember which one I wore last time. He cannot. Mademoiselle says it was the Blue, and offers to make slight alterations to Black-and-gold which will, she says, render it unrecognisable. I accept, and she cuts large pieces out of the back of it. I say *Pas trop décolletée* and she replies intelligently *Je comprends, Madame ne désire pas se voir nue au salon.*

(Query: Have not the French sometimes a very strange way of expressing themselves, and will this react unfavourably on Vicky?)

Tell Robert about the distinguished literary friends, but do not mention *Symphony in Three Sexes.* He makes no answer.

Have absolutely decided that if Lady B. should introduce us to distinguished literary friends, or anyone else, as Our Agent, and Our Agent's Wife, I shall at once leave the house.

Tell Robert this. He says nothing. (*Mem.*: Put evening shoes out of window to see if fresh air will remove smell of petrol.)

November 25th. — Go and get hair cut and have mani-cure in the morning, in honour of Lady B.'s dinner-party. Should like new pair of evening stockings, but depressing communication from Bank, still maintaining that I am overdrawn, prevents this, also rather unpleas-antly worded letter from Messrs. Frippy and Coleman requesting payment of overdue account by return of post. Think better not to mention this to Robert, as bill for coke arrived yesterday, also reminder that Rates are much overdue, therefore write civilly to Messrs. F. and

C. to the effect that cheque follows in a few days. (Hope they may think I have temporarily mislaid chequebook.)

Black-and-gold as rearranged by Mademoiselle very satisfactory, but am obliged to do my hair five times owing to wave having been badly set. Robert unfortunately comes in just as I am using brand-new and expensive lipstick, and objects strongly to result.

(Query: If Robert could be induced to go to London rather oftener, would he perhaps take broader view of these things?)

Am convinced we are going to be late, as Robert has trouble in getting car to start, but he refuses to be agitated. Am bound to add that subsequent events justify this attitude, as we arrive before anybody else, also before Lady B. is down. Count at least a dozen Roman hyacinths growing in bowls all over the drawing-room. (Probably grown by one of the gardeners, whatever Lady B. may say. Resolve not to comment on them in any way, but am conscious that this is slightly ungenerous.)

Lady B. comes down wearing silver lace frock that nearly touches the floor all round, and has new waist-line. This may or not be becoming, but has effect of making everybody else's frock look out-of-date.

Nine other people present besides ourselves, most of them staying in house. Nobody is introduced. Decide that a lady in what looks like blue tapestry is probably responsible for *Symphony in Three Sexes*.

Just as dinner is announced Lady B. murmurs to me: "I've put you next to Sir William. He's interested in *water-supplies*, you know, and I thought you'd like to talk to him about local conditions."

Find, to my surprise, that Sir W. and I embark almost at once on the subject of Birth Control. Why or how this topic presents itself cannot say at all, but greatly prefer it to water-supplies. On the other side of the table, Robert is sitting next to *Symphony in Three Sexes*. Hope he is enjoying himself.

I talk to pale young man with horn-rimmed glasses, sitting at my left hand, about Jamaica, where neither of us has ever been. This leads—but cannot say how—to stag-hunting, and eventually to homeopathy. (*Mem.*: Interesting, if time permitted, to trace train of thought leading on from one topic to another. Second, and most disquieting idea: perhaps no such train of thought exists.) Just as we reach interchange of opinions about growing cucumbers under glass, Lady B. gets up.

Go into the drawing-room, and all exclaim how nice it is to see the fire. Room very cold. (Query: Is this good for the bulbs?) Lady in blue tapestry takes down her hair, which she says she is growing, and puts it up again. We all begin to talk about hair.

Discover, in the course of the evening, that the blue tapestry has nothing whatever to do with literature, but is a Government Sanitary Inspector, and that *Symphony in Three Sexes* was written by pale young man with glasses. Lady B. says, Did I get him on to the subject of *perversion*, as he is always so amusing about it? I reply evasively.

Men come in, and we are herded into billiard-room (just as drawing-room seems to be getting slightly warmer), where Lady B. inaugurates unpleasant game of skill with billiard balls, involving possession of a Straight Eye, which most of us do not possess. Robert does well at this. Am thrilled, and feel it to be more satisfactory way of acquiring distinction than even authorship of *Symphony in Three Sexes*.

Congratulate Robert on the way home, but he makes no reply.

November 26th. — Robert says at breakfast that he thinks we are no longer young enough for late nights.

Frippy and Coleman regret that they can no longer allow account to stand over, but must request favour of a cheque by return, or will be compelled, with utmost regret, to take Further Steps. Have written to Bank to transfer Six Pounds, thirteen shillings, and tenpence from Deposit Account to Current. (This leaves Three Pounds, seven shillings, and twopence, to keep Deposit Account open). Decide to put off paying milk book till next month, and to let cleaners have something on account instead of full settlement. This enables me to send F. and C. cheque, post-dated Dec. 1st, when allowance becomes due. Financial instability very trying.

December 1st. — Cable from dear Rose saying she lands at Tilbury on 10th. Cable back welcome, and will meet her Tilbury, 10th. Tell Vicky that her godmother, my dearest friend, is returning home after three years in America. Vicky says: "Oh, will she have a present for me?" Am disgusted with her mercenary attitude and complain to Mademoiselle, who replies *Si la Sainte Vierge revenait sur la terre, madame, ce serait notre petite Vicky.* Do not at all agree with this. Moreover, in other moods Mademoiselle first person to refer to Vicky as *ce petit démon enragé.*

(Query: Are the Latin races always as sincere as one would wish them to be?)

December 3rd.—Radio from dear Rose, landing Plymouth 8th, after all. Send return message, renewed welcomes, and will meet her Plymouth.

Robert adopts unsympathetic attitude and says This is Waste of Time and Money. Do not know if he means cables, or journey to meet ship, but feel sure better not to enquire. Shall go to Plymouth on 7th. (*Mem.*: Pay grocer's book before I go, and tell him last lot of ginger-nuts were soft. Find out first if Ethel kept tin properly shut.)

December 8th.—*Plymouth.* Arrived last night, terrific storm, ship delayed. Much distressed at thought of Rose, probably suffering severe sea-sickness. Wind howls round hotel, which shakes, rain lashes against window-pane all night. Do not like my room and have unpleasant idea that someone may have committed a murder in it. Mysterious door in corner which I feel conceals a corpse. Remember all the stories I have read to this effect, and cannot sleep. Finally open mysterious door and find large cupboard, but no corpse. Go back to bed again.

Storm worse than ever in the morning, am still more distressed at thought of Rose, who will probably have to be carried off ship in state of collapse.

Go round to Shipping Office and am told to be on docks at ten o'clock. Having had previous experience of this, take fur coat, camp-stool, and copy of longest book I can find, and camp myself on docks. Rain stops.

Other people turn up and look enviously at camp-stool. Very old lady in black totters up and down till I feel guilty, and offer to give up camp-stool to her. She replies: "Thank you, thank you, but my Daimler is outside, and I can sit in that when I wish to do so."

Policeman informs me that tender is about to start for ship, if I wish to go on board. Remove self and camp-stool to tender.

Very, very unpleasant half-hour follows. Camp-stool shows tendency to slide about all over the place, and am obliged to abandon book for the time being.

Numbers of men of seafaring aspect walk about and look at me. One of them asks Am I a good sailor? No, I am not. Presently ship appears, apparently suddenly rising up from the middle of the waves, and ropes are dangled in every direction.

Catch glimpse of Rose from strange angles as tender heaves up and down. Gangway eventually materialises, and self and camp-stool achieve the ship.

Dear Rose most appreciative of effort involved by coming to meet her, but declares herself perfectly good sailor, and slept all through last night's storm. Try hard not to feel unjustly injured about this.

December 9th.—Rose staying here two days before going on to London. Says All American houses are Always Warm, which annoys Robert. He says in return that All American houses are Grossly Overheated and Entirely Airless. Impossible not to feel that this would carry more weight if Robert had ever been to America. Rose also very insistent about efficiency of American Telephone Service, and inclined to ask for glasses of cold water at breakfast time—which Robert does not approve of.

Otherwise dear Rose entirely unchanged and offers to put me up in her West-End flat as often as I like to come to London. Accept gratefully. (*N.B.* How very different to old school-friend Cissie Crabbe, with bed-sitting-room and gas-ring in Norwich! But should not like to think myself in any way a snob.)

On Rose's advice, bring bulb-bowls up from cellar and put them in drawing-room. Several of them perfectly visible, but somehow do not look entirely healthy. Rose thinks too much watering. If so, Cissie Crabbe entirely to blame. (*Mem.*: Either move bulb-bowls upstairs, or tell Ethel to show Lady Boxe into morning-room, if she calls. Cannot possibly enter into further discussion with her concerning bulbs.)

December 10th.—Robert, this morning, complains of insufficient breakfast. Cannot feel that porridge, scrambled eggs, toast, marmalade, scones, brown bread, and coffee give adequate grounds for this, but admit that porridge is slightly burnt. How impossible ever to encounter burnt porridge without vivid recollections of Jane Eyre at Lowood School, say I parenthetically! This literary allusion not a success. Robert suggests ringing for Cook, and have greatest difficulty in persuading him that this course utterly disastrous.

Read Life and Letters of distinguished woman recently dead, and am struck, as so often, by difference between her correspondence and that of less distinguished women. Immense and affectionate letters from celebrities on every other page, epigrammatic notes from literary and political acquaintances, poetical assurances of affection and admiration from husband, and even infant children. Try to imagine Robert writing in similar strain in the (improbable) event of my becoming celebrity, but fail. Dear Vicky equally unlikely to commit her feelings (if any) to paper.

Robin's letter arrives by second post, and am delighted to have it as ever, but cannot feel that laconic information about boy—unknown to me—called Baggs, having been swished, and Mr. Gompshaw, visiting master, being kept away by Sore Throat is on anything like equal footing with lengthy and picturesque epistles received almost daily by subject of biography, whenever absent from home.

Remainder of mail consists of one bill from chemist—(*Mem.*: Ask Mademoiselle why *two* tubes of toothpaste within ten days)—illiterate postcard from piano-tuner, announcing visit to-morrow, and circular concerning True Temperance.

Inequalities of Fate very curious. Should like, on this account, to believe in Reincarnation. Spend some time picturing to myself completely renovated state of affairs, with, amongst other improvements, total reversal of relative positions of Lady B. and myself.

(Query: Is thought on abstract questions ever a waste of time?)

December 11th.—Robert, still harping on topic of yesterday's breakfast, says suddenly Why Not a Ham? to which I reply austerely that a ham is on order, but will not appear until arrival of R.'s brother William and his wife, for Christmas visit. Robert, with every manifestation of horror, says Are William and Angela coming to us for *Christmas*? This attitude absurd, as invitation was given months ago, at Robert's own suggestion.

(Query here becomes unavoidable: Does not a misplaced optimism exist, common to all mankind, leading on to false conviction that social engagements, if dated sufficiently far ahead, will never really materialise?)

Vicky and Mademoiselle return from walk with small white-and-yellow kitten, alleged by them homeless and starving. Vicky fetches milk, and becomes excited. Agree that kitten shall stay "for to-night," but feel that this is weak.

(*Mem.*: Remind Vicky to-morrow that Daddy does not like cats.) Mademoiselle becomes very French, on subject of cats generally, and am obliged to check her. She is *blessée*, and all three retire to schoolroom.

December 12th.—Robert says out of the question to keep stray kitten. Existing kitchen cat more than enough. Gradually modifies this attitude under Vicky's pleadings. All now depends on whether kitten is male or female. Vicky and Mademoiselle declare this is known to them, and kitten already christened Napoleon. Find myself unable to enter into discussion on the point in French. The gardener takes opposite view to Vicky's and Mademoiselle's. They thereupon re-christen the kitten, seen playing with an old tennis ball, as Helen Wills, after international champion.

Robert's attention, perhaps fortunately, diverted by mysterious trouble with the water-supply. He says The Ram has Stopped. (This sounds to me Biblical.)

Give Mademoiselle a hint that H. Wills should not be encouraged to put in injudicious appearances downstairs.

December 13th.—Ram resumes activities. Helen Wills still with us.

December 14th.—Very stormy weather, floods out and many trees prostrated at inconvenient angles. Call from Lady Boxe, who says that she is off to the South of France next week, as she Must have Sunshine. She asks Why I do not go there too, and likens me to piece of chewed string, which I feel to be entirely inappropriate and rather offensive figure of speech, though perhaps kindly meant.

Why not just pop into the train, enquires Lady B., pop across France, and pop out into Blue Sky, Blue Sea, and Summer Sun? Could make perfectly comprehensive reply to this, but do not do so, question of expense having evidently not crossed Lady B.'s horizon. (*Mem.*: Interesting subject for debate at Women's Institute, perhaps: That Imagination is incompatible with Inherited Wealth. On second thoughts, though, fear this has a socialistic trend.)

Reply to Lady B. with insincere professions of liking England very much even in the Winter. She begs me not to let myself become parochially-minded.

Departure of Lady B. with many final appeals to me to reconsider South of France. Make civil pretence, which deceives neither of us, of wavering, and promise to ring her up in the event of a change of mind.

(Query: Cannot many of our moral lapses from

Truth be frequently charged upon the tactless per-sistence of others?)

December 15th, London. — Come up to dear Rose's flat for two days' Christmas shopping, after prolonged discussion with Robert, who maintains that All can equally well be done by Post.

Take early train so as to get in extra afternoon. Have with me Robert's old leather suit-case, own ditto in fibre, large quantity of chrysanthemums done up in brown paper for Rose, small packet of sandwiches, handbag, fur coat in case weather gets colder, book for train, and illustrated paper kindly presented by Made-moiselle at the station. (Query suggests itself: Could not some of these things have been dispensed with, and if so which?)

Bestow belongings in the rack, and open illustrated paper with sensation of leisured opulence, derived from unwonted absence of all domestic duties.

Unknown lady enters carriage at first stop, and takes seat opposite. She has expensive-looking luggage in moderate quantity and small red morocco jewel-case, also brand-new copy, without library label, of *Life of Sir Edward Marshall-Hall.* Am reminded of Lady B. and have recrudescence of Inferiority Complex.

Roused from unprofitable considerations by agita-tion on the part of elderly gentleman in corner seat, who says that, upon his soul, he is being dripped upon. Everybody looks at ceiling, and Burberry female makes a vague reference to unspecified "pipes" which she declares often "go like that". Someone else madly sug-gests turning off the heat. Elderly gentleman refuses all explanations and declares that *It comes from the rack*. We all look with horror at Rose's chrysanthemums, from which large drips of water descend regularly. Am overcome with shame, remove chrysanthemums, apologise to elderly gentleman, and sit down again opposite to superior unknown, who has remained glued to *Sir E. Marshall-Hall* throughout, and reminds me of Lady B. more than ever.

(*Mem.*: Speak to Mademoiselle about officiousness of thrusting flowers into water unasked, just before wrapping up.)

Immerse myself in illustrated weekly. Am informed by it that Lord Toto Finch (inset) is responsible for camera-study (herewith) of the Loveliest Legs in Los Angeles, belonging to well-known English Society girl, near relation (by the way) of famous racing peer, father of well-known Smart Set twins (portrait overleaf).

(Query: Is our popular Press going to the dogs?)

Turn attention to short story, but gave it up on being directed, just as I become interested, to page *xlvii b*, which I am quite unable to locate. Become involved instead with suggestions for Christmas Gifts. I want my gifts, the writer assures me, to be individual and yet appropriate—beautiful, and yet enduring. Let originality of thought, she says, add character to trifling offering. Would not many of my friends welcome suggestion of a course of treatment at Beauty Parlour in Piccadilly to be placed to my account?

Cannot visualise myself making this offer to Our Vicar's Wife, still less her reception of it, and decide to confine myself to one-and-sixpenny calendar with picture of sunset on Scaw Fell, as usual.

(Indulge, on the other hand, in a few moments' idle phantasy, in which I suggest to Lady B. that she should accept from me as a graceful and appropriate Christmas gift, a course of Reducing Exercises accompanied by Soothing and Wrinkle-eradicating Face Massage.)

This imaginative exercise brought to a conclusion by arrival.

Obliged to take taxi from station, mainly owing to chrysanthemums (which would not combine well with two suitcases and fur coat on moving stairway, which I distrust and dislike anyhow, and am only too apt to make conspicuous failure of Stepping Off with Right Foot foremost)—but also partly owing to fashionable locality of Rose's flat, miles removed from any Underground.

Kindest welcome from dear Rose, who is most appreciative of chrysanthemums. Refrain from mentioning unfortunate incident with elderly gentleman in train.

December 19th.—Find Christmas shopping very exhausting. Am paralysed in the Army and Navy Stores on discovering that List of Xmas Presents is lost, but eventually run it to earth in Children's Books Department. While there choose book for dear Robin, and wish for the hundredth time that Vicky had been less definite about wanting Toy Greenhouse and *nothing else.* This apparently unprocurable.

December 20th.—Return home. One bulb in partial flower, but not satisfactory.

December 23rd.—Meet Robin at the Junction. He has lost his ticket, parcel of sandwiches, and handkerchief, but produces large wooden packing-case, into which little shelf has been wedged. Understand that this represents result of Carpentry Class—expensive "extra" at school—and is a Christmas present. Will no doubt appear on bill in due course.

Much touched at enthusiastic greeting between Robin and Vicky. Mademoiselle says *Ah, c'est gentil!* and produces a handkerchief, which I think exaggerated, especially as in half-an-hour's time she comes to me with complaint that R. and V. have gone up into the rafters and are shaking down plaster from ceiling. Remonstrate with them from below.

Arrival of William and Angela, at half-past three. Should like to hurry up tea, but feel that servants would be annoyed, so instead offer to show them their rooms, which they know perfectly well already. We exchange news about relations. Robin and Vicky appear. Angela says that they have grown. Can see by her expression that she thinks them odious, and very badly brought-up. She tells me about the children in the last house she stayed at. All appear to have been miracles of cleanliness, intelligence, and charm. A. also adds, most unnecessarily, that they are musical, and play the piano nicely.

(*Mem.*: A meal the most satisfactory way of entertaining any guest. Should much like to abridge the interval between tea and dinner—or else to introduce supplementary collation in between.)

At dinner we talk again about relations, and ask one another if anything is ever heard of poor Frederick nowadays, and how Mollie's marriage is turning out, and whether Grandmamma is thinking of going to the

East Coast again this summer. Am annoyed because Robert and William sit on in the dining-room until nearly ten o'clock, which makes the servants late.

Xmas Day. — Festive, but exhausting, Christmas. Robin and Vicky delighted with everything, and spend much of the day eating. Vicky presents her Aunt Angela with small square of canvas on which blue donkey is worked in cross-stitch. Do not know whether to apologise for this or not, but eventually decide better to say nothing, and hint to Mademoiselle that other design might have been preferable.

The children perhaps rather too much *en évidence*, as Angela, towards tea-time, begins to tell me that the little Maitlands have such a delightful nursery, and always spend entire day in it except when out for long walks with governess and dogs.

William asks if that Mrs. Somers is one of the *Dorsetshire* lot — the woman who knows about Bees.

Make a note that I really must call on Mrs. S. early next week. Read up something about Bees before going.

Turkey and plum-pudding cold in the evening, to give servants a rest. Angela looks at bulbs and says What made me think they would be in flower for Christmas? Do not reply to this, but suggest early bed for us all.

December 27th. — Departure of William and Angela. Children's party this afternoon, too large and elaborate. Mothers stand about it in black hats and talk to one another about gardens, books, and difficulty of getting servants to stay in the country. Tea handed about the hall in a detached way, while children are herded into another room. Vicky and Robin behave well, and I compliment them on the way home, but am informed later by Mademoiselle that she has found large collection of chocolate biscuits in pocket of Vicky's party-frock.

(*Mem.*: Would it be advisable to point out to Vicky that this constitutes failures in intelligence, as well as in manners, hygiene, and common honesty?)

January 1st, 1930.—We give a children's party ourselves. Very, very exhausting, performance greatly complicated by stormy weather, which keeps half the guests away, and causes grave fears as to arrival of the conjurer.

Decide to have children's tea in the dining-room, grown-ups in the study, and clear the drawing-room for games and conjurer. Minor articles of drawing-room furniture moved up to my bedroom, where I continually knock myself against them. Bulb-bowls greatly in everybody's way and are put on widow-ledges in passage, at which Mademoiselle says *Tiens! ça fait un drôle d'effet, ces malheureux petits brins de verdure!* Do not like this description at all.

The children from neighbouring Rectory arrive too early, and are shown into completely empty drawing-room. Entrance of Vicky, in new green party-frock, with four balloons, saves situation.

(Query: What is the reason that clerical households are always unpunctual, invariably arriving either first, or last, at any gathering to which bidden?)

Am struck by variety of behaviour amongst mothers,

some so helpful in organising games and making suggestions, others merely sitting about. (*N.B.* For sake of honesty, should rather say *standing* about, as supply of chairs fails early.) Resolve always to send Robin and Vicky to parties without me, if possible, as children without parents infinitely preferable from point of view of hostess. Find it difficult to get "Oranges and Lemons" going, whilst at same time appearing to give intelligent attention to remarks from visiting mother concerning Exhibition of Italian Pictures at Burlington House. Find myself telling her how marvellous I think them, although in actual fact have not yet seen them at all. Realise that this mis-statement should be corrected at once, but omit to do so, and later find myself involved in entirely unintentional web of falsehood. Should like to work out how far morally to blame for this state of things, but have not time.

Conjurer arrives late, but is a success with children. Ends up with presents from a bran-tub, in which more bran is spilt on carpet, children's clothes, and house generally, than could ever have been got into tub originally. Think this odd, but have noticed similar phenomenon before.

Guests depart between seven and half-past, and Helen Wills and the dog are let out by Robin, having been shut up on account of crackers, which they dislike.

Robert and I spend evening helping servants to restore order, and trying to remember where ash-trays, clock, ornaments and ink were put for safety.

January 3rd.—Hounds meet in the village. Robert agrees to take Vicky on the pony. Robin, Mademoiselle, and I walk to the Post Office to see the start, and Robin talks about Oliver Twist, making no reference whatever to hunt from start to finish, and viewing horses, hounds and huntsmen with equal detachment. Am impressed at his non-suggestibility, but feel that some deep Freudian significance may lie behind it all. Feel also that Robert would take very different view of it.

Meet quantities of hunting neighbours, who say to Robin, "Aren't you riding *too*?" which strikes one as lacking in intelligence, and ask me if we have lost many trees lately, but do not wait for answer, as what they really want to talk about is the number of trees they have lost themselves.

Mademoiselle looks at hounds and says *Ah, ces bons chiens!* also admires horses, *quelles bêtes superbes*—but prudently keeps well away from all, in which I follow her example.

Vicky looks nice on pony, and I receive compliments about her, which I accept in an off-hand manner, tinged with incredulity, in order to show that I am a modern mother and should scorn to be foolish about my children.

Hunt moves off, Mademoiselle remarking *Voilà bien le sport anglais!* Robin says: "Now can we go home?" and eats milk-chocolate. We return to the house and I write order to the Stores, post-card to the butcher, two letters about Women's Institutes, one about Girl Guides, note to the dentist asking for appointment next week, and make memorandum in engagement book that I *must* call on Mrs. Somers at the Grange.

Am horrified and incredulous at discovery that these occupations have filled the entire morning.

Robert and Vicky return late, Vicky plastered with mud from head to foot but unharmed. Mademoiselle removes her, and says no more about *le sport anglais*.

January 5th.—Rose, in the kindest way, offers to take me as her guest to special dinner of famous Literary Club if I will come up to London for the night. Celebrated editor of literary weekly paper in the chair, spectacularly successful author of famous play as guest of honour. Principal authors, poets, and artists from— says Rose—all over the world, expected to be present.

Spend much of the evening talking to Robert about this. Put it to him: (*a*) That no expense is involved beyond 3rd-class return ticket to London; (*b*) that in another twelve years Vicky will be coming out, and it is therefore incumbent on me to Keep in Touch with People; (*c*) that this is an opportunity that will never occur again; (*d*) that it isn't as if I were asking him to come too. Robert says nothing to (*a*) or (*b*) and only "I should hope not" to (*c*), but appears slightly moved by (*d*). Finally says he supposes I must do as I like, and very likely I shall meet some old friends of my Bohemian days when living with Rose in Hampstead.

Am touched by this, and experience passing wonder if Robert can be feeling slightly jealous. This fugitive idea dispelled by his immediately beginning to speak about failure of hot water this morning.

January 7th.—Rose takes me to Literary Club dinner. I wear my Blue. Am much struck by various young men who have defiantly put on flannel shirts and no ties, and brushed their hair up on end. They are mostly accompanied by red-headed young women who wear printed crêpe frocks and beads. Otherwise, everyone in evening dress.

Am placed at dinner next to celebrated best-seller, who tells me in the kindest way how to evade paying super-tax. Am easily able to conceal from him the fact that I am not at present in a position to require this information.

Rose handsomely pays for my dinner as well as her own.

Young gentleman is introduced to me by Rose—(she saying in rapid murmur that he is part-author of a one-act play that has been acted three times by a Repertory company in Jugoslavia.) It turns out later that he has met Lady Boxe, who struck him, he adds immediately, as a poisonous woman. We then get on well together. (Query: Is not a common hate one of the strongest links in human nature? Answer, most regrettably, in the affirmative.)

Very, very distinguished Novelist approaches me (having evidently mistaken me for someone else), and talks amiably. She says that she can only write between twelve at night and four in the morning, and not always then. When she cannot write, she plays the organ. Should much like to ask whether she is married—but get no opportunity of asking that or anything else. She tells me about her sales. She tells me about her last book. She tells me about her new one. She says that there are many people here to whom she *must* speak, and pursues well-known Poet—who does not, however, allow her to catch up with him. Can understand this.

Move about after dinner, and meet acquaintance whose name I have forgotten, but connect with literature. I ask if he has published anything lately. He says that his work is not, and never can be, for publication. Thought passes through my mind to the effect that this attitude might with advantage be adopted by many others. Do not say so, however, and we talk instead about Rebecca West, the progress of aviation, and the case for and against stag-hunting.

Rose, who has been discussing psychiatry as practised in the U.S.A. with Danish journalist, says Am I ready to go? We depart by nearest Tube, and sit up till one o'clock discussing our fellow-creatures, with special reference to those seen and heard this evening. Rose says I ought to come to London more often and suggests that outlook requires broadening.

January 9th.—Came home yesterday. Robin and Mademoiselle no longer on speaking terms, owing to involved affair centring round a broken window-pane. Vicky, startlingly, tells me in private that she has learnt a new Bad Word, but does not mean to use it. Not now, anyway, she disquietingly adds.

Cook says she hopes I enjoyed my holiday, and it is very quiet in the country. I leave the kitchen before she has time to say more, but am only too well aware that this is not the last of it.

Write grateful letter to Rose, at the same time explaining difficulty of broadening my outlook by further time spent away from home, just at present.

January 14th.—I have occasion to observe, not for the first time, how extraordinary plain a cold can make one look. Cook assures me that colds always run through the house and that she has herself been suffering from sore throat for weeks, but is never one to make a fuss. (Query: Is this meant to imply that similar fortitude should be, but is not, displayed by me?) Mademoiselle says she *hopes* children will not catch my cold, but that both sneezed this morning. I run short of handkerchiefs.

January 16th. — We all run short of handkerchiefs.

January 17th. — Mademoiselle suggests butter-muslin. There is none in the house. I say that I will go out and buy some. Mademoiselle says, "No, the fresh air gives pneumonia." Feel that I ought to combat this un-British attitude, but lack energy, especially when she adds that she will go herself — *Madame, j'y cours.* She puts on black kid gloves, buttoned boots with pointed tips and high heels, hat with little feather in it, black jacket and several silk neckties, and goes, leaving me to amuse Robin and Vicky, both in bed. Twenty minutes after she has started, I remember it is early-closing day.

Go up to night-nursery and offer to read Lamb's *Tales from Shakespeare*. Vicky says she prefers *Pip, Squeak, and Wilfred*. Robin says that he would like *Gulliver's Travels*. Compromise on *Grimm's Fairy Tales*, although slightly uneasy as to their being in accordance with best modern ideals. Both children take immense interest in story of highly undesirable Person who wins fortune, fame, and beautiful Princess by means of lies, violence, and treachery. Feel sure that this must have disastrous effect on both in years to come.

Our Vicar's Wife calls before Mademoiselle returns. Go down to her, sneezing, and suggest that she had better not stay. She says, much better not, and she won't keep me a minute. Tells me long story about the Vicar having a stye on one eye. I retaliate with Cook's sore throat. This leads to draughts, the heating apparatus in church, and news of Lady Boxe in South of France. Our Vicar's Wife has had a picture postcard from her (which she produces from bag), with small cross marking bedroom window of hotel. She says, It's rather interesting, isn't it? to which I reply Yes, it is, very, which is not in the least true. (*N.B.* Truth-telling in everyday life extraordinarily difficult. Is this personal, and highly deplorable, idiosyncrasy, or do others suffer in the same way? Have momentary impulse to put this to Our Vicar's Wife, but decide better not.)

How, she says, are the dear children, and how is my husband? I reply suitably, and she tells me about cinnamon, Vapex, gargling with glycerine of thymol, blackcurrant tea, onion broth, Friar's Balsam, linseed poultices, and thermogene wool. I sneeze and say Thank you—thank you very much, a good many times. She goes, but turns back at the door to tell me about wool next the skin, nasal douching, and hot milk last thing at night. I say Thank you, again.

On returning to night-nursery, find that Robin has unscrewed top of hot-water bottle in Vicky's bed, which apparently contained several hundred gallons of tepid water, now distributed through and through pillows, pyjamas, sheets, blankets, and mattresses of both. I ring for Ethel, who helps me to reorganise entire situation and says It's like a hospital, isn't it, trays up and down stairs all day long, and all this extra work.

January 20th.—Take Robin, now completely restored, back to school. I say good-bye with hideous brightness, and cry all the way back to the station.

January 22nd.—Robert startles me at breakfast by asking if my cold—which he has hitherto ignored—is better. I reply that it has gone. Then why, he asks, do I look like that? Refrain from asking like what, as I know only too well. Feel that life is wholly unendurable, and decide madly to get a new hat.

Visit four linen-drapers and try on several dozen hats. Look worse and worse in each one, as hair gets wilder and wilder, and expression paler and more harassed. Decide to get myself shampooed and waved before doing any more, in hopes of improving the position.

Hairdresser's assistant says, It's a pity my hair is losing all its colour, and have I ever thought of having it touched up? After long discussion, I do have it touched up, and emerge with mahogany-coloured head. Hairdresser's assistant says this will wear off "in a few days". I am very angry, but all to no purpose. Return home in old hat, showing as little hair as possible, and keep it on till dressing time—but cannot hope to conceal my shame at dinner.

January 25th.—Attend a Committee Meeting in the village to discuss how to raise funds for Village Hall. Am asked to take the chair. Begin by saying that I know how much we all have this excellent object at heart, and that I feel sure there will be no lack of suggestions as to best method of obtaining requisite sum of money. Pause for suggestions, which is met with deathlike silence. I say, There are so many ways to choose from— implication being that I attribute silence to plethora of ideas, rather than to absence of them. (*Note*: Curious and rather depressing, to see how frequently the pursuit of Good Works leads to apparently unavoidable duplicity.) Silence continues, and I say Well, twice, and Come, come, once. At last extract a suggestion of a concert from Mrs. L. (whose son plays the violin) and a whist-drive from Miss P. (who won Ladies' First Prize at the last one). Florrie P. suggests a dance and is at once reminded that it will be Lent. She says that Lent isn't what it was. Her mother says the Vicar is one that holds with Lent, and always has been. Someone else says That reminds her, has anyone heard that old Mr. Small passed away last night? We all agree that eighty-six is a great age. Mrs. L. says that on her mother's side of the family, there is an aunt of ninety-eight. Still with us, she adds. The aunt's husband, on the other hand, was gathered just before his sixtieth birthday. Everyone says, You can't ever *tell*, not really. There is a suitable pause before we go back to Lent and the Vicar. General opinion that a concert isn't like a dance, and needn't—says Mrs. L.—interfere.

On this understanding, we proceed. Various familiar items—piano solo, recitation, duet, and violin solo from Master L.—are all agreed upon. Someone says that Mrs. F. and Miss H. might do a duologue, and has to be reminded that they are no longer on speaking terms

owing to strange behaviour of Miss H. about her bantams. Ah, says Mrs. S., it wasn't only *bantams* was at
the bottom of it, there's two sides to every question.

Meeting ends at about five o'clock. Our Vicar's Wife
walks home with me, and tells me that I look tired. I ask
her to come in and have tea. No, she says, no, it's too
kind of me, but she must go on to the far end of the
parish. She remains standing at the gate telling me about
old Small—eighty-six a great age—till quarter-to-six,
when she departs, saying that she cannot *think* why I
am looking so tired.

February 11th.—Hear that Lady Boxe has returned
from South of France and is entertaining house-party.
She sends telephone message by the butler, asking me to
tea to-morrow. I accept. (Why?)

February 12th.—Insufferable behaviour of Lady B.
Find large party, all of whom are directed at front door
to go to the Hard Courts, where, under inadequate
shelter, in Arctic temperature, all are compelled to
watch young men in white flannels keeping themselves
warm by banging a little ball against a wall. Lady B.
wears an emerald-green leather coat with fur collar and
cuffs. I, having walked down, have on ordinary coat and
skirt, and freeze rapidly. Find myself next unknown
lady who talks wistfully about the tropics. Can well
understand this. Past five o'clock before we are allowed
to go in to tea, by which time am only too well aware
that my face is blue and my hands purple. Lady B. asks
me at tea how the children are, and adds, to the table
at large, that I am "A Perfect Mother". Am naturally

avoided, conversationally, after this, by everybody at the tea-table. Later on, Lady B. tells us about South of France. She quotes repartees made by herself in French, and then translates them.

(Unavoidable Query presents itself here: Would a verdict of Justifiable Homicide delivered against their mother affect future careers of children unfavourably?)

Discuss foreign travel with unknown, but charming, lady in black. We are delighted with one another—or so I confidently imagine—and she begs me to go and see her if I am ever in her neighbourhood. I say that I will—but am well aware that courage will fail me when it comes to the point. Pleasant sense of mutual sympathy suddenly and painfully shattered by my admitting—in reply to direct enquiry—that I am *not* a gardener—which the lady in black *is*, to an extent that apparently amounts to monomania. She remains charming, but quite ceases to be delighted with me. I feel discouraged and think I had better go.

Lady B. says, shall she ring for my car? Refrain from replying that no amount of ringing will bring my car to the door all by itself, and say instead that I walked. Lady B. exclaims that this is Impossible, and that I am Too Marvellous, Altogether. Take my leave before she can add that I am such a Perfect Countrywoman, which I feel is coming next.

Get home—still chilled to the bone owing to enforced detention at Hard Court—and tell Robert what I think of Lady B. He makes no answer, but I feel he agrees.

Mademoiselle says *Tiens! Madame a mauvaise mine. On dirait un cadavre. . . .*

Feel that this is kindly meant, but do not care about the picture that it conjures up.

Say good-night to Vicky, looking angelic in bed, and ask what she is thinking about, lying there. She disconcertingly replies with briskness: "Oh, Kangaroos and things."

(*Note*: The workings of the infant mind very, very difficult to follow, sometimes. Mothers by no means infallible.)

February 16th.—Informed by Ethel, as she calls me in the morning, that Helen Wills has had six kittens, of which five survive.

Cannot imagine how I shall break this news to Robert. Reflect—not for the first time—that all workings of Nature are most singular.

February 21st.—Remove bulb-bowls, with what is left of bulbs, to greenhouse. Tell Robert that I hope to do better another year. He replies, Another year, better not waste my money. This reply depresses me, moreover weather continues Arctic, and have by no means recovered from effects of Lady B.'s so-called hospitality.

Vicky and Mademoiselle spend much time in boot-cupboard, where Helen Wills is established with five kittens. Robert still unaware of what has happened, but cannot hope this ignorance will continue. Must, however, choose suitable moment for revelation—which is unlikely to occur to-day owing to bath-water having been cold again this morning.

Lady B. calls in the afternoon—not, as might have been expected, to see if I am in bed with pneumonia, but to ask if I will help at a Bazaar early in May. Further enquiry reveals that it is in aid of the Party Funds. I say What Party? (Am well aware of Lady B.'s political views, but resent having it taken for granted that mine are the same—which they are not.)

Lady B. says she is Surprised. Later on she says Look at the Russians, and even, Look at the Pope. I find myself telling her to Look at Unemployment—none of which gets us any farther. Am relieved when tea comes in, and still more so when Lady B. says she really mustn't wait, as she has to call on such a number of Tenants. She asks after Robert, and I think seriously of replying that he is out receiving the Oath of Allegiance from all the vassals on the estate, but decide that this would be undignified.

Escort Lady B. to the hall-door. She tells me that the oak dresser would look better on the other side of the hall, and that it is a mistake to put mahogany and walnut in the same room. Her last word is that she will Write about the bazaar. Relieve my feelings by waving small red flag belonging to Vicky, which is lying on the hall-stand, and saying *A la lanterne!* as chauffeur drives off. Rather unfortunately, Ethel chooses this moment to walk through the hall. She says nothing, but looks astonished.

February 22nd.—Gloom prevails, owing to Helen Wills having elected, with incredible idiocy, to introduce progeny, one by one, to Robert's notice at late hour last night, when he was making final round of the house.

Send Mademoiselle and Vicky on errand to the village whilst massacre of the innocents takes place in pail of water in backyard. Small ginger is allowed to survive. Spend much time in thinking out plausible story to account to Vicky for disappearance of all the rest. Mademoiselle, when informed privately of what has happened, tells me to leave Vicky to her—which I gladly agree to do—and adds that *les hommes manquent de cœur*. Feel that this is leading us in the direction of a story which I have heard before, and do not wish to hear again, regarding *un mariage échoué* arranged years ago for Mademoiselle by her parents, in which negotiations broke down owing to mercenary attitude of *le futur*. Break in with hasty enquiry regarding water-tightness or otherwise of Vicky's boots.

(Query: Does incessant pressure of domestic cares vitiate capacity for human sympathy? Fear that it does, but find myself unable to attempt reformation in this direction at present.)

February 24th.—Robert and I lunch with Our Member and his wife. I sit next elderly gentleman who talks about stag-hunting and tells me that there is Nothing Cruel about it. The *Stag likes it,* and it is an honest, healthy, thoroughly *English* form of sport. I say Yes, as anything else would be waste of breath, and turn to Damage done by recent storms, New arrivals in the neighbourhood, and Golf-links at Budleigh Salterton. Find that we get back to stag-hunting again in next to no time, and remain there for the rest of lunch.

Can hear Robert's neighbour, sitting opposite in cochineal three-piece suit, telling him about her chilblains. Robert civil, but does not appear unduly concerned. (Perhaps three-piece cochineal thinks that he is one of those people who feel more than they can express?) She goes on to past appendicitis, present sciatica, and threat of colitis in the near future. Robert still unmoved.

Ladies retire to the drawing-room and gather round quite inadequate fire. Coffee. I perform my usual sleight-of-hand, transferring large piece of candy-sugar from saucer to handbag, for Vicky's benefit. (Query: Why do people living in same neighbourhood as myself obtain without difficulty minor luxuries that I am totally unable to procure? Reply to this, if pursued to logical conclusion, appears to point to inadequate housekeeping on my part.)

Entrance of males. I hear my neighbour at lunch beginning all over again about stag-hunting, this time addressed to his hostess, who is well-known supporter of the R.S.P.C.A.

As we take our leave with customary graceful speeches, clasp of handbag unfortunately gives way, and piece of candy-sugar falls, with incredible noise and violence, on to the parquet, and is pursued with officious zeal and determination by all present except myself.

Very, very difficult moment. . . .

Robert on the whole takes this well, merely enquiring on the way home if I suppose that we shall ever be asked inside the house again.

February 28th.—Notice, and am gratified by, appearance of large clump of crocuses near the front gate. Should like to make whimsical and charming reference to these, and try to fancy myself as "Elizabeth of the

German Garden", but am interrupted by Cook, saying that the Fish is here, but he's only brought cod and haddock, and the haddock doesn't smell any too fresh, so what about cod?

Have often noticed that Life is like that.

March 3rd.—Vicky, after Halma, enquires abruptly whether, if she died, I should cry. I reply in the affirmative. But, she says, should I cry really *hard?* Should I roar and scream? Decline to commit myself to any such extravagant demonstrations, at which Vicky displays a tendency to hurt astonishment. I speak to Mademoiselle and say that I hope she will discourage anything in Vicky that seems to verge upon the morbid. Mademoiselle requires a translation of the last word, and, after some consideration, I suggest *dénaturé*, at which she screams dramatically and crosses herself, and assures me that if I knew what I was saying, I should *en reculer d'effroi.*

We decide to abandon the subject.

Our Vicar's Wife calls for me at seven o'clock and we go to a neighbouring Women's Institute at which I have, rather rashly, promised to speak. On the way there, Our Vicar's Wife tells me that the secretary of the Institute is liable to have a heart attack at any minute and must on no account exert herself, or be allowed to get over-excited. Even a violent fit of laughing, she adds impressively, might carry her off in a moment.

Hastily revise my speech and remove from it two funny stories. After this it is a shock to find that the programme for the evening includes dancing and a game of General Post. I ask Our Vicar's Wife what would happen if the secretary *did* get a heart attack, and she replies mysteriously, Oh, she always carries Drops in her handbag. The thing to do is to keep an eye on her handbag. This I do nervously throughout the evening, but fortunately no crisis supervenes.

I speak, am thanked, and asked if I will judge a Darning Competition. This I do, in spite of inward misgivings that few people are less qualified to give any opinion about darning than I am. I am thanked again and given tea and a doughnut. We all play General Post and get very heated. Signal success of the evening when two stout and elderly members collide in the middle of the room, and both fall heavily to the floor together. This, if anything, will surely bring on a heart attack, and am prepared to make a rush at the handbag, but nothing happens. We all sing the National Anthem, and Our Vicar's Wife says she does hope the lights of her two-seater are in order, and drives me home. We are relieved, and surprised, to find that the lights, all except the rear one, *are* in order, although rather faint.

March 4th.—Ethel gives notice. Cook says this is so unsettling, she thinks she had better go too. Despair invades me. Write five letters to Registry Offices.

March 7th.—No hope.

March 8th.—Cook relents, so far as to say that she will stay until I am suited. Feel inclined to answer that, in that case, she had better make up her mind to a lifetime spent together—but naturally refrain. Spend exhausting day in Plymouth chasing mythical house-parlourmaids.

Meet Lady B., who says the servant difficulty, in reality, is non-existent. She has **NO** trouble. It is a question of knowing how to treat them. Firmness, she says, but at the same time one must be human. Am I human? she asks. Do I understand that they want occasional diversion, just as I do myself? I lose my head and reply No, that it is my custom to keep my servants chained up in the cellar when their work is done. This flight of satire rather spoilt by Lady B. laughing heartily, and saying that I am always so amusing. Well, she adds, we shall no doubt see one another at lunch-time at the Duke of Cornwall Hotel, where alone it is possible to get a decent meal. I reply with ready cordiality that no doubt we shall, and go and partake of my usual lunch of baked beans and a glass of water in small and obscure café.

Unavoidable Query, of painfully searching character, here presents itself: If Lady B. had invited me as her guest to lunch at the D. of C. Hotel, should I have accepted? Am conscious of being heartily tired of baked beans and water, which in any case do not really serve to support one through long day of shopping and servant-hunting. Moreover, am always ready to See Life, in hotels or anywhere else. On the other hand, am aware that self-respect would suffer severely through accepting five-shillings-worth of luncheon from Lady B. Ponder this problem of psychology in train on the way home, but reach no definite conclusion.

March 9th.—Cannot hear of a house-parlourmaid. Ethel, on the other hand, can hear of at least a hundred situations, and opulent motor-cars constantly dash up to front door, containing applicants for her services. Cook more and more unsettled. If this goes on, shall go to London and stay with Rose, in order to visit Agencies.

Meet Barbara Blenkinsop, wearing new tweed, in village—nice bright girl, but long to suggest she should have adenoids removed. She says, Will I be an Angel and look in on her mother, now practically an invalid? I reply warmly Of course I will, not really meaning it, but remember that we are now in Lent and suddenly decide to go at once. Admire the new tweed. Barbara says It *is* rather nice, isn't it, and adds—a little strangely—that it came out of John Barker's Sale Catalogue, under four guineas, and only needed letting out at the waist and taking in a bit on the shoulders. Especially, she adds elliptically, now that skirts are longer again.

Barbara goes to Evening Service, and I go to look in on her mother, whom I find in shawls, sitting in an armchair reading—rather ostentatiously—enormous *Life of Lord Beaconsfield*. I ask how she is, and she shakes her head and enquires if I should ever guess that her pet name amongst her friends once used to be Butterfly? (This kind of question always so difficult, as either affirmative or negative reply apt to sound unsympathetic. Feel it would hardly do to suggest that Chrysalis, in view of the shawls, would now be more appropriate.) However, says Mrs. Blenkinsop with a sad smile, it is never her way to dwell upon herself and her own troubles. She just sits there, day after day, always ready to sympathise in the little joys and troubles of others, and I would hardly believe how unfailingly these are brought to her. People say, she adds deprecatingly, that just her smile does them good. She does not know, she says, what they mean. (Neither do I.)

After this, there is a pause, and I feel that Mrs. B. is waiting for me to pour out my little joys and troubles. Perhaps she hopes that Robert has been unfaithful to me, or that I have fallen in love with the Vicar.

Am unable to rise to the occasion, so begin instead to talk about Barbara's new tweed. Mrs. Blenkinsop at once replies that, for her part, she has never given up all those little feminine touches that make All the Difference. A ribbon here, a flower there. This leads to a story about what was once said to her by a friend, beginning "It's so wonderful, dear Mrs. Blenkinsop, to see the trouble you always take on behalf of others", and ending with Mrs. B.'s own reply, to the effect that she is only A useless Old Woman, but that she has many, many friends, and that this must be because her motto has always been: Look Out and Not In: Look Up and Not Down: Lend a Hand.

Conversation again languishes, and I have recourse to *Lord Beaconsfield*. What, I ask, does Mrs. B. feel about him? She feels, Mrs. B. replies, that he was a most Remarkable Personality. People have often said to Mrs. B., Ah, how lonely it must be for you, alone here, when dear Barbara is out enjoying herself with other young things. But Mrs. B.'s reply to this is No, no. She is never alone when she has Her Books. Books, to her, are *Friends*. Give her Shakespeare or Jane Austen, Meredith or Hardy, and she is Lost—lost in a world of her own. She sleeps so little that most of her nights are spent in reading. Have I any idea, asks Mrs. B., what it is like to hear every hour, every half-hour, chiming out all through the night? I have no idea whatever, since am invariably obliged to struggle with overwhelming sleepiness from nine o'clock onwards, but do not like to tell her this, so take my departure.

Reach home totally unbenefited by this visit, and with strange tendency to snap at everybody I meet.

March 10th.—Still no house-parlourmaid, and write to ask Rose if I can go to her for a week. Also write to old Aunt Gertrude in Shropshire to enquire if I may send Vicky and Mademoiselle there on a visit, as this will make less work in house while we are short-handed.

March 11th.—Rose wires that she will be delighted to put me up. Cook, very unpleasantly, says, "I'm sure I hope you'll enjoy your holiday, mum". Am precluded from making the kind of reply I should *like* to make, owing to grave fears that she should also give notice. Tell her instead that I hope to "get settled" with a house-parlourmaid before my return. Cook looks utterly incredulous and says she is sure she hopes so too, because really, things have been so unsettled lately. Pretend not to hear this and leave the kitchen.

March 12th.—Collect major portion of my wardrobe and dispatch to address mentioned in advertisement pages of *Time and Tide* as prepared to pay Highest Prices for Outworn Garments, cheque by return. Have gloomy foreboding that six penny stamps by return will more adequately represent value of my contribution, and am thereby impelled to add Robert's old shooting-coat and mackintosh, and least reputable woollen sweater. Customary struggle ensues between frank and straightforward course of telling Robert what I have done, and less straightforward, but more practical, decision to keep complete silence on the point and let him make discovery for himself after parcel has left the house. Conscience, as usual, is defeated, but nevertheless unsilenced.

March 13th. — Vicky and Mademoiselle leave in order to pay visit to Aunt Gertrude. Mademoiselle becomes sentimental and says *Ah, déjà je languis pour notre retour!* As total extent of her absence at this stage is about half-an-hour, and they have three weeks before them, feel that this is not a spirit to be encouraged. See them into the train, when Mademoiselle at once produces eau-de-Cologne in case either, or both, should be ill, and come home again. House resembles the tomb, and the gardener says that Miss Vicky seems such a little bit of a thing to be sent right away like that, and it isn't as if she could write and *tell* me how she was getting on, either.

Go to bed feeling like a murderess.

March 14th. — Rather inadequate Postal Order arrives, together with white tennis coat trimmed with rabbit, which — says accompanying letter — is returned as being unsaleable. Should like to know *why*.

March 15th. — Robert discovers absence of ancient mackintosh. Says that he would "rather have lost a hundred pounds"—which I know to be untrue. Unsuccessful evening follows. Cannot make up my mind whether to tell him at once about shooting-coat and sweater, and get it all over in one, or leave him to find out for himself when present painful impression has had time to die away. Ray of light pierces impenetrable gloom when Robert is driven to enquire if I can tell him "a word for *calmer* in seven letters" and I, after some thought, suggest "*serener*"—which he says will do, and returns to *Times* Crossword Puzzle. Later he asks for famous mountain in Greece, but does not accept my too hasty offer of Mount Atlas, nor listen to interesting explanation as to associative links between Greece, Hercules, and Atlas, which I proffer. After going into it at some length, I perceive that Robert is not attending and retire to bed.

March 17th.—Travel up to London with Barbara Blenkinsop—(wearing new tweed)—who says she is going to spend a fortnight with old school-friend at Streatham and is looking forward to Italian Art Exhibition. I say that I am, too, and ask after Mrs. B. Barbara says that she is Wonderful.

I ask Barbara to tea at my club one day next week, she accepts, and we part.

Met by Rose, who has a new hat, and says that *no one* is wearing a brim, which discourages me—partly because I have nothing *but* brims, and partly because I know only too well that I shall look my worst without one. Confide this fear to Rose, who says, Why not go to well-known Beauty Culture Establishment, and have course of treatment there? I look at myself in the glass, see much room for improvement, and agree to this, only stipulating that all shall be kept secret as the grave, as could not tolerate the idea of Lady B.'s comments, should she ever come to hear of it. Make appointment by telephone.

Rose's cook, as usual, produces marvellous dinner, and I remember with shame and compassion that Robert, at home, is sitting down to minced beef and macaroni cheese, followed by walnuts.

Rose says that she is taking me to dinner to-morrow with distinguished woman-writer who has marvellous collection of Jade, to meet still more distinguished Professor (female) and others. Decide to go and buy an evening dress to-morrow, regardless of overdraft.

March 18th. — Visit several Registry Offices, and am told that maids do not like the country — which I know already — and that the wages I am offering are low. Come away from there depressed, and decide to cheer myself up by purchasing evening dress — which I cannot afford — with present-day waist — which does not suit me. Select the Brompton Road, as likely to contain what I want, and crawl up it, scrutinising windows. Come face-to-face with Barbara Blenkinsop, who says, *How* extraordinary we should meet here, to which I reply that that is so often the way, when one comes to London, and plunge into elegant establishment with expensive-looking garments in the window.

Try on five dresses, but find judgement of their merits very difficult, as hair gets wilder and wilder, and nose more devoid of powder. Am also worried by extraordinary and tactless tendency of saleswoman to emphasise the fact that all the colours I like are very trying by daylight, but will be less so at night. Finally settle on silver tissue with large bow, stipulate for its immediate delivery, am told that this is impossible, reluctantly agree to carry it away with me in cardboard box, and go away wondering if it wouldn't have been better to choose the black chiffon instead.

Hope that Beauty Parlour experiment may enhance self-respect, at present at rather low ebb, but am cheered by going into Fuller's and sending boxes of chocolates to Robin and Vicky respectively. Add peppermint creams for Mademoiselle by an afterthought, as otherwise she may find herself *blessée*. Lunch on oxtail soup, lobster mayonnaise, and cup of coffee, as being menu farthest removed from that obtainable at home.

Beauty Parlour follows. Feel that a good deal could be written on this experience, and even contemplate— in connection with recent observations exchanged between Barbara B. and myself—brightening the pages of our Parish Magazine with result of my reflections, but on second thoughts abandon this, as unlikely to appeal to the Editor (Our Vicar).

Am received by utterly terrifying person with dazzling complexion, indigo-blue hair, and orange nails, presiding over reception-room downstairs, but eventually passed on to extremely pretty little creature with auburn bob and charming smile. Am reassured. Am taken to discreet curtained cubicle and put into long chair. Subsequent operations, which take hours and hours, appear to consist of the removal of hundreds of layers of dirt from my face. (These discreetly explained away by charming operator as the result of "acidity".)

She also plucks away portions of my eyebrows. Very, very painful operation.

Eventually emerge more or less unrecognisable, and greatly improved. Lose my head, and buy Foundation Cream, rouge, powder, lipstick. Foresee grave difficulty in reconciling Robert to the use of these appliances, but decide not to think about this for the present.

March 19th.—Rose takes me to dine with talented group of her friends, connected with Feminist Movement. I wear new frock, and for once in my life am satisfied with my appearance (but still regret great-aunt's diamond ring, now brightening pawnbroker's establishment back-street Plymouth). Am, however, compelled to make strong act of will in order to banish all recollection of bills that will subsequently come in from Beauty Parlour and dressmaker. Am able to succeed in this largely owing to charms of distinguished Feminists, all as kind as possible, including well-known Professor concerning whom I have previously consulted Rose as to the desirability of reading up something about Molecules or other kindred topic, for conversational purposes.

Rose and I take our leave just before midnight, sharing taxi with very well-known woman dramatist. (Should much like Lady B. to know this, and have every intention of making casual mention to her of it at earliest possible opportunity.)

March 20th.—A letter from dear Robin, forwarded from home, arrives to-night. He says, wouldn't a motor tour in the Easter holidays be great fun, and a boy at school called Briggs is going on one. (Briggs is the only son of millionaire parents, owning two Rolls-Royces and any number of chauffeurs.) Feel that it would be unendurable to refuse this trustful request, and decide that I can probably persuade Robert into letting me drive the children to the far side of the county in the old Standard. Can call this modest expedition a motor tour if we stay the night at a pub and return the next day.

At the same time realise that, financial situation being what it is, and moreover time rapidly approaching when great-aunt's diamond ring must either be redeemed, or relinquished for ever, there is nothing for it but to approach Bank on subject of an overdraft.

Am never much exhilarated at this prospect, and do not in the least find that it becomes less unpleasant with repetition, but rather the contrary. Experience customary difficulty in getting to the point, and Bank Manager and I discuss weather, political situation, and probable starters for the Grand National with passionate suavity for some time. Inevitable pause occurs, and we look at one another across immense expanse of pink blotting-paper. Irrelevant impulse rises in me to ask if he has other supply, for use, in writing-table drawer, or if fresh pad is brought in whenever a client calls. (Strange divagations of the human brain under the stress of extreme nervousness presents itself here as interesting topic for speculation. Should like to hear opinion of Professor met last night on this point. Subject far preferable to Molecules.)

Long, and rather painful, conversation follows. Bank Manager kind, but if he says the word "security" once, he certainly says it twenty times. Am, myself, equally insistent with "temporary accommodation only", which I think sounds thoroughly business-like, and at the same time optimistic as to speedy repayment. Just as I think we are over the worst, Bank Manager reduces me to spiritual pulp by suggesting that we should see how the Account Stands at the Moment. Am naturally compelled to agree to this with air of well-bred and detached amusement, but am in reality well aware that the Account Stands—or, more accurately, totters—on a Debit Balance of Thirteen Pounds, two shillings, and tenpence. Large sheet of paper, bearing this impressive statement, is presently brought in and laid before us.

Negotiations resumed.

Eventually emerge into the street with purpose accomplished, but feeling completely unstrung for the day. Rose is kindness personified, produces Bovril and an excellent lunch, and agrees with me that it is All Nonsense to say that Wealth wouldn't mean Happiness, because we know quite well that it *would*.

March 21st.—Express to Rose serious fear that I shall lose my reason if no house-parlourmaid materialises. Rose, as usual, sympathetic, but can suggest nothing that I have not already tried. We go to a Sale in order to cheer ourselves up, and I buy yellow linen tennis-frock—£1 9s. 6d.—on strength of newly-arranged over-draft, but subsequently suffer from the conviction that I am taking the bread out of the mouths of Robin and Vicky.

March 22nd. — Completely amazed by laconic postcard from Robert to say that local Registry Office can supply us with house-parlour*man*, and if I am experiencing difficulty in finding anyone, had we not better engage him? I telegraph back Yes, and then feel that I have made a mistake, but Rose says No, and refuses to let me rush out and telegraph again, for which, on subsequent calmer reflection, I feel grateful to her — and am sure that Robert would be still more so, owing to well-authenticated masculine dislike of telegrams.

Spend the evening writing immense letter to Robert enclosing list of duties of house-parlourman. (Jib at thought of being called by him in the mornings with early tea, and consult Rose, who says boldly, Think of waiters in Foreign Hotels! — which I do, and am reminded at once of many embarrassing episodes which I would rather forget.) Also send detailed instructions to Robert regarding the announcement of this innovation to Cook. Rose again takes up modern and fearless attitude, and says that Cook, mark her words, will be delighted.

I spend much of the night thinking over the whole question of running the house successfully, and tell myself — not by any means for the first time — that my abilities are very, very deficient in this direction. Just as the realisation of this threatens to overwhelm me altogether, I fall asleep.

March 26th. — Return home. Try to tell Robert all about London, but Aladdin lamp flares up, which interferes, and have also to deal with correspondence concerning Women's Institute Monthly Meeting, replacement of broken bedroom tumblers—attributed to Ethel—disappearance of one pyjama-jacket and two table-napkins in the wash, and instructions to house-parlourman concerning his duties. (*Mem.*: Must certainly make it crystal-clear that acceptable formula, when receiving an order, is not "Right-oh!" Cannot, at the moment, think how to word this, but must work it out, and then deliver with firmness and precision.)

Robert very kind about London, but perhaps rather more interested in my having met Barbara Blenkinsop —which, after all, I can do almost any day in the village —than in my views on theatres or remarkable increase of traffic in recent years. Tell Robert by degrees about my new clothes. He asks when I expect to wear them, and I reply that one never knows—which is only too true—and conversation closes.

March 28th.—Read admirable, but profoundly discouraging, article in weekly paper relating to Bernard Shaw's women, but applying to most of us. Realise— not for the first time—that intelligent women can perhaps best perform their duty towards their own sex by devastating process of telling them the truth about themselves. At the same time, cannot feel that I shall really enjoy hearing it. Ultimate paragraph of article, moreover, continues to haunt me most unpleasantly with reference to own undoubted vulnerability where Robin and Vicky are concerned. Have very often wondered if Mothers are not rather A Mistake altogether, and now definitely come to the conclusion that they *are*.

April 2nd.—Barbara calls. Can she, she says, speak to me in *confidence*? I assure her that she can, and at once put Helen Wills and kitten out of the window in order to establish confidential atmosphere. Sit, seething with excitement, in the hope that I am at least going to be told that Barbara is engaged. Try to keep this out of sight, and to maintain expression of earnest and sympathetic attention only, whilst Barbara says that it is sometimes very difficult to know which way Duty lies, that she has always thought a true woman's highest vocation is home-making, and that the love of a Good Man is the crown of life. I say Yes, Yes, to all of this. (Discover, on thinking it over, that I do not agree with any of it, and am shocked at my own extraordinary duplicity.)

Barbara at length admits that Crosbie Carruthers, a man she met in town, has asked her to marry him—he did it, she says, at the Zoo—and go out with him as his wife to the Himalayas. This, says Barbara, is where all becomes difficult. She may be old-fashioned—no doubt she is—but can she leave her mother alone? No, she cannot. Can she, on the other hand, give up dear Crosbie, who has never loved a girl before, and says that he never will again? No, she cannot.

Barbara weeps. I kiss her. Robert comes in, he talks of swine-fever, all further confidences become impossible. Barbara takes her leave immediately after tea, only asking if I could look in on her mother and have a Little Talk? I reluctantly agree to do so, and she mounts her bicycle and rides off. Robert says, That girl holds herself well, but it's a pity she has those ankles.

April 4th.—Go to see old Mrs. Blenkinsop. She is, as usual, swathed in shawls, but has exchanged *Lord Beaconsfield* for *Froude and Carlyle.* She says that I am very good to come and see a poor old woman, and that she often wonders how it is that so many of the younger generation seem to find their way to her by instinct. Is it, she suggests, because her *heart* has somehow kept young, in spite of her grey hair and wrinkles, ha-ha-ha, and so she has always been able to find the Silver Lining, she is thankful to say. I circuitously approach the topic of Barbara. Mrs. B. at once says that the young are very hard and selfish. This is natural, perhaps, but it saddens her. Not on her own account—no, no, no—but because she cannot bear to think of what Barbara will have to suffer from remorse when it is Too Late.

Feel a strong inclination to point out that this is *not* finding the Silver Lining, but refrain. Long monologue from old Mrs. B. follows. Main points that emerge are: (*a*) That Mrs. B. has not got very many more years to spend amongst us; (*b*) that all her life has been given up to others, but that she deserves no credit for this, as it is just the way she is made; (*c*) that all she wants is to see her Barbara happy, and it matters nothing at all that she herself should be left alone and helpless in her old age, and no one is to give a thought to that for a moment. Finally, that it has never been her way to think of herself or of her own feelings. People have often said to her that they believe she *has* no self—simply none at all.

Pause, which I do not attempt to fill, ensues.

We return to Barbara, and Mrs. B. says it is very natural that a girl should be wrapped up in her own little concerns. I feel that we are getting no farther, and boldly introduce the name of Crosbie Carruthers. Terrific effect on Mrs. B., who puts her hand on her heart, leans back, and begins to gasp and turn blue. She is sorry, she pants, to be so foolish, but it is now many nights since she has had any sleep at all, and the strain is beginning to tell. I must forgive her. I hastily do forgive her, and depart.

Very, very unsatisfactory interview.

Am told, on my way home, by Mrs. S. of the *Cross and Keys*, that a gentleman is staying there who is said to be engaged to Miss Blenkinsop, but the old lady won't hear of it, and he seems such a nice gentleman too, though perhaps not quite as young as some, and do I think the Himalayas would be All Right if there was a baby coming along? Exchange speculations and comments with Mrs. S. for some time before recollecting that the whole thing is supposed to be private, and that in any case gossip is undesirable.

Am met at home by Mademoiselle with intelligent enquiry as to the prospects of Miss Blenkinsop's immediate marriage, and the attitude adopted by Mrs. B. *Le cœur d'une mère*, says Mademoiselle sentimentally. Even the infant Vicky suddenly demands if that gentleman at the *Cross and Keys* is really Miss Blenkinsop's True Love? At this, Mademoiselle screams, *Ah, nom Dieu, ces enfants anglais!* and is much upset at impropriety of Vicky's language.

Even Robert enquires What All This Is about Barbara Blenkinsop? I explain, and he returns—very, very briefly—that old Mrs. Blenkinsop ought to be Shot—

which gets us no farther, but meets with my entire approval.

April 10th.—Entire parish now seething with the *affaire* Blenkinsop. Old Mrs. B. falls ill, and retires to bed. Barbara bicycles madly up and down between her mother and the garden of the *Cross and Keys*, where C. C. spends much time reading copies of *The Times of India* and smoking small cigars. We are all asked by Barbara What she Ought to Do, and all give different advice. Deadlock appears to have been reached, when C. C. suddenly announces that he is summoned to London and must have an answer One Way or the Other immediately.

Old Mrs. B.—who has been getting better and taking Port—instantly gets worse again and says that she will not long stand in the way of dear Barbara's happiness.

Period of fearful stress sets in, and Barbara and C. C. say Good-bye in the front sitting-room of the *Cross and Keys*. They have, says Barbara in tears, parted For Ever, and Life is Over, and will I take the Guides' Meeting for her to-night—which I agree to do.

April 12th.—Return of Robin for the holidays. He has a cold, and, as usual, is short of handkerchiefs. I write to the Matron about this, but have no slightest hope of receiving either handkerchiefs or rational explanation of their disappearance.

Receive a letter from Mary K. with postscript: Is it true that Barbara Blenkinsop is engaged to be married? and am also asked the same question by Lady B., who looks in on her way to some ducal function on the other side of the county. Have no time in which to enjoy being in the superior position of bestowing information, as Lady B. at once adds that *she* always advises girls to marry, no matter what the man is like, as any husband is better than none, and there are not nearly enough to go round.

I immediately refer to Rose's collection of distinguished Feminists, giving her to understand that I know them all well and intimately, and have frequently discussed the subject with them. Lady B. waves her hand—(in elegant white kid, new, not cleaned)—and declares That may be all very well, but if they could have got *husbands* they wouldn't *be* Feminists. I instantly assert that all have had husbands, and some two or three. This may or may not be true, but have seldom known stronger homicidal impulse. Final straw is added when Lady B. amiably observes that *I*, at least, have nothing to complain of, as she always thinks Robert such a safe, respectable husband for *any* woman. Her car moves off, leaving her with, as usual, the last word.

Evolve in my own mind merry fantasy in which members of the Royal Family visit the neighbourhood and honour Robert and myself by becoming our guests at luncheon. (Cannot quite fit house-parlourman into this scheme, but gloss over that aspect of the case.) Robert has just been raised to the peerage, and I am, with a slight and gracious inclination of the head, taking precedence of Lady B. at large dinner-party, when Vicky comes in to say that the Scissor-Grinder is at the door, and if we haven't anything to grind, he'll be pleased to attend to the clocks or rivet any china.

Look for Robin and eventually find him with the cat, shut up into totally unventilated linen-cupboard, eating cheese which he says he found on the back stairs.

(Undoubtedly, a certain irony can be found in the fact that I have recently been appointed to new Guardians Committee, and am expected to visit Workhouse, etc., with particular reference to children's quarters, in order that I may offer valuable suggestions on questions of hygiene and general welfare of inmates. . . . Can only hope that fellow-members of the Committee will never be inspired to submit my own domestic arrangements to similar inspection.)

April 14th.—Cook electrifies me by asking me if I have heard that Miss Barbara Blenkinsop's engagement is on again, it's all over the village. The gentleman, she says, came down by the 8.45 last night, and is at the *Cross and Keys.* As it is exactly 9.45 A.M. when she tells me this, I ask how she knows? Cook merely repeats that It is All Over the Village, and that Miss Barbara will quite as like as not be married by special licence, and old Mrs. B. is in such a way as never was. Am disconcerted to find that Cook and I have been talking our heads off for the better part of forty minutes before I remember again that gossip is both undignified and undesirable.

Similar information also reaches us from six different quarters in the village. No less than three motor-cars and two bicycles are to be seen outside old Mrs. B.'s cottage, but no one emerges, and I am obliged to suggest that Our Vicar's Wife should come home with me to lunch. This she does, after many demurs, and gets cottage-pie—(too much onion)—rice-shape, and stewed prunes. Should have sent to the farm for cream, if I had known.

April 15th.—Old Mrs. Blenkinsop reported to have Come Round. Elderly unmarried female Blenkinsop, referred to as Cousin Maud, has suddenly materialised, and offered to live with her—Our Vicar has come out boldly in support of this scheme—and Crosbie Carruthers has given Barbara engagement ring with three stones, said to be rare Indian Topazes, and has gone up to town to Make Arrangements.

April 18th.—Receive visit from Barbara, who begs that I will escort her to London for quiet and immediate wedding. Am obliged to refuse, owing to bad colds of Robin and Vicky, general instability of domestic staff, and customary unsatisfactory financial situation. Offer then passed on to Our Vicar's Wife, who at once accepts it. I undertake, however, at Barbara's urgent request, to look in as often as possible on her mother. Will I, adds Barbara, make it clear that she is not losing a Daughter, but only gaining a Son, and two years will soon be over, and at the end of that time dear Crosbie will bring her home to England? I recklessly commit myself to doing anything and everything, and write to the Army and Navy Stores for a luncheon-basket, to give as wedding-present to Barbara. The Girl Guides present her with a sugar-castor and a waste-paper basket embossed with raffia flowers. Lady B. sends a chafing-dish with a card bearing illegible and far-fetched joke connected with Indian curries. We all agree that this is not in the least amusing. Mademoiselle causes Vicky to present Barbara with small tray-cloth, on which two hearts are worked in cross-stitch.

April 19th. — Both children simultaneously develop incredibly low complaint known as "pink-eye" that everyone unites in telling me is peculiar to the more saliently neglected and under-fed section of the juvenile population in the East End of London.

Vicky has a high temperature and is put to bed, while Robin remains on his feet, but is not allowed out of doors until present cold winds are over. I leave Vicky to Mademoiselle and *Les Mémoires d'un Âne* in the night-nursery, and undertake to amuse Robin downstairs. He says that he has a Splendid Idea. This turns out to be that I should play the piano, whilst he simultaneously sets off the gramophone, the musical-box, and the chiming clock.

I protest.

Robin implores, and says It will be just like an Orchestra. (Shade of Dame Ethel Smyth, whose Reminiscences I have just been reading!) I weakly yield, and attack, *con spirito*, "The Broadway Melody" in the key of C Major. Robin, in great excitement, starts the clock, puts "Mucking About the Garden" on the gramophone, and winds up the musical-box, which tinkles out the Waltz from *Florodora* in a tinny sort of way, and no recognisable key. Robin springs about and cheers. I watch him sympathetically and keep down, at his request, the loud pedal.

The door is flung open by house-parlourman, and Lady B. enters, wearing brand-new green Kasha with squirrel collar, and hat to match, and accompanied by military-looking friend.

Have no wish to record subsequent few minutes, in which I endeavour to combine graceful greetings to Lady B. and the military friend with simple and yet dignified explanation of singular state of affairs presented to them, and unobtrusive directions to Robin to switch off musical-box and gramophone and betake himself and his pink-eye upstairs. (Should not have minded quite so much if it had been "Classical Memories", which I also possess, or even a Layton and Johnstone duet.)

Military friend tactfully pretends absorption in the nearest bookcase until this is over, when he emerges with breezy observation concerning *Bulldog Drummond*.

Lady B. at once informs him that he must not say that kind of thing to *me*, as I am so Very Literary. After this, the military friend looks at me with unconcealed horror, and does not attempt to speak to me again.

On the whole, am much relieved when the call is over.

April 20th. — Vicky develops unmistakable measles, and doctor says that Robin may follow suit any day. Infection must have been picked up at Aunt Gertrude's, and shall write and tell her so.

Extraordinary and nightmare-like state of affairs sets in, and I alternate between making lemonade for Vicky and telling her the story of *Frederick and the Picnic* upstairs, and bathing Robin's pink-eye with boracic lotion and reading *The Coral Island* to him downstairs.

Mademoiselle is *dévouée* in the extreme, and utterly

refuses to let anyone but herself sleep in Vicky's room, but find it difficult to understand exactly on what principle it is that she persists in wearing a *peignoir* and *pantoufles* day and night alike. She is also unwearied in recommending very strange *tisanes*, which she proposes to brew herself from herbs—fortunately unobtainable—in the garden.

Robert, in this crisis, is less helpful than I could wish, and takes up characteristically masculine attitude that We are All Making a Great Fuss about Very Little, and the whole thing has been got up for the express purpose of putting him to inconvenience—(which, however, it does not do, as he stays out all day, and insists on having dinner exactly the same as usual every evening).

Vicky incredibly and alarmingly good, Robin almost equally so in patches, but renders himself unpopular by leaving smears of plasticine, pools of paint-water, and even blots of ink on much of the furniture.

Weather very cold and rainy, and none of the fires will burn up. Cannot say why this is, but it adds considerably to condition of gloom and exhaustion which I feel to be gaining upon me hourly.

April 25th.—Vicky recovering slowly, Robin showing no signs of measles. Am myself victim of curious and unpleasant form of chill, no doubt due to over-fatigue.

May 7th.—Resume Diary after long and deplorable interlude, vanquished chill having suddenly reappeared with immense force and fury, and revealed itself as measles. Robin, on same day, begins to cough, and expensive hospital nurse materialises and takes complete charge. She proves kind and efficient, and brings me messages from the children, and realistic drawing from Robin entitled: "Ill person being eaten up by jerms".

Robert, the nurse, and I decide in conclave that the children shall be sent to Bude for a fortnight with Nurse, and Mademoiselle given a holiday in which to recover from her exertions. I am to join the Bude party when doctor permits.

Robert goes to make this announcement to the nursery, and comes back with fatal news that Mademoiselle is *blessée*, and that the more he asks her to explain, the more monosyllabic she becomes. Am not allowed either to see her or to write explanation and soothing note, and am far from reassured by Vicky's report that Mademoiselle, bathing her, has wept, and said that in England there are hearts of stone.

May 12th.—Further interlude, this time owing to trouble with the eyes. The children and hospital nurse depart on the 9th, and I am left to gloomy period of total inactivity and lack of occupation. Get up after a time and prowl about in kind of semi-ecclesiastical darkness, further intensified by enormous pair of tinted spectacles. One and only comfort is that I cannot see myself in the glass. Two days ago, decide to make great effort and come down for tea, but nearly relapse, and go straight back to bed again at sight of colossal demand for the Rates, confronting me on hall-stand without so much as an envelope between us.

(*Mem.*: This sort of thing so very unlike picturesque convalescence in a novel, when heroine is gladdened by sight of spring flowers, sunshine, and what not. No mention ever made of Rates, or anything like them.)

Miss the children very much, and my chief companion is kitchen cat, a hard-bitten animal with only three and a half legs and a reputation for catching and eating a nightly average of three rabbits. We get on well together until I have recourse to the piano, when he invariably yowls and asks to be let out. On the whole, am obliged to admit that he is probably right, for I have forgotten all I ever knew, and am reduced to playing popular music by ear, which I do badly.

May 13th — Regrettable, but undeniable ray of amusement lightens general murk on hearing report, through Robert, that Cousin Maud Blenkinsop possesses a Baby Austin, and has been seen running it all round the parish with old Mrs. B., shawls and all, beside her. (It is many years since Mrs. B. gave us all to understand that if she so much as walked across the room unaided, she would certainly fall down dead.)

May 15th. — Our Vicar's Wife, hearing that I am no longer in quarantine, comes to enliven me. Greet her with an enthusiasm to which she must, I fear, be unaccustomed, as it appears to startle her. Endeavour to explain it (perhaps a little tactlessly) by saying that I have been alone so long . . . Robert out all day . . . children at Bude . . . and end up with quotation to the effect that I never hear the sweet music of speech, and start at the sound of my own. Can see by the way Our Vicar's Wife receives this that she does not recognise it as a quotation, and believes the measles to have affected my brain. (Query: Perhaps she is right?) More normal atmosphere established by a plea from Our Vicar's Wife that kitchen cat may be put out of the room. It is, she knows, very foolish of her, but the presence of a cat makes her feel faint. Her grandmother was exactly the same. Put a cat into the same room as her grandmother, hidden under the sofa if you liked, and in two minutes the grandmother would say: "I believe there's a cat in this room", and at once turn queer. I hastily put kitchen cat out of the window, and we agree that heredity is very odd.

Incredible number of births, marriages, and deaths appear to have taken place in the parish in the last four weeks; also Mrs. W. has dismissed her cook and cannot get another one, Our Vicar has written a letter about Drains to the local paper and it has been put in, and Lady B. has been seen in a new car. To this Our Vicar's Wife adds rhetorically: Why not an aeroplane, she would like to know? (Why not, indeed?)

Finally a Committee Meeting has been held—at which, she interpolates hastily, I was much missed—and a Garden Fête arranged, in aid of funds for Village Hall. It would be so nice, she adds optimistically, if the Fête could be held *here*. I agree that it would, and stifle a misgiving that Robert may not agree. In any case, he knows, and I know, and Our Vicar's Wife knows, that Fête will have to take place here, as there isn't anywhere else.

Our Vicar's Wife suddenly discovers that it is six o'clock, exclaims that she is shocked, and attempts *fausse sortie*, only to return with urgent recommendation to me to try Valentine's Meat Juice, which once practically, under Providence, saved Our Vicar's uncle's life. Story of uncle's illness, convalescence, recovery, and subsequent death at the age of eighty-one, follows. Am unable to resist telling her, in return, about wonderful effect of Bemax on Mary Kellway's youngest, and this leads—curiously enough—to the novels of Anthony Trollope, death of the Begum of Bhopal, and scenery in the Lake Country.

At twenty minutes to seven, Our Vicar's Wife is again shocked, and rushes out of the house. She meets Robert on the doorstep and stops to tell him that I am as thin as a rake, and a very bad colour, and the eyes, after measles, often give rise to serious trouble. Robert, so far as I can hear, makes no answer to any of it, and Our Vicar's Wife finally departs.

(Query here suggests itself: Is not silence frequently more efficacious than the utmost eloquence? Answer probably yes. Must try to remember this more often than I do.)

May 16th.—But for disappointing children, should be much tempted to abandon scheme for my complete restoration to health at Bude. Weather icy cold, self feeble and more than inclined to feverishness, and Mademoiselle, who was to have come with me, and helped with children, now writes that she is *désolée*, but has developed *une angine*. Do not know what this is, and have alarming thoughts about Angina Pectoris, but dictionary reassures me. I say to Robert: "After all, shouldn't I get well just as quickly at home?" He replies briefly: "Better go," and I perceive that his mind is made up. After a moment he suggests—but without real conviction—that I might like to invite Our Vicar's Wife to come with me. I reply with a look only, and suggestion falls to the ground.

Further demand for the Rates arrives, and Cook sends up jelly once more for lunch. I offer it to Helen Wills, who gives one heave, and turns away. Feel that this would more than justify me in sending down entire dish untouched, but Cook will certainly give notice if I do, and cannot face possibility.

Go to sleep in the afternoon, and awake sufficiently restored to do what I have long contemplated, and Go Through my clothes. Result so depressing that I wish I had never done it. Have nothing fit to wear, and if I had, should look like a scarecrow in it at present. Send off parcel with knitted red cardigan, two evening dresses (much too short for present mode), three out-of-date hats, and tweed skirt that bags at the knees, to Jumble Sale. Make out a list of all the new clothes I require, get pleasantly excited about them, am again confronted with the Rates, and put the list in the fire.

May 17th.—Robert drives me to North Road station to catch train for Bude. Temperature has fallen again, and I ask Robert if it is below zero. He replies briefly and untruthfully that the day will get warmer as it goes on, and no doubt Bude will be one blaze of sunshine. We arrive early, and sit on a bench on the platform next to a young woman with a cough, who takes one look at me and then says: "Dreadful, isn't it?" Cannot help feeling that she has summarised the whole situation quite admirably. Journey ensues, and proves chilly and exhausting. Rain lashes at the windows, and every time carriage door opens—which is often—gust of icy wind, mysteriously blowing in two opposite directions at once, goes up my legs and down back of my neck. Have not told children by what train I am arriving, so no one meets me, not even bus on which I had counted. Am, however, secretly thankful, as this gives me an excuse for taking a taxi. Reach lodgings at rather uninspiring hour of 2.45, too early for tea or bed, which constitute present summit of my ambitions. Uproarious welcome from children, both in blooming health and riotous spirits, makes up for everything.

May 19th.—Recovery definitely in sight, although almost certainly retarded by landlady's inspiration of sending up a nice jelly for supper on evening of arrival. Rooms reasonably comfortable—(except for extreme cold, which is, says landlady, quite unheard-of at this or any other time of year)—all is linoleum, pink and gold china, and enlarged photographs of females in lace collars and males with long moustaches and bow ties. Robin, Vicky, and the hospital nurse—retained at vast expense as a temporary substitute for Mademoiselle—have apparently braved the weather and spent much time on the Breakwater. Vicky has also made friends with a little dog, whose name she alleges to be "Baby", a gentleman who sells papers, another gentleman who drives about in a Sunbeam, and the head-waiter from the Hotel. I tell her about Mademoiselle's illness, and after a silence she says "Oh!" in tones of brassy indifference, and resumes topic of little dog "Baby". Robin, from whom I cannot help hoping better things, makes no comment except "Is she?" and immediately adds a request for a banana.

May 23rd.—Sudden warm afternoon, children take off their shoes and dash into pools, landlady says that it's often like this on the *last* day of a visit to the sea, she's noticed, and I take brisk walk over the cliffs, wearing thick tweed coat, and really begin to feel quite warm at the end of an hour. Pack suit-case after children are in bed, register resolution never to let stewed prunes and custard form part of any meal ever again as long as I live, and thankfully write postcard to Robert, announcing time of our arrival at home to-morrow.

May 28th.—Mademoiselle returns, and is greeted with enthusiasm—to my great relief. She has on new black and white check skirt, white blouse with frills, black kid gloves, embroidered in white on the backs, and black straw hat almost entirely covered in purple violets, and informs me that the whole outfit was made by herself at a total cost of one pound, nine shillings, and fourpence-halfpenny. The French undoubtedly thrifty, and gifted in using a needle, but cannot altogether stifle conviction that a shade less economy might have produced better results.

She presents me, in the kindest way, with a present in the shape of two blue glass flower-vases, of spiral construction, and adorned with gilt knobs at many unexpected points. Vicky receives a large artificial-silk red rose, which she fortunately appears to admire, and Robin a small affair in wire that is intended, says Mademoiselle, to extract the stones out of cherries.

(*Mem.*: Interesting to ascertain number of these ingenious contrivances sold in a year.)

Am privately rather overcome by Mademoiselle's generosity, and wish that we could reach the level of the French in what they themselves describe as *petits soins*.

May 30th.—Receive telephone invitation to lunch with the Frobishers on Sunday. I accept, less because I want to see them than because a change from domestic roast beef and gooseberry-tart always pleasant; moreover, absence makes work lighter for the servants. (*Mem.*: Candid and intelligent self-examination as to motive, etc., often leads to very distressing revelations.)

Constrained by conscience, and recollection of promise to Barbara, to go and call on old Mrs. Blenkinsop. Receive many kind enquiries in village as to my complete recovery from measles, but observe singular tendency on part of everybody else to treat this very serious affliction as a joke.

Find old Mrs. B.'s cottage in unheard-of condition of hygienic ventilation, no doubt attributable to Cousin Maud. Windows all wide open, and casement curtains flapping in every direction, very cold east wind more than noticeable. Mrs. B.—(surely fewer shawls than formerly?)—sitting quite close to open window, and not far from equally open door, seems to have turned curious shade of pale-blue, and shows tendency to shiver. Room smells strongly of furniture polish and black-lead. Fireplace, indeed, exhibits recent handsome application of the latter, and has evidently not held fire for days past. Old Mrs. B. more silent than of old, and makes no reference to silver linings and the like. (Can spirit of optimism have been blown away by living in continual severe draught?) Cousin Maud comes in almost immediately. Have met her once before, and say so, but she makes it clear that this encounter left no impression, and has entirely escaped her memory. Am convinced that Cousin Maud is one of those people who pride themselves on always speaking the truth. She is wearing brick-red sweater—feel sure she knitted it herself—tweed skirt, longer at the back than in front—and large row of pearl beads. Has very hearty and emphatic manner, and uses many slang expressions.

I ask for news of Barbara, and Mrs. B.—(voice a mere bleat, by comparison with Cousin Maud's)—says that the dear child will be coming down once more before she sails, and that continued partings are the lot of the Aged, and to be expected. I begin to hope that she is approaching her old form, but all is stopped by Cousin Maud, who shouts out that we're not to talk Rot, and it's a jolly good thing Barbara has got Off the Hooks at last, poor old girl.

Take my leave feeling depressed. Old Mrs. B. rolls her eyes at me as I say good-bye and mutters something about not being here much longer, but this is drowned by hearty laughter from Cousin Maud, who declares that she is Nothing but an old Humbug and will See Us All Out.

Am escorted to the front gate by Cousin Maud, who tells me what a topping thing it is for old Mrs. B. to be taken out of herself a bit, and asks if it isn't good to be Alive on a bracing day like this? Should like to reply that it would be far better for some of us to be dead, in my opinion, but spirit for this repartee fails me, and

I weakly reply that I know what she means. I go away before she has time to slap me on the back, which I feel certain will be the next thing.

June 1st.—Sunday lunch with the Frobishers, and four guests staying in the house with them—introduced as, apparently, Colonel and Mrs. Brightpie—(which seems impossible)—Sir William Reddie—or Ready, or Reddy, or perhaps even Reddeigh—and My sister Violet. Latter quite astonishingly pretty, and wearing admirable flowered tussore that I, as usual, mentally try upon myself, only to realise that it would undoubtedly suggest melancholy saying concerning mutton dressed as lamb.

The Colonel sits next to me at lunch, and we talk about fishing, which I have never attempted, and look upon as cruelty to animals, but this, with undoubted hypocrisy and moral cowardice, I conceal. Robert has My sister Violet, and I hear him at intervals telling her about the pigs, which seems odd, but she looks pleased, so perhaps is interested.

Conversation suddenly becomes general, as topic of present-day Dentistry is introduced by Lady F. We all, except Robert, who eats bread, have much to say.

(*Mem.*: Remember to direct conversation into similar channel, when customary periodical deathly silence descends upon guests at my own table.)

Weather is wet and cold, and had confidently hoped to escape tour of the garden, but this is not to be, and directly lunch is over we rush out into the damp. Boughs drip on to our heads and water squelches beneath our feet, but rhododendrons and lupins undoubtedly very magnificent, and references to Ruth Draper not more numerous than usual.

I find myself walking with Mrs. Brightpie (?), who evidently knows all that can be known about a garden. Fortunately she is prepared to originate all the comments herself, and I need only say, "Yes, isn't that an attractive variety?" and so on.

After prolonged inspection, we retrace steps, and this time find myself with Sir William R. and Lady F. talking about grass. Realise with horror that we are now making our way towards the *stables*. Nothing whatever to be done about it, except keep as far away from the horses as possible, and refrain from any comment whatever, in hopes of concealing that I know nothing about horses except that they frighten me. Robert, I notice, looks sorry for me, and places himself between me and terrifying-looking animal that glares out at me from loose-box and curls up its lip. Feel grateful to him, and eventually leave stables with shattered nerves and soaking wet shoes. Exchange customary graceful farewells with host and hostess, saying how much I have enjoyed coming.

(Query here suggests itself, as often before: Is it utterly impossible to combine the amenities of civilisation with even the minimum of honesty required to satisfy the voice of conscience? Answer still in abeyance at present.)

Robert goes to Evening Service, and I play Halma with Vicky. She says that she wants to go to school, and produces string of excellent reasons why she should do so. I say that I will think it over, but am aware, by previous experience, that Vicky has almost miraculous aptitude for getting her own way, and will probably succeed in this instance as in others.

Rather depressing Sunday supper—cold beef, baked potatoes, salad, and depleted cold tart—after which I write to Rose, the Cleaners, the Army and Navy Stores, and the County Secretary of the Women's Institute, and Robert goes to sleep over the *Sunday Pictorial*.

June 3rd.—Astounding and enchanting change in the weather, which becomes warm. I carry chair, writing-materials, rug, and cushion into the garden, but am called in to have a look at the Pantry Sink, please, as it seems to have blocked itself up. Attempted return to garden frustrated by arrival of note from the village concerning Garden Fête arrangements, which requires immediate answer, necessity for speaking to the butcher on the telephone, and sudden realisation that Laundry List hasn't yet been made out, and the Van will be here at eleven.

Shortly after this, Mrs. S. arrives from the village, to collect jumble for Garden Fête, which takes time. After lunch, sky clouds over, and Mademoiselle and Vicky kindly help me to carry chair, writing-materials, rug, and cushion into the house again.

Robert receives letter by second post announcing death of his godfather, aged ninety-seven, and decides to go to the funeral on 5th June.

(*Mem.*: Curious, but authenticated fact, that a funeral is the only gathering to which the majority of men ever go willingly. Should like to think out why this should be so, but must instead unearth top-hat and other accoutrements of woe and try if open air will remove smell of naphthalene.)

June 7th.—Receive letter—(Why, in Heaven's name, not telegram?)—from Robert, to announce that godfather has left him Five Hundred Pounds. This strikes me as so utterly incredible and magnificent that I shed tears of pure relief and satisfaction. Mademoiselle comes in, in the midst of them, and on receiving explanation kisses me on both cheeks and exclaims *Ah, je m'en doutais! Voilà bien ce bon Saint Antoine!* Can only draw conclusion that she has, most touchingly, been petitioning Heaven on our behalf, and very nearly weep again at the thought.

June 9th.—Return, yesterday, of Robert, and have every reason to believe that, though neither talkative nor exuberant, he fully appreciates newly achieved stability of financial position. He warmly concurs in my suggestion that great-aunt's diamond ring should be retrieved from Plymouth pawnbroker's in time to figure at our next excitement, which is the Garden Fête, and I accordingly hasten to Plymouth by earliest available bus.

Not only do I return with ring—(pawnbroker, after a glance at the calendar, congratulates me on being just in time)—but have also purchased new hat for myself, many yards of material for Vicky's frocks, a Hornby train for Robin, several gramophone records, and a small mauve bag for Mademoiselle. All give the utmost satisfaction, and I furthermore arrange to have hot lobster and fruit salad for dinner—these, however, not a great success with Robert, unfortunately, and he suggests—though kindly—that I was perhaps thinking more of my own tastes than of his, when devising this form of celebration. Must regretfully acknowledge truth in this.

June 12th.—Nothing spoken of but weather for Fête, at moment propitious—but who can say whether similar conditions will prevail on 17th?—relative merits of having the Tea laid under the oak trees or near the tennis-court, outside price that can be reasonably asked for articles on Jumble Stall, desirability of having Ice-cream combined with Lemonade Stall, and the like. Date fortunately coincides with Robin's half-term, and I feel that he must and shall come home for the occasion. Expense, as I point out to Robert, now nothing to us. He yields. I become reckless, have thoughts of a House-party, and invite Rose to come down from London. She accepts.

June 17th.—Entire household rises practically at dawn, in order to take part in active preparations for Garden Fête. Mademoiselle reported to have refused breakfast in order to put final stitches in embroidered pink satin boot-bag for Fancy Stall, which she has, to my certain knowledge, been working at for the past six weeks. At ten o'clock Our Vicar's Wife dashes in to ask what I think of the weather, and to say that she cannot stop a moment. At eleven she is still here, and has been joined by several stall-holders, and tiresome local couple called White, who want to know if there will be a Tennis Tournament, and if not, is there not still time to organise one?

I reply curtly in the negative to both suggestions and they depart, looking huffed. Our Vicar's Wife says that this may have lost us their patronage at the Fête altogether, and that Mrs. White's mother, who is staying with them, is said to be rich, and might easily have been worth a couple of pounds to us.

Diversion fortunately occasioned by unexpected arrival of solid and respectable-looking claret-coloured motor-car, from which Barbara and Crosbie Carruthers emerge. Barbara is excited; C. C. remains calm but looks benevolent. Our Vicar's Wife screams, and throws a pair of scissors wildly into the air. (They are eventually found in Bran Tub, containing Twopenny Dips, and are the cause of much trouble, as small child who fishes them out maintains them to be *bona fide* dip and refuses to give them up.)

Sudden arrival of Cissie Crabbe on way to Land's End (wearing curious wool hat which I at once feel would look better on Jumble Stall) is followed by cold lunch. Just as tinned pineapple and junket stage is passed, Robin informs me that there are people beginning to arrive, and we all disperse in desperate haste and excitement, to reappear in best clothes. I wear red foulard and new red hat, but find—as usual—that every petticoat I have in the world is either rather too long or much too short. Mademoiselle comes to the rescue and puts safety-pins in shoulder-straps, one of which becomes unfastened later and causes me great suffering. Rose, also as usual, looks nicer than anybody else in delightful green delaine. Cissie Crabbe also produces reasonably attractive dress, but detracts from effect with numerous scarab rings, cameo brooches, tulle scarves, enamel buckles, and barbaric necklaces. More-over, she clings (I think mistakenly) to little wool hat, which looks odd.

Lady Frobisher arrives—ten minutes too early—to open Fête, and is walked about by Robert until Our Vicar says, Well, he thinks perhaps that we are now all gathered together. . . . (Have profane impulse to add "*In the sight of God*", but naturally stifle it.) Lady F. is poised gracefully on little bank under the chestnut tree, Our Vicar beside her, Robert and myself modestly retiring a few paces behind, Our Vicar's Wife kindly, but mistakenly, trying to induce various unsuitable people to mount bank—which she humorously refers to as the Platform—when all is thrown into confusion by sensational arrival of colossal Bentley containing Lady B.—in sapphire-blue and pearls—with escort of fashionable creatures, male and female, apparently dressed for Ascot.

"Go on, go on!" says Lady B., waving hand in white kid glove, and dropping small jewelled bag, lace parasol, and embroidered handkerchief as she does so. Great confusion while these articles are picked up and restored, but at last we do go on, and Lady F. says what a pleasure it is to her to be here to-day, what a desirable asset a Village Hall is, and much else to the same effect. Our Vicar thanks her for coming here to-day—so many claims upon her time—Robert seconds him with almost incredible brevity—someone else thanks Robert and myself for throwing open these magnificent grounds—(tennis-court, three flower borders, and microscopic shrubbery)—I look at Robert, who shakes his head, thus obliging me to make necessary reply myself, and

Our Vicar's Wife, with undeniable presence of mind, darts forward and reminds Lady F. that she has forgotten to declare the Fête open. This is at once done, and we disperse to stalls and side-shows.

Everyone buys nobly, unsuitable articles are raffled —(raffling illegal, winner to pay sixpence)—guesses are made as to contents of sealed boxes, number of currants in large cake, weight of bilious-looking ham, and so on. Band arrives, is established on lawn, and plays selections from *The Geisha*. Sports, tea, and dancing on the tennis-lawn all successful—(except possibly from point of view of future tennis-parties)—and even Robin and Vicky do not dream of eating final icecream cornets, and retiring to bed, until ten o'clock.

Robert, Rose, Cissie Crabbe, Helen Wills, and myself all sit in the drawing-room in pleasant state of exhaustion, and congratulate ourselves and one another. Robert has information, no doubt reliable, but source remains mysterious, to the effect, that we have Cleared Three Figures. All, for the moment, is *couleur-de-rose*.

June 23rd.—Tennis-party at wealthy and elaborate house, to which Robert and I now bidden for the first time. (Also, probably, the last.) Immense opulence of host and hostess at once discernible in fabulous display of deck-chairs, all of complete stability and miraculous cleanliness. Am introduced to youngish lady in yellow, and serious young man with horn-rimmed spectacles. Lady in yellow says at once that she is sure I have a lovely garden. (Why?)

Elderly, but efficient-looking, partner is assigned to me, and we play against the horn-rimmed spectacles and agile young creature in expensive crêpe-de-chine. Realise at once that all three play very much better tennis than I do. Still worse, realise that *they* realise this. Just as we begin, my partner observes gravely that he ought to tell me he is a left-handed player. Cannot imagine what he expects me to do about it, lose my head, and reply madly that That is Splendid.

Game proceeds, I serve several double-faults, and elderly partner becomes graver and graver. At beginning of each game he looks at me and repeats score with fearful distinctness, which, as it is never in our favour, entirely unnerves me. At "Six-*one*" we leave the court and silently seek chairs as far removed from one another as possible. Find myself in vicinity of Our Member, and we talk about the Mace, peeresses in the House of Lords—on which we differ—winter sports, and Alsatian dogs.

Robert plays tennis, and does well.

At tea, am struck, as usual, by infinite superiority of other people's food to my own.

Conversation turns upon Lady B. and everyone says she is really very kind-hearted, and follows this up by anecdotes illustrating all her less attractive qualities. Youngish lady in yellow declares that she met Lady B. last week in London, face three inches thick in new sunburn-tan. Can quite believe it. Feel much more at home after this, and conscious of new bond of union cementing entire party. Sidelight thus thrown upon human nature regrettable, but not to be denied. Even tennis improves after this. Serve fewer double-faults, but still cannot quite escape conviction that whoever plays with me invariably loses the set—which I cannot believe to be mere coincidence.

Suggest to Robert, on the way home, that I had better give up tennis altogether, to which, after long silence—during which I hope he is perhaps evolving short speech that shall be at once complimentary and yet convincing—he replies that he does not know what I could take up instead. As I do not know either, the subject is dropped, and we return home in silence.

June 27th.—Cook says that unless I am willing to let her have the Sweep, she cannot possibly be responsible for the stove. I say that of course she can have the Sweep. If not, Cook returns, totally disregarding this, she really can't say what won't happen. I reiterate my complete readiness to send the Sweep a summons on the instant, and Cook continues to look away from me and to repeat that unless I *will* agree to having the Sweep in, there's no knowing.

This dialogue—cannot say why—upsets me for the remainder of the day.

June 30th.—The Sweep comes, and devastates the entire day. Bath-water and meals are alike cold, and soot appears quite irrelevantly in portions of the house totally removed from sphere of Sweep's activities. Am called upon in the middle of the day to produce twelve-and-sixpence in cash, which I cannot do. Appeal to everybody in the house, and find that nobody else can, either. Finally Cook announces that the Joint has just come and can oblige at the back door, if I don't mind its going down in the book. I do not, and the Sweep is accordingly paid and disappears on a motor-bicycle.

July 3rd.—Breakfast enlivened by letter from dear Rose written at, apparently, earthly paradise of blue sea and red rocks, on South Coast of France. She says that she is having complete rest, and enjoying congenial society of charming group of friends, and makes unprecedented suggestion that I should join her for a fortnight. I am moved to exclaim—perhaps rather thoughtlessly—that the most wonderful thing in the world must be to be a childless widow—but this is met by unsympathetic silence from Robert, which recalls me to myself, and impels me to say that that isn't in the *least* what I meant.

(*Mem.*: Should often be very, very sorry to explain exactly what it is that I *do* mean, and I am in fact conscious of deliberately avoiding self-analysis on many occasions. Do not propose, however, to go into this now or at any other time.)

I tell Robert that if it wasn't for the expense, and not having any clothes, and the servants, and leaving Vicky, I should think seriously of Rose's suggestion. Why, I enquire rhetorically, should Lady B. have a monopoly of the South of France? Robert replies, Well—and pauses for such a long while that I get agitated, and have mentally gone through the Divorce Court with him, before he ends up by saying Well, again, and picking up the *Western Morning News*. Feel—but do not say—that this, as contribution to discussion, is inadequate.

I re-read Rose's letter, and feel that I have here opportunity of a lifetime. Suddenly hear myself exclaiming passionately that Travel broadens the Mind, and am immediately reminded of Our Vicar's Wife, who frequently makes similar remark before taking Our Vicar to spend fortnight's holiday in North Wales.

Robert finally says Well, again—this time tone of voice slightly more lenient—and then asks if it is quite impossible for his bottle of Eno's to be left undisturbed on bathroom shelf?

I at once and severely condemn Mademoiselle as undoubted culprit, although guiltily aware that original suggestion probably emanated from myself. And what, I add, about the South of France? Robert looks astounded, and soon afterwards leaves the dining-room without having spoken.

I deal with my correspondence, omitting Rose's letter. Return to drawing-room and find Robert asleep behind *The Times.* Read Rose's letter all over again, and am moved to make list of clothes that I should require if I joined her, estimate of expenses—financial situation, though not scintillating, still considerably brighter than usual, owing to recent legacy—and even Notes, on back of envelope, of instructions to be given to Mademoiselle, Cook, and the tradespeople, before leaving.

July 6th.—Decide definitely on joining Rose at Ste. Agathe, and write and tell her so. Die now cast, and Rubicon crossed—or rather will be, on achieving farther side of the Channel. Robert, on the whole, takes lenient view of entire project, and says he supposes that nothing else will satisfy me, and better not count on really hot weather promised by Rose but take good supply of woollen underwear. Mademoiselle is sympathetic, but theatrical, and exclaims *C'est la Ste. Vierge qui a tout arrangé!* which sounds like a travel agency, and shocks me.

July 12th.—Pay farewell calls, and receive much good advice. Our Vicar says that it is madness to drink water anywhere in France, unless previously boiled and filtered; Our Vicar's Wife shares Robert's distrust as to climate, and advises Jaeger next the skin, and also offers loan of small travelling medicine-chest for emergencies. Discussion follows as to whether Bisulphate of Quinine is, or is not, dutiable article, and is finally brought to inconclusive conclusion by Our Vicar's pronouncing definitely that, in *any case*, Honesty is the Best Policy.

Old Mrs. Blenkinsop—whom I reluctantly visit whenever I get a letter from Barbara saying how grateful she is for my kindness—adopts quavering and enfeebled manner, and hopes she may be here to welcome me home again on my return, but implies that this is not really to be anticipated. I say Come, come, and begin well-turned sentence as to Mrs. B.'s wonderful vitality, when Cousin Maud bounces in, and inspiration fails me on the spot. What Ho! says Cousin Maud—(or at least, produces the effect of having said it, though possibly slang slightly more up-to-date than this—but not much)—What is all this about our cutting a dash on the Lido or somewhere, and leaving our home to take care of itself? Talk about the Emancipation of Females, says Cousin Maud. Should like to reply that no one, except herself, ever *does* talk about it—but feel this might reasonably be construed as uncivil, and do not want to upset unfortunate old Mrs. B., whom I now regard as a victim pure and simple. Ignore Cousin Maud, and ask old Mrs. B. what books she would advise me to take. Amount of luggage strictly limited, both as to weight and size, but could manage two very long ones, if in pocket editions, and another to be carried in coat-pocket for journey.

Old Mrs. B.—probably still intent on thought of approaching dissolution—suddenly says that there is nothing like the Bible—suggestion which I feel might more properly have been left to Our Vicar. Naturally, give her to understand that I agree, but do not commit myself further. Cousin Maud, in a positive way that annoys me, recommends No book At All, especially when crossing the sea.

We touch on literature in general—old Mrs. B. observes that much that is published nowadays seems to her unnecessary, and why so much Sex in everything? —Cousin Maud says that books collect dust, anyway. I take my leave. Am embraced by old Mrs. B. (who shows tendency to have one of her old-time Attacks, but is briskly headed off it by Cousin Maud) and slapped on the back by Cousin Maud in familiar and extremely offensive manner.

Walk home, and am overtaken by well-known blue Bentley, from which Lady B. waves elegantly and commands chauffeur to stop. He does so, and Lady B. says, Get in, Get in, never mind muddy boots—which makes me feel like a plough-boy. Good works, she supposes, have been taking me plodding round the village as usual? The way I go on, day after day, is too marvellous. Reply with utmost distinctness that I am just on the point of starting for the South of France, where I am joining party of distinguished friends. (This is not entirely untrue, since dear Rose has promised introduction to many interesting acquaintances, including Viscountess.)

Really, says Lady B., why not go at the right time of year? Or why not go all the way by sea?—yachting too marvellous. Or why not, again, make it Scotland, instead of France?

Do not reply to any of all this, and request to be put down at the corner. This is done, and Lady B. waves directions to chauffeur to drive on, but subsequently stops him again and leans out to say that she can find out all about quite inexpensive *pensions* for me if I like. I do *not* like, and we part finally.

July 14th.—Question of books to be taken abroad undecided till late hour last night. Robert says, Why take any? and Vicky proffers *Les Malheurs de Sophie*, which she puts into the very bottom of my suit-case, whence it is extracted with some difficulty by Mademoiselle later. Finally decide on *Little Dorrit* and *The Daisy Chain*, with *Jane Eyre* in coat-pocket. Should prefer to be the kind of person who is inseparable from volume of Keats, or even Jane Austen, but cannot compass this.

July 15th.—*Mem.*: Remind Robert before starting that Gladys's wages due on Saturday. Speak about having my room turned out. Speak about laundry. Speak to Mademoiselle about Vicky's teeth, glyco-thymoline, Helen Wills *not* on bed, and lining of tussore coat. Write butcher. Wash hair.

July 17th.—Robert sees me off by early train for London, after scrambled and agitating departure, exclusively concerned with frantic endeavours to induce suit-case to shut. This is at last accomplished, but leaves me with conviction that it will be at least equally difficult to induce it to open again. Vicky bids me cheerful, but affectionate, good-bye and then shatters me at eleventh hour by enquiring trustfully if I shall be home in time to read to her after tea? As entire extent of absence has already been explained to her in full, this enquiry merely senseless—but serves to unnerve me badly, especially as Mademoiselle ejaculates *Ah! la pauvre chère mignonne!* into the blue.

(*Mem.*: The French very often carried away by emotionalism to wholly preposterous lengths.)

Cook, Gladys, and the gardener stand at hall-door and hope that I shall enjoy my holiday, and Cook adds a rider to the effect that It seems to be blowing up for a gale, and for her part, she has always had a Norror of death by drowning. On this, we drive away.

Arrive at station too early—as usual—and I fill in time by asking Robert if he will telegraph if anything happens to the children, as I could be back again in twenty-four hours. He only enquires in return whether I have my passport. Am perfectly aware that passport is in my small purple dressing-case, where I put it a week ago, and have looked at it two or three times every day ever since—last time just before leaving my room forty-five minutes ago. Am nevertheless mysteriously impelled to open hand-bag, take out key, unlock small purple dressing-case, and verify presence of passport all over again.

(Query: Is not behaviour of this kind well known in therapeutic circles as symptomatic of mental derangement? Vague but disquieting association here with singular behaviour of Dr. Johnson in London streets—but too painful to be pursued to a finish.)

Arrival of train, and I say good-bye to Robert, and madly enquire if he would rather I gave up going at all. He rightly ignores this altogether.

(Query: Would not extremely distressing situation arise if similar impulsive offer were one day to be accepted? This gives rise to unavoidable speculation in regard to sincerity of such offers, and here again, issue too painful to be frankly faced, and am obliged to shelve train of thought altogether.)

Turn my attention to fellow-traveller—distrustful-looking woman with grey hair—who at once informs me that door of lavatory—opening out of compartment—has defective lock, and will *not* stay shut. I say Oh, in tone of sympathetic concern, and shut door. It remains shut. We watch it anxiously, and it flies open again. Later on, fellow-traveller makes fresh attempt, with similar result. Much of the journey spent in this exercise. I observe thoughtfully that Hope springs eternal in the human breast, and fellow-traveller looks more distrustful than ever. She finally says in despairing tones that Really, it isn't what she calls very nice, and lapses into depressed silence. Door remains triumphantly open.

Drive from Waterloo to Victoria, take out passport in taxi in order to Have It Ready, then decide safer to put it back again in dressing-case, which I do. (Dr. Johnson recrudesces faintly, but is at once dismissed.)

Observe with horror that trees in Grosvenor Gardens are swaying with extreme violence in stiff gale of wind.

Change English money into French at Victoria Station, where superior young gentleman in little kiosk refuses to let me have anything smaller than one-hundred-franc notes. I ask what use *that* will be when it comes to porters, but superior young gentleman remains adamant. Infinitely competent person in blue and gold, labelled Dean & Dawson, comes to my rescue, miraculously provides me with change, says Have I booked a seat, pilots me to it, and tells me that he represents the best-known Travel Agency in London. I assure him warmly that I shall never patronise any other—which is true—and we part with mutual esteem.

Journey to Folkestone entirely occupied in looking out of train window and seeing quite large trees bowed to earth by force of wind. Cook's words recur most unpleasantly. Also recall various forms of advice received, and find it difficult to decide between going instantly to the Ladies' Saloon, taking off my hat, and lying down Perfectly Flat—(Mademoiselle's suggestion)—or Keeping in the Fresh Air at All Costs and Thinking about Other Things—(course advocated on a postcard by Aunt Gertrude). Choice taken out of my hands by discovery that Ladies' Saloon is entirely filled, within five minutes of going on board, by other people, who have all taken off their hats and are lying down Perfectly Flat.

Return to deck, sit on suit-case, and decide to Think about Other Things. Schoolmaster and his wife, who are going to Boulogne for a holiday, talk to one another across me about University Extension Course, and appear to be superior to the elements. I take out *Jane Eyre* from coat-pocket—partly in faint hope of impressing them, and partly to distract my mind—but remember Cousin Maud, and am forced to conclusion that she may have been right. Perhaps advice equally correct in respect of repeating poetry? Can think of nothing whatever except extraordinary damp chill which appears to be creeping over me. Schoolmaster suddenly says to me: "Quite all *right*, aren't you?" To which I reply, Oh yes, and he laughs in a bright and scholastic way, and talks about the Matterhorn. Although unaware of any conscious recollection of it, find myself inwardly repeating curious and ingenious example of alliterative verse, committed to memory in my schooldays.

Attain Boulogne at last, discover reserved seat in train, am told by several officials whom I question that we do, or alternatively, do not, change when we reach Paris, give up the elucidation of the point for the moment, and demand—and obtain—small glass of brandy, which restores me.

July 18th, at Ste. Agathe.—Vicissitudes of travel very strange, and am struck—as often—by enormous dissimilarity between journeys undertaken in real life, and as reported in fiction. Can remember very few novels in which train journey of any kind does not involve either (*a*) hectic encounter with member of opposite sex, leading to tense emotional issue; (*b*) discovery of murdered body in hideously battered condition, under circumstances which utterly defy detection; (*c*) elopement between two people each of whom is married to somebody else, culminating in severe disillusionment, or lofty renunciation.

Nothing of all this enlivens my own peregrinations, but on the other hand, the night not without incident.

Second-class carriage full, and am not fortunate enough to obtain corner-seat. American young gentleman sits opposite, and elderly French couple, with talkative friend wearing blue beret, who trims his nails with a pocket-knife and tells us about the state of the wine-trade.

I have dusty and elderly mother in black on one side, and her two sons—names turn out to be Guguste and Dédé—on the other. (Dédé looks about fifteen, but wears socks, which I think a mistake, but must beware of insularity.)

Towards eleven o'clock we all subside into silence, except the blue beret, who is now launched on tennis-champions, and has much to say about all of them. American young gentleman looks uneasy at mention of any of his compatriots, but evidently does not understand enough French to follow blue beret's remarks—which is as well.

Just as we all—except indefatigable beret, now eating small sausage-rolls—drop one by one into slumber, train stops at station and fragments of altercation break out in corridor concerning admission, or otherwise, of someone evidently accompanied by large dog. This is opposed by masculine voice repeating steadily, at short intervals, *Un chien n'est pas une personne*, and heavily backed by assenting chorus, repeating after him *Mais non, un chien n'est pas une personne*.

To this I fall asleep, but wake a long time afterwards, to sounds of appealing enquiry, floating in from corridor: *Mais voyons—n'est-ce pas qu'un chien n'est pas une personne?*

The point still unsettled when I sleep again, and in the morning no more is heard, and I speculate in vain as to whether owner of the *chien* remained with him on the station, or is having *tête-à-tête* journey with him in separate carriage altogether. Wash inadequately, in extremely dirty accommodation provided, after waiting some time in lengthy queue. Make distressing discovery that there is no way of obtaining breakfast until train halts at Avignon. Break this information later to American young gentleman, who falls into deep distress and says that he does not know the French for grapefruit. Neither do I, but am able to inform him decisively that he will not require it.

Train is late, and does not reach Avignon till nearly ten. American young gentleman has a severe panic, and assures me that if he leaves the train it will start without him. This happened once before at Davenport, Iowa. In order to avoid similar calamity on this occasion, I offer to procure him a cup of coffee and two rolls, and successfully do so—but attend first to my own requirements. We all brighten after this, and Guguste announces his intention of shaving. His mother screams, and says *Mais c'est fou*—with which I privately agree—and everybody else remonstrates with Guguste (except Dédé, who is wrapped in gloom), and points out that the train is rocking, and he will cut himself. The blue beret goes so far as to predict that he will decapitate himself, at which everybody screams.

Guguste remains adamant, and produces shaving apparatus and a little mug, which is given to Dédé to hold. We all sit round in great suspense, and Guguste is supported by one elbow by his mother, while he conducts operations to a conclusion which produces no perceptible change whatever in his appearance.

After this excitement, we all suffer from reaction, and sink into hot and dusty silence. Scenery gets rocky and sandy, with heat-haze shimmering over all, and occasional glimpses of bright blue-and-green sea.

At intervals train stops, and ejects various people. We lose the elderly French couple—who leave a Thermos behind them and have to be screamed at by Guguste from the window—and then the blue beret, eloquent to the last, and turning round on the platform to bow as train moves off again. Guguste, Dédé, and the mother remain with me to the end, as they are going on as far as Antibes. American young gentleman gets out when I do, but lose sight of him altogether in excitement of meeting Rose, charming in yellow embroidered linen. She says that she is glad to see me, and adds that I look a Rag—which is true, as I discover on reaching hotel and looking-glass—but kindly omits to add that I have smuts on my face, and that petticoat has mysteriously descended two and half inches below my dress, imparting final touch of degradation to general appearance.

She recommends bath and bed, and I agree to both, but refuse proffered cup of tea, feeling this would be altogether too reminiscent of English countryside, and quite out of place. I ask, insanely, if letters from home are awaiting me—which, unless they were written before I left, they could not possibly be. Rose enquires after Robert and the children, and when I reply that I feel I ought not really to have come away without them, she again recommends bed. Feel that she is right, and go there.

July 23rd.—Cannot avoid contrasting deliriously rapid flight of time when am on holiday with very much slower passage of days, and even hours, in other and more familiar surroundings.

(*Mem.*: This disposes once and for all of fallacy that days seem long when spent in complete idleness. They seem, on the contrary, very much longer when filled with ceaseless activities.)

Rose—always so gifted in discovering attractive and interesting friends—is established in circle of gifted—and in some cases actually celebrated—personalities. We all meet daily on rocks, and bathe in sea. Temperature and surroundings very, very different to those of English Channel or Atlantic Ocean, and consequently find myself emboldened to the extent of quite active swimming. Cannot, however, compete with Viscountess, who dives, or her friend, who has unique and very striking method of doing back-fall into the water. Am, indeed, led away by spirit of emulation into attempting dive on one solitary occasion, and am convinced that I have plumbed the depths of the Mediterranean—have doubts, in fact, of ever leaving it again—but on enquiring of extremely kind spectator—(famous Headmistress)—How I went In, she replies gently: About level with the Water, she thinks—and we say no more about it.

July 25th.—Vicky writes affectionately, but briefly—Mademoiselle at greater length, and quite illegibly, but evidently full of hopes that I am enjoying myself. Am touched, and send each a picture-postcard. Robin's letter, written from school, arrives later, and contains customary allusions to boys unknown to me, also information that he has asked two of them to come and stay with him in the holidays, and has accepted invitation to spend a week with another. Postscript adds straightforward enquiry, Have I bought any chocolate yet?

I do so forthwith.

July 26th.—Observe in the glass that I look ten years younger than on arrival here, and am gratified. This, moreover, in spite of what I cannot help viewing as perilous adventure recently experienced in (temporarily) choppy sea, agitated by *vent d'est,* in which no one but Rose's Viscountess attempts to swim. She indicates immense and distant rock, and announces her intention of swimming to it. I say that I will go too. Long before we are half-way there, I know that I shall never reach it, and hope that Robert's second wife will be kind to the children. Viscountess, swimming calmly, says, Am I all right? I reply, Oh quite, and am immediately submerged.

(Query: Is this a Judgement?)

Continue to swim. Rock moves farther and farther away. I reflect that there will be something distinguished about the headlines announcing my demise in such exalted company, and mentally frame one or two that I think would look well in local paper. Am just turning my attention to paragraph in our Parish

Magazine when I hit a small rock, and am immediately submerged again. Mysteriously rise again from the foam—though not in the least, as I know too well, like Venus.

Death by drowning said to be preceded by mental panorama of entire past life. Distressing reflection which very nearly causes me to sink again. Even *one* recollection from my past, if injudiciously selected, disconcerts me in the extreme, and cannot at all contemplate entire series. Suddenly perceive that space between myself and rock has actually diminished. Viscountess —who has kept near me and worn slightly anxious expression throughout—achieves it safely, and presently find myself grasping at sharp projections with tips of my fingers and bleeding profusely at the knees. Perceive that I have been, as they say, Spared.

(*Mem.*: Must try and discover for what purpose if any.)

Am determined to take this colossal achievement as a matter of course, and merely make literary reference to Byron swimming the Hellespont—which would sound better if said in less of a hurry, and when not obliged to gasp, and spit out several gallons of water.

Minor, but nerve-racking, little problem here suggests itself: What substitute for a pocket-handkerchief exists when sea-bathing? Can conceive of no occasion —except possibly funeral of nearest and dearest— when this homely little article more frequently and urgently required. Answer, when it comes, anything but satisfactory.

I say that I am cold—which is true—and shall go

back across the rocks. Viscountess, with remarkable tact, does not attempt to dissuade me, and I go.

July 27th. — End of holiday quite definitely in sight, and everyone very kindly says, Why not stay on? I refer, in return, to Robert and the children—and add, though not aloud, the servants, the laundry, the Women's Institute, repainting the outside of bath, and the state of my overdraft. Everyone expresses civil regret at my departure, and I go so far as to declare recklessly that I shall be coming back next year—which I well know to be unlikely in the extreme.

Spend last evening sending picture-postcards to everyone to whom I have been intending to send them ever since I started.

July 29th, London. — Return journey accomplished under greatly improved conditions, travelling first-class in company with one of Rose's most distinguished friends. (Should much like to run across Lady B. by chance in Paris or elsewhere, but no such gratifying coincidence supervenes. Shall take care, however, to let her know circles in which I have been moving.)

Boat late, train even more so, last available train for west of England has left Paddington long before I reach Victoria, and am obliged to stay night in London. Put through long-distance call to tell Robert this, but line is, as usual, in a bad way, and all I can hear is "What?" As Robert, on his side, can apparently hear even less, we do not get far. I find that I have no money, in spite of having borrowed from Rose—expenditure, as invariably happens, has exceeded estimate—but confide all to Secretary of my club, who agrees to trust me, but adds, rather disconcertingly—"as it's for one night only".

July 30th.—Readjustment sometimes rather difficult, after absence of unusual length and character.

July 31st.—The beginning of the holidays signalled, as usual, by the making of appointments with dentist and doctor. Photographs taken at Ste. Agathe arrive, and I am—perhaps naturally—much more interested in them than anybody else appears to be. (Bathing dress shows up as being even more becoming than I thought it was, though hair, on the other hand, not at its best—probably owing to salt water.) Notice, regretfully, how much more time I spend in studying views of myself, than on admirable group of delightful friends, or even beauties of Nature, as exemplified in camera studies of sea and sky.

Presents for Vicky, Mademoiselle, and Our Vicar's Wife all meet with acclamation, and am gratified. Blue flowered chintz frock, however, bought at Ste. Agathe for sixty-three francs, no longer becoming to me, as sunburn fades and original sallowness returns to view. Even Mademoiselle, usually so sympathetic in regard to clothes, eyes chintz frock doubtfully, and says *Tiens! On dirait un bal masqué.* As she knows, and I know, that the neighbourhood never has, and never will, run to *bals masqués*, this equals unqualified condemnation of blue chintz, and I remove it in silence to farthest corner of the wardrobe.

August 1st. — Return of Robin, who has grown, and looks pale. He has also purchased large bottle of brilliantine, and applied it to his hair, which smells like inferior chemist's shop. Do not like to be unsympathetic about this, so merely remain silent while Vicky exclaims rapturously that it is *lovely* — which is also Robin's own opinion. They get excited and scream, and I suggest the garden. Robin says that he is hungry, having had no lunch. Practically — he adds conscientiously. "Practically" turns out to be packet of sandwiches, two bottles of atrocious liquid called Cherry Ciderette, slab of milk chocolate, two bananas purchased on journey, and small sample tin of cheese biscuits, swopped by boy called Sherlock for Robin's last year's copy of *Pop's Annual.*

Customary rather touching display of affection between Robin and Vicky much to the fore, and am sorry to feel that repeated experience of holidays has taught me not to count for one moment upon its lasting more than twenty-four hours — if that.

(Query: Does motherhood lead to cynicism? This contrary to every convention of art, literature, or morality, but cannot altogether escape conviction that answer may be in the affirmative.)

August 2nd. — Noteworthy what astonishing difference made in entire household by presence of one additional child. Robert finds one marble — which he unfortunately steps upon — mysterious little empty box with hole in bottom, and half of torn sponge on the stairs, and says, This house is a perfect Shambles — which I think excessive. Mademoiselle refers to sounds emitted by Robin, Vicky, the dog, and Helen Wills—all, apparently, gone mad together in the hayloft—as *tohu-bohu*. Very expressive word.

Meal-times, especially lunch, very, very far from peaceful. From time to time remember, with pained astonishment, theories subscribed to in pre-motherhood days, as to inadvisability of continually saying Don't, incessant fault-finding, and so on. Should now be sorry indeed to count number of times that I find myself forced to administer these and similar checks to the dear children.

Rose writes cheerfully, still in South of France—sky still blue, rocks red, and bathing as perfect as ever. Experience curious illusion of receiving communication from another world, visited many æons ago, and dimly remembered. Weather abominable, and customary difficulty experienced of finding indoor occupation for children that shall be varied, engrossing, and reasonably quiet. Cannot imagine what will happen if these conditions still prevail when visiting school-fellow—Henry by name—arrives. I ask Robin what his friend's tastes are, and he says, Oh, anything. I enquire if he likes cricket, and Robin replies, Yes, he expects so. Does he care for reading? Robin says that he does not know. I give it up, and write to Army and Navy Stores for large tin of Picnic Biscuits.

Messrs. R. Sydenham, and two unknown firms from places in Holland, send me little books relating to indoor bulbs. R. Sydenham particularly optimistic, and, though admitting that failures *have* been known, pointing out that all, without exception, have been owing to neglect of directions on page twenty-two. Immerse myself in page twenty-two, and see that there is nothing for it but to get R. Sydenham's Special Mixture for growing R. Sydenham's Special Bulbs.

Mention this to Robert, who does not encourage scheme in any way, and refers to last November. Cannot at the moment think of really good answer, but shall probably do so in church on Sunday, or in other surroundings equally inappropriate for delivering it.

August 3rd.—Difference of opinion arises between Robin and his father as to the nature and venue of former's evening meal, Robin making sweeping assertions to the effect that All Boys of his Age have Proper Late Dinner downstairs, and Robert replying curtly More Fools their Parents, which I privately think unsuitable language for use before children. Final and unsatisfactory compromise results in Robin's coming nightly to the dining-room and partaking of soup, followed by interval, and ending with dessert, during the whole of which Robert maintains disapproving silence and I talk to both at once on entirely different subjects.

(Life of a wife and mother sometimes very wearing.)

Moreover, Vicky offended at not being included in what she evidently looks upon as nightly banquet of Lucullan magnificence, and covertly supported in this rebellious attitude by Mademoiselle. Am quite struck by extraordinary persistence with which Vicky, day after day, enquires *Why* can't she stay up to dinner too? and equally phenomenal number of times that I reply with unvarying formula that Six years old is too young, darling.

Weather cold and disagreeable, and I complain.

Robert asserts that it is really quite warm, only I don't take enough exercise. Have often noticed curious and prevalent masculine delusion, to the effect that sympathy should never, on any account, be offered when minor ills of life are in question.

August 7th. — Local Flower Show takes place. We walk about in Burberrys, on wet grass, and say that it might have been much worse, and look at the day they had last week at West Warmington! Am forcibly reminded of what I have heard of Ruth Draper's admirable sketch of country Bazaar, but try hard not to think about this. Our Vicar's Wife takes me to look at the school-children's needlework, laid out in tent amidst onions, begonias, and other vegetable products. Just as I am admiring pink cotton camisole embroidered with mauve pansies, strange boy approaches me and says, If I please, the little girl isn't very well, and can't be got out of the swing-boat, and will I come, please. I go, Our Vicar's Wife following, and saying — absurdly — that it must be the heat, and those swing-boats have always seemed to her very dangerous ever since there was a fearful accident at her old home, when the whole thing broke down, and seven people were killed and a good many of the spectators injured. A relief, after this, to find Vicky merely green in the face, still clinging obstinately to the ropes and disregarding two men below saying Come along out of it, missie, and Now then, my dear, and Mademoiselle in terrific state of agitation, clasping her hands and pacing backwards and forwards, uttering many Gallic ejaculations and adjurations to the saints. Robin has removed himself to farthest corner of the ground, and is feigning interest in immense cart-horse tied up in red ribbons.

(*N.B.* Dear Robin perhaps not so utterly unlike his father as one is sometimes tempted to suppose.)

I tell Vicky, very, very shortly, that unless she descends instantly, she will go to bed early every night for a week. Unfortunately, tremendous outburst of "Land of Hope and Glory" from brass band compels me to say this in undignified bellow, and to repeat it three times before it has any effect, by which time quite large crowd has gathered round. General outburst of applause when at last swing-boat is brought to a stand-still, and Vicky—mottled to the last degree—is lifted out by man in check coat and tweed cap, who says *Here* we are, Amy Johnson! to fresh applause.

Vicky removed by Mademoiselle, not a moment too soon. Our Vicar's Wife says that children are all alike, and it may be a touch of ptomaine poisoning, one never knows, and why not come and help her judge decorated perambulators?

Meet several acquaintances and newly-arrived Miss Pankerton, who has bought small house in village, and on whom I have not yet called. She wears pince-nez and is said to have been at Oxford. All I can get out of her is that the whole thing reminds her of Dostoeffsky.

Feel that I neither know nor care what she means. Am convinced, however, that I have not heard the last of either Miss P. or Dostoeffsky, as she assures me that she is the most unconventional person in the whole world, and never stands on ceremony. If she meets an affinity, she adds, she knows it directly, and then noth-ing can stop her. She just follows the impulse of the moment, and may as like as not stroll in for breakfast, or be strolled in upon for after-dinner coffee. Am quite unable to contemplate Robert's reaction to Miss P. and Dostoeffsky at breakfast, and bring the conversation to an end as quickly as possible.

Find Robert, Our Vicar, and neighbouring squire, looking at horses. Our Vicar and neighbouring squire talk about the weather, but do not say anything new. Robert says nothing.

Get home towards eight o'clock, strangely exhausted, and am discouraged at meeting both maids just on their way to the Flower-Show Dance. Cook says encouragingly that the potatoes are in the oven, and everything else on the table, and she only hopes Pussy hasn't found her way in, on account of the butter. Eventually do the washing-up, while Mademoiselle puts children to bed, and I afterwards go up and read *Tanglewood Tales* aloud.

(Query, mainly rhetorical: Why are non-professional women, if married and with children, so frequently referred to as "leisured"? Answer comes there none.)

August 8th.—Frightful afternoon, entirely filled by call from Miss Pankerton, wearing hand-woven blue jumper, wider in front than at the back, very short skirt, and wholly incredible small black beret. She smokes cigarettes in immense holder, and sits astride the arm of the sofa.

(*N.B.* Arm of the sofa not at all calculated to bear any such strain, and creaks several times most alarmingly. Must remember to see if anything can be done about it, and in any case manœuvre Miss P. into sitting elsewhere on subsequent visits, if any.)

Conversation very, very literary and academic, my own part in it being mostly confined to saying that I haven't yet read it, and, It's down on my library list, but hasn't come, so far. After what feels like some hours of this, Miss P. becomes personal, and says that I strike her as being a woman whose life has never known fulfilment. Have often thought exactly the same thing myself, but this does not prevent my feeling entirely furious with Miss P. for saying so. She either does not perceive, or is indifferent to, my fury, as she goes on to ask accusingly whether I realise that I have no *right* to let myself become a domestic beast of burden, with no interests beyond the nursery and the kitchen. What, for instance, she demands rousingly, have I read within the last two years? To this I reply weakly that I have read *Gentlemen Prefer Blondes*, which is the only thing I seem able to remember, when Robert and the tea enter simultaneously. Curious and difficult interlude follows, in the course of which Miss P. talks about the N.U.E.C.—(cannot imagine what this is, but pretend to know all about it)—and the situation in India, and Robert either says nothing at all, or contradicts her very briefly and forcibly. Miss P. finally departs, saying that she is determined to scrape all the barnacles off me before she has done with me, and that I shall soon be seeing her again.

August 9th.—The child Henry deposited by expensive-looking parents in enormous red car, who dash away immediately, after one contemptuous look at house, garden, self, and children. (Can understand this, in a way, as they arrive sooner than expected, and Robin, Vicky, and I are all equally untidy owing to prolonged game of Wild Beasts in the garden.)

Henry unspeakably immaculate in grey flannel and red tie—but all is discarded when parents have departed, and he rapidly assumes disreputable appearance and loud, screeching tones of complete at-homeness.

August 10th.—See Miss Pankerton through Post Office window and have serious thoughts of asking if I may just get under the counter for a moment, or retire into back premises altogether, but am restrained by presence of children, and also interesting story, embarked upon by Postmistress, concerning extraordinary decision of Bench, last Monday week, as to Separation Order applied for by Mrs. W. of the *Queen's Head.* Just as we get to its being well known that Mr. W. once threw hand-painted plate with view of Teignmouth right across the bedroom—absolutely right *across* it, from end to end, says Postmistress impressively—we are invaded by Miss P., accompanied by two sheep-dogs and some leggy little boys.

Little boys turn out to be nephews, paying visit, and are told to go and make friends with Robin, Henry, and Vicky—at which all exchange looks of blackest hatred, with regrettable exception of Vicky, who smirks at the tallest nephew, who takes no notice. Miss P. pounces on Henry and says to me Is this my boy, his eyes are so exactly like mine she'd have known him anywhere. Nobody contradicts her, although I do not feel pleased, as Henry, in my opinion, entirely undistinguished-looking child.

We all surge out of Post Office together, and youngest Pankerton nephew suddenly remarks that at *his* home the water once came through the bathroom floor into the dining-room. Vicky says Oh, and all then become silent again until Miss P. tells another nephew not to twist the sheep-dog's tail like that, and the nephew, looking astonished, says in return, Why not? to which Miss P. rejoins, Noel, that will *Do*.

We part with Pankertons at the cross-roads, but not before Miss P. has accepted invitation to picnic, and added that her brother will be staying with her then, and a dear friend who Writes, and that she hopes that will not be too large a party. I say No, not at all, and feel that this settles the question of buying another half-dozen picnic plates and enamel mugs, and better throw in a new Thermos as well, otherwise not a hope of things going round. That, says Miss P., will be delightful, and shall they bring their own sandwiches?—at which I exclaim in horror, and she says Really? and I say Really, with equal emphasis but quite different inflection, and we part.

Robin says he does not know why I asked them to the picnic, and I stifle impulse to reply that neither do I, and Henry tells me all about hydraulic lifts.

Send children upstairs to wash for lunch, and call out several times that they must hurry up or they will be late, but am annoyed when gong, eventually, is sounded by Gladys nearly ten minutes after appointed hour. Cannot decide whether I shall, or shall not, speak about this, and am preoccupied all through roast lamb and mint sauce, but forget about it when fruit-salad is reached, as Cook has disastrously omitted banana and put in loganberries.

August 13th.—I tell Cook about the picnic lunch—for about ten people, say I—which sounds less than if I just said "ten" straight out—but she is not taken in by this, and at once declares that there isn't anything to make sandwiches of, that she can see, and butcher won't be calling till the day after to-morrow, and then it'll be scrag-end for Irish stew. I perceive that the moment has come for taking up absolutely firm stand with Cook, and surprise us both by suddenly saying Nonsense, she must order chicken from farm, and have it cold for sandwiches. It won't go round, Cook protests—but feebly—and I pursue advantage and advocate supplementary potted meat and hard-boiled eggs. Cook utterly vanquished, and I leave kitchen triumphant, but am met in the passage outside by Vicky, who asks in clarion tone (easily audible in kitchen and beyond) if I know that I threw cigarette-end into drawing-room grate, and that it has lit the fire all by itself.

August 15th.—Picnic takes place under singular and rather disastrous conditions.

Sky is grey, but not necessarily threatening, and glass has not fallen unreasonably. All is in readiness when Miss Pankerton (wearing Burberry, green knitted cap, and immense yellow gloves) appears in large Ford car which brims over with nephews, sheep-dogs, and a couple of men. Latter resolve themselves into the Pankerton brother—who turns out to be from Vancouver—and the friend who Writes—very tall and pale, and is addressed by Miss P. in a proprietary manner as "Jahsper".

After customary preliminaries about weather, much time is spent in discussing arrangements in cars. All the children show tendency to wish to sit with their own relations rather than anybody else, except Henry, who says simply that the hired car looks much the best, and may he sit in front with the driver, please. All is greatly complicated by presence of the sheep-dogs, and Robert offers to shut them into an outhouse for the day, but Miss Pankerton replies that this would break their hearts, bless them, and they can just pop down anywhere amongst the baskets. (In actual fact, both eventually pop down on Mademoiselle's feet, and she looks despairing, and presently asks if I have by any chance a little bottle of eau-de-Cologne with me—which I naturally haven't.)

Picnic baskets, as usual, weigh incredible amount, and Thermos flasks stick up at inconvenient angles and run into our legs. (I quote "John Gilpin", rather aptly, but nobody pays any attention.)

When we have driven about ten miles, rain begins, and goes on and on. Cars are stopped, and we find that two schools of thought exist, one—of which Miss P. is leader—declaring that we are Running out of It, and the other—headed by the Vancouver brother and heavily backed by Robert—that we are Running into It. Miss P.—as might have been expected—wins, and we proceed; but Run into It more and more. By the time destination is reached, we have Run into It to an extent that makes me wonder if we shall ever Run out of It.

Lunch has to be eaten in three bathing huts, hired by Robert, and the children become hilarious and fidgety. They also ask riddles—mostly very old and foolish ones—and Miss P. looks annoyed, and says See if it has stopped raining—which it hasn't. I feel that she and the children must, at all costs, be kept apart, and tell Robert in urgent whisper that, rain or no rain, they must go out.

They do.

Miss Pankerton becomes expansive, and suddenly remarks to Jahsper that *Now* he can see what she meant, about positively Victorian survivals still to be found in English family life. At this, Vancouver brother looks aghast—as well he may—and dashes out into the wet. Jahsper says Yerse, Yerse, and sighs, and I at once institute vigorous search for missing plate, which creates a diversion.

Subsequently the children bathe, get wetter than ever, drip all over the place, and are dried—Mademoiselle predicts death from pneumonia for all—and we seek the cars once more. One sheep-dog is missing, but eventually recovered in soaking condition, and is gathered on to united laps of Vicky, Henry, and a nephew. I lack energy to protest, and we drive away.

Beg Miss P., Jahsper, brother, nephews, sheep-dogs, and all, to come in and get dry and have tea, but they have the decency to refuse, and I make no further effort, but watch them depart with untold thankfulness.

(Should be sorry to think impulses of hospitality almost entirely dependent on convenience, but cannot altogether escape suspicion that this is so.)

Robert extremely forbearing on the whole, and says nothing worse than Well!—but this very expressively.

August 16th.—Robert, at breakfast, suddenly enquires if that nasty-looking fellow does anything for a living. Instinct at once tells me that he means Jahsper, but am unable to give him any information, except that Jahsper writes, which Robert does not appear to think is to his credit. He goes so far as to say that he hopes yesterday's rain may put an end to him altogether—but whether this means to his presence in the neighbourhood, or to his existence on this planet, am by no means certain, and prefer not to enquire. Ask Robert instead if he did not think, yesterday, about Miss Edgeworth, Rosamond and the Party of Pleasure, but this wakens no response, and conversation—such as it is—descends once more to level of slight bitterness about the coffee, and utter inability to get really satisfactory bacon locally. This is only brought to a close by abrupt entrance of Robin, who remarks without preliminary: "Isn't Helen Wills going to have kittens almost at once? Cook thinks so."

Can only hope that Robin does not catch exact wording of short ejaculation with which his father receives this.

August 18th.—Pouring rain, and I agree to let all three children dress up, and give them handsome selection from my wardrobe for the purpose. This ensures me brief half-hour uninterrupted at writing-table, where I deal with baker—brown bread far from satisfactory—Rose—on a picture-postcard of Backs at Cambridge, which mysteriously appears amongst stationery—Robin's Headmaster's wife—mostly about stockings, but Boxing may be substituted for Dancing in future—and Lady Frobisher, who would be so delighted if Robert and I would come over for tea whilst there is still something to be seen in the garden. (Do not like to write back and say that I would far rather come when there is nothing to be seen in the garden, and we might enjoy excellent tea in peace—so, as usual, sacrifice truth to demands of civilisation.)

Just as I decide to tackle large square envelope of thin blue paper, with curious purple lining designed to defeat anyone endeavouring to read letter within—which would anyhow be impossible, as Barbara Carruthers always most illegible—front-door bell rings.

Door opens, and Miss Pankerton is shown in, followed—it seems to me reluctantly—by Jahsper. Miss P. has on military-looking cape, and beret as before, which strikes me as odd combination, and anyhow cape looks to me as though it might drip rain-drops on furniture, and I beg her to take it off. This she does with rather spacious gesture—(Can she have been seeing *The Three Musketeers* at local cinema?)—and unfortunately one end of it, apparently heavily weighted, hits Jahsper in the eye. Miss P. is very breezy and off-hand about this, but Jahsper, evidently in severe pain, falls into deep dejection, and continues to hold large yellow crêpe-de-chine handkerchief to injured eye for some time. Am distracted by wondering whether I ought to ask him if he would like to bathe it—which would involve taking him up to bathroom, probably untidy—and trying to listen intelligently to Miss P., who is talking about Proust.

This leads, by process that I do not follow, to a discussion on Christian names, and Miss P. says that All Flower Names are Absurd. Am horrified to hear myself replying, senselessly, that I think Rose is a pretty name, as one of my greatest friends is called Rose—to which Miss P. rightly answers that that, really, has nothing to do with it, and Jahsper, still dabbing at injured eye, contributes austere statement to the effect that only the Russians really understand Beauty in Nomenclature. Am again horrified at hearing myself interject *"Ivan Ivanovitch"* in entirely detached and irrelevant manner, and really begin to wonder if mental weakness is overtaking me. Moreover, am certain that I have given Miss P. direct lead in the direction of Dostoeffsky, about whom I do not wish to hear, and am altogether unable to converse.

Entire situation is, however, revolutionised by totally unexpected entrance of Robin—staggering beneath my fur coat and last summer's red crinoline straw hat—Henry, draped in blue kimono, several scarfs belonging to Mademoiselle, old pair of fur gloves, with scarlet school-cap inappropriately crowning all—and Vicky, wearing nothing whatever but small pair of green silk knickerbockers and large and unfamiliar black felt hat put on at rakish angle.

Completely stunned silence overtakes us all, until Vicky, advancing with perfect aplomb, graciously says, "How do you do?" and shakes hands with Jahsper and Miss P. in turn, and I succeed in surpassing already well-established record for utter futility, by remarking that They have been Dressing Up.

Greatest possible relief when Miss P. declares that they must go, otherwise they will miss the Brahms Concerto on the wireless. I hastily agree that this would never do, and tell Robin to open the door. Just as we all cross the hall, Gladys is inspired to sound the gong for tea, and I am compelled to say, Won't they stay and have some? but Miss P. says she never takes anything at all between lunch and dinner, thanks, and Jahsper pretends he hasn't heard me and makes no reply whatever.

August 25th. — Am displeased by Messrs. R. Sydenham, who have besought me, in urgently worded little booklet, to Order Bulbs Early, and when I do so — at no little inconvenience, owing to customary pressure of holidays — reply on a postcard that order will be forwarded "when ready". Have serious thoughts of cancelling the whole thing. Cannot very well do this, however, owing to quite recent purchase of coloured bowls from Woolworth's, as being desirable additions to existing collection of odd pots, dented enamel basins, large red glass jam-dish, and dear grandmamma's disused willow-pattern foot-bath.

Departure of the boy Henry — who says that he has enjoyed himself, which I hope is true — accompanied by Robin, who is to be met and extracted from train at Salisbury by uncle of boy with whom he is to stay.

Vicky, Mademoiselle, and I wave good-bye from hall door — rain pouring down as usual — and Vicky seems a thought depressed at remaining behind. This tendency greatly enhanced by Mademoiselle's exclamation on retiring into the house once more—*On dirait un tombeau!*

Second post brings letter from Barbara in the Himalayas, which gives me severe shock of realising that I haven't yet read her last one, owing to lack of time and general impression that it is illegibly scrawled and full of allusions to native servants. Remorsefully open this one, perceive with relief that it is quite short and contains nothing that looks like native servants, but very interesting piece of information, rather circuitously worded by dear Barbara, but still quite beyond misunderstanding. I tell Mademoiselle, who says *Ah, comme c'est touchant!* and at once wipes her eyes—display which I think excessive.

Robert, to whom I also impart news, goes to the other extreme and makes no comment except "I daresay". On the other hand, Our Vicar's Wife calls, for the express purpose of asking whether I think it will be a boy or a girl, and of suggesting that we should at once go together and congratulate old Mrs. Blenkinsop. I remind her that Barbara stipulates in letter for secrecy, and Our Vicar's Wife says, Of course, of course—it had slipped her memory for the moment—but surely old Mrs. B. must know all about it? However, she concedes that dear Barbara may perhaps not wish her mother to know that we know, just yet, and concludes with involved quotation from Thomas à Kempis about exercise of discretion.

August 28th.—Picnic, and Cook forgets to put in the sugar. Postcard from Robin's hostess says that he has arrived, but adds nothing as to his behaviour, or impression that he is making, which makes me feel anxious.

September 1st.—Postcard from the station announces arrival of parcel, that I at once identify as bulbs, with accompanying Fibre, Moss, and Charcoal mixture. Suggest that Robert should fetch them this afternoon, but he is unenthusiastic, and says to-morrow, when he will be meeting Robin and school-friend, will do quite well.

(*Mem.*: Very marked difference between the sexes is male tendency to procrastinate doing practically everything in the world except sitting down to meals and going up to bed. Should like to purchase little painted motto: *Do it now*, so often on sale at inferior stationers' shops, and present it to Robert, but on second thoughts quite see that this would not conduce to domestic harmony, and abandon scheme at once.)

Think seriously about bulbs, and spread sheets of newspaper on attic floor to receive them and bowls. Resolve also to keep careful record of all operations, with eventual results, for future guidance. Look out notebook for the purpose, and find small green booklet, with mysterious references of which I can make neither head nor tail, in own handwriting on two first pages. Spend some time in trying to decide what I could have meant by: Kp. p. in sh. twice p. w. *without fail* or: Hell H. *not* 12" by 8" Washable f.c. to be g'd, but eventually give it up, and tear out two first pages of little green book, and write BULBS and to-morrow's date in capital letters.

September 2nd.—Robert brings home Robin, and friend called Micky Thompson, from station, but has unfortunately forgotten to call for the bulbs. Micky Thompson is attractive and shows enchanting dimple whenever he smiles, which is often.

(*Mem.*: Theory that mothers think their own children superior to any others Absolute Nonsense. Can see only too plainly that Micky easily surpasses Robin and Vicky in looks, charm, and good manners—and am very much annoyed about it.)

September 10th.—Unbroken succession of picnics, bathing expeditions, and drives to Plymouth Café in search of ices. Mademoiselle continually predicts catastrophes to digestions, lungs, or even brains—but none materialise.

September 11th.—Departure of Micky Thompson, but am less concerned with this than with Robert's return from station, this time accompanied by bulbs and half-bushel of Fibre, Moss, and Charcoal. Devote entire afternoon to planting these, with much advice from Vicky and Robin, and enter full details of transaction in little green book. Prepare to carry all, with utmost care, into farthest and darkest recess of attic, when Vicky suddenly announces that, Helen Wills is there already with six brand-new kittens.

Am obliged to leave bulbs in secondary corner of attic, owing to humane scruples about disturbing H. Wills and family.

September 20th.—Letter from County Secretary of adjoining County, telling me that she knows how busy I am—which I'm certain she doesn't—but Women's Institutes of Chick, Little March, and Crimpington find themselves in terrible difficulty owing to uncertainty about next month's speaker. Involved fragments about son coming, or not coming, home on leave from Patagonia, and daughter ill—but not dangerously—at Bromley, Kent—follow. President is away—(further fragment, about President being obliged to visit aged relative while aged relative's maid is on holiday)—and County Secretary does not know what to do. What she does do, however, is to suggest that I should be prepared to come and speak at all three Institute meetings, if—as she rather strangely puts it—the worst comes to the worst. Separate half-sheet of paper gives details about dates, times, and bus between Chick and Little March, leading on to doctor's sister's two-seater, at cross-roads between Little March and Crimpington Hill. At Crimpington, County Secretary concludes triumphantly, I shall be put up for the night by Lady Magdalen Crimp—always so kind, and such a friend to the Movement—at Crimpington Hall. *P.S.* Travel talks always popular, but anything I like will be delightful. Chick very keen about Folk Lore, Little March more on the Handicraft side. *But anything I like. P.P.S.* Would I be so kind as to judge Recitation Competition at Crimpington?

I think this over for some time, and decide to write and say that I will do it, as Robin will have returned to school next week, and should like to distract my mind. Tell Mademoiselle casually that I may be going on a short tour, speaking, and she is suitably impressed. Vicky enquires: "Like a menagerie, mummie?" which seems to me very extraordinary simile, though innocently meant. I reply, "No, not in the least like a menagerie," and Mademoiselle adds, officiously, "More like a mission." Am by no means at one with her here, but have no time to go further into the subject, as Gladys summons me to prolonged discussion with the Laundry.

Go up to attic and inspect bulb-bowls, but nothing to be seen. Cannot decide whether they require water or not, but think perhaps better be on the safe side, so give them some. Make note in little green book to this effect, as am determined to keep full record of entire procedure.

September 24th.—Frightful welter of packing, putting away, and earnest consultations of School List, for Robin's return to school. Robin gives everybody serious injunctions about not touching anything *whatever* in his bedroom—which looks like inferior pawnbroking establishment at stocktaking time—and we all more or less commit ourselves to leaving it alone till Christmas holidays—which is completely out of the question.

He is taken away by Robert in the car, looking forlorn and infantile, and Vicky roars. I beseech her to desist at once, but am rebuked by Mademoiselle, who says *Ah, elle a tant de cœur!* in tone which implies that she cannot say as much for myself.

October 1st.—Tell Robert about proposed short tour to Chick, Little March, and Crimpington, on behalf of

W.I.s. He says little, but that little not very enthusiastic. I spend many hours—or so it seems—looking out Notes for Talks, and trying to remember anecdotes that shall be at once funny and suitable. (This combination rather unusual.)

Pack small bag, search frantically all over writing-table, bedroom and drawing-room for W.I. Badge—which is at last discovered by Mademoiselle in remote corner of drawer devoted to stockings—and take my departure. Robert drives me to station, and I beg that he will keep an eye on the bulbs whilst I am away.

October 2nd.—Bus from Chick conveys me to Little March, after successful meeting last night, at which I discourse on Amateur Theatricals, am applauded, thanked by President in the chair—name inaudible—applauded once more, and taken home by Assistant Secretary, who is putting me up for the night. We talk about the Movement—Annual Meeting at Blackpool perhaps a mistake, why not Bristol or Plymouth?—difficulty of thinking out new Programmes for monthly meetings, and really magnificent performance of Chick at recent Folk-dancing Rally, at which Institute members called upon to go through "Gathering Peascods" no less than three times—two of Chick's best performers, says Assistant Secretary proudly, being grandmothers. Just as Assistant Secretary—who is unmarried and lives in nice little cottage—has escorted me to charming little bedroom, she remembers that I am eventually going on to Crimpington, and embarks on interesting scandal about two members of Institute there, and unaccountable disappearance of one member's name from Committee. This keeps us up till eleven o'clock, when she begs me to say nothing whatever about her having mentioned the affair, which was all told her in strictest confidence, and we part.

Reach Little March, via the bus—which is old, and rattles—in time for lunch. Doctor's sister meets me— elderly lady with dog—and talks about hunting. Meeting takes place at three o'clock, in delightful Hut, and am impressed by business-like and efficient atmosphere. Doctor's sister, in the chair, introduces me—unluckily my name eludes her at eleventh hour, but I hastily supply it and she says, "Of course, of course"—and I launch out into A Visit to Switzerland. As soon as I have finished, elderly member surges up from front row and says that this has been particularly interesting to *her*, as she once lived in Switzerland for nearly fourteen years and knows every inch of it from end to end. (My own experience confined to six weeks round and about Lucerne, ten years ago.)

We drink cups of tea, eat excellent buns, sing several Community Songs and Meeting comes to an end. Doctor's sister's two-seater, now altogether home-like, receives me once again, and I congratulate her on Institute. She smiles and talks about hunting.

Evening passes off quietly, doctor comes in—elderly man with two dogs—he also talks about hunting, and we all separate for bed at ten o'clock.

October 3rd.—Part early from doctor, sister, dogs, and two-seater, and proceed by train to Crimpington, as Meeting does not take place till afternoon, and have no wish to arrive earlier than I need. Curious cross-country journey with many stops, and one change involving long and draughty wait that I enliven by cup of Bovril.

Superb car meets me, with superb chauffeur who despises me and my bag at sight, but is obliged to drive us both to Crimpington Hall. Butler receives me, and I am conducted through immense and chilly hall with stone flags to equally immense and chilly drawing-room, where he leaves me. Very small fire is lurking behind steel bars at far end of room, and I make my way to it past little gilt tables, large chairs, and sofas, cabinets apparently lined with china cups and lustre tea-pots, and massive writing-tables entirely furnished with hundreds of photographs in silver frames. Butler suddenly reappears with *The Times*, which he hands to me on small salver. Have already read it from end to end in the train, but feel obliged to open it and begin all over again. He looks doubtfully at the fire, and I hope he is going to put on more coal, but instead he goes away, and is presently replaced by Lady Magdalen Crimp, who is about ninety-five and stone-deaf. She wears black, and large fur cape—as well she may. She produces trumpet, and I talk down it, and she smiles and nods, and has evidently not heard one word—which is just as well, as none of them worth hearing. After some time she suggests my room, and we creep along slowly for about quarter of a mile, till first floor is reached, and vast bedroom with old-fashioned four-poster in the middle of it. Here she leaves me, and I wash, from little brass jug of tepid water, and note—by no means for the first time—that the use of powder, when temperature has sunk below a certain level, merely casts extraordinary azure shade over nose and chin.

Faint hope of finding fire in dining-room is extinguished on entering it, when, I am at once struck by its resemblance to a mausoleum. Lady M. and I sit down at mahogany circular table, she says Do I mind a Cold Lunch? I shake my head, as being preferable to screaming "No" down trumpet—though equally far from the truth—and we eat rabbit-cream, coffee-shape and Marie biscuits.

Conversation spasmodic and unsatisfactory, and I am reduced to looking at portraits on wall, of gentlemen in wigs and ladies with bosoms, also objectionable study of dead bird, dripping blood, lying amongst oranges and other vegetable matter. (Should like to know what dear Rose, with her appreciation of Art, would say to this.) Later we adjourn to drawing-room—fire now a mere ember—and Lady M. explains that she is not going to the Meeting, but Vice-President will look after me, and she hopes I shall enjoy Recitation Competition—some of our members really very clever, and one in particular, so amusing in dialect. I nod and smile, and continue to shiver, and presently car fetches me away to village. Meeting is held in reading-room, which seems to me perfect paradise of warmth, and I place myself as close as possible to large oil-stove. Vice-President—very large and expansive in blue—conducts everything successfully, and I deliver homily about What Our Children Read, which is kindly received. After tea—delightfully hot, in fact scalds me, but I welcome it—Recitation Competition takes place, and have to rivet my attention on successive members, who mount a little platform and declaim in turns. We begin with not very successful rendering of verses hitherto unknown to me, entitled "Our Institute", and which turn out to be original composition of reciter. This followed by "Gunga Din" and very rousing poem about Keeping the Old Flag Flying. Elderly member then announces "The Mine" and is very dramatic and impressive, but not wholly intelligible, which I put down to Dialect. Finally award first place to "The Old Flag", and second to "The Mine", and present prizes. Am unfortunately inspired to observe that dialect poems are always so interesting, and it then turns out that "The Mine" wasn't in dialect at all. However, too late to do anything about it.

Meeting is prolonged, for which I am thankful, but finally can no longer defer returning to arctic regions of Crimpington Hall. Lady M. and I spend evening cowering over grate, and exchanging isolated remarks, and many nods and smiles, across ear-trumpet. Finally I get into enormous four-poster, covered by very inadequate supply of blankets, and clutching insufficiently heated hot-water bottle.

October 5th.—Develop really severe cold twenty-four hours after reaching home. Robert says that all Institutes are probably full of germs—which is both unjust and ridiculous.

October 17th.—Surprising invitation to evening party— Dancing, 9.30—at Lady B.'s. Cannot possibly refuse, as Robert has been told to make himself useful there in various ways; moreover, entire neighbourhood is evidently being polished off, and see no object in raising question as to whether we have, or have not, received invitation. Decide to get new dress, but must have it made locally, owing to rather sharply worded enquiry from London shop which has the privilege of serving me, as to whether I have not overlooked overdue portion of account. (Far from overlooking it, have actually been kept awake by it at night.) Proceed to Plymouth, and get very attractive black taffeta, with little pink and blue posies scattered over it. Mademoiselle removes, and washes, Honiton lace from old purple velvet every-night tea-gown, and assures me that it will be *gentil à croquer* on new taffeta. Also buy new pair black evening-shoes, but shall wear them every evening for at least an hour in order to ensure reasonable comfort at the party.

Robert begs that I will order dinner at home exactly as usual, and make it as substantial as possible, so as to give him every chance of keeping awake at party, and I agree that this would indeed appear desirable.

October 19th.—Rumour that Lady B.'s party is to be in Fancy Dress throws entire neighbourhood into consternation. Our Vicar's Wife comes down on gardener's wife's bicycle—borrowed, she says, for greater speed and urgency—and explains that, in her position she does not think that fancy dress would do at all—unless perhaps *poudré,* which, she asserts, is different, but takes ages to brush out afterwards. She asks what I am going to do, but am quite unable to enlighten her, as black taffeta already completed. Mademoiselle, at this, intervenes, and declares that black taffeta can be transformed by a touch into Dresden China Shepherdess *à ravir*. Am obliged to beg her not to be ridiculous, nor attempt to make me so, and she then insanely suggests turning black taffeta into costume for (*a*) Mary Queen of Scots, (*b*) Mme. de Pompadour, (*c*) Cleopatra.

I desire her to take Vicky for a walk; she is *blessée*, and much time is spent in restoring her to calm.

Chaos prevails, when Robert enters, is frenziedly appealed to by Our Vicar's Wife, and says Oh, didn't he say so? one or two people *have* had "Fancy Dress" put on invitation cards, as Lady B.'s own house-party intends to dress up, but no such suggestion has been made to majority of guests.

Our Vicar's Wife and I agree at some length that, really, nobody in this world *but* Lady B. would behave like this, and we have very good minds not to go near her party. Robert and I then arrange to take Our Vicar and his wife with us in car to party, she is grateful, and goes.

October 23rd. — Party takes place. Black taffeta and Honiton lace look charming and am not dissatisfied with general appearance, after extracting two quite unmistakably grey hairs. Vicky goes so far as to say that I look Lovely, but enquires shortly afterwards why old people so often wear black — which discourages me.

Received by Lady B. in magnificent Eastern costume, with pearls dripping all over her, and surrounded by bevy of equally bejewelled friends. She smiles graciously and shakes hands without looking at any of us, and strange fancy crosses my mind that it would be agreeable to bestow on her sudden sharp shaking, and thus compel her to recognise existence of at least one of guests invited to her house. Am obliged, however, to curb this unhallowed impulse, and proceed quietly into vast drawing-room, at one end of which band is performing briskly on platform.

Our Vicar's Wife—violet net and garnets—recognises friends, and takes Our Vicar away to speak to them. Robert is imperatively summoned by Lady B.— (Is she going to order him to take charge of cloak-room, or what?)—and I am greeted by an unpleasant-looking Hamlet, who suddenly turns out to be Miss Pankerton. Why, she asks accusingly, am I not in fancy dress? It would do me all the good in the world to give myself over to the Carnival spirit. It is what I *need*.

Lady B.'s house-party, all in expensive disguises and looking highly superior, dance languidly with one another, and no introductions take place.

It later becomes part of Robert's duty to tell everyone that supper is ready, and we all flock to buffet in dining-room, and are given excellent sandwiches and unidentified form of cup. Lady B.'s expensive-looking house-party nowhere to be seen, and Robert tells me in gloomy aside that he thinks they are in the library, having champagne. I express charitable—and improbable—hope that it may poison them, to which Robert merely replies, Hush, not so loud—but should not be surprised to know that he agrees with me.

Final, and most unexpected, incident of the evening is when I come upon old Mrs. Blenkinsop, all over black jet and wearing martyred expression, sitting in large armchair underneath platform, and exactly below energetic saxophone. She evidently has not the least idea how to account for her presence there, and saxophone prevents conversation, but can distinguish something about Maud, and not getting between young things and their pleasure, and reference to old Mrs. B. not having very much longer to spend amongst us. I smile and nod my head, then feel that this may look unsympathetic, so frown and shake it, and am invited to dance by male Frobisher—who talks about old furniture and birds. House-party reappear, carrying balloons, which they distribute like buns at a school-feast, and party proceeds until midnight.

Band then bursts into Auld Lang Syne and Lady B. screams Come along, Come along, and all are directed to form a circle. Am horrified to realise that I am myself on one side clasping hand of particularly offensive young male specimen of house-party, and on the other that of Lady B. We all shuffle round to well-known strains, and sing For *Ole* Lang Syne, For *Ole* Lang Syne, over and over again, since no one appears to know any other words, and relief is general when this exercise is brought to a close.

Lady B., evidently fearing that we shall none of us know when she has had enough of us, then directs band to play National Anthem, which is done, and she receives our thanks and farewells.

Go home, and on looking at myself in the glass am much struck with undeniable fact that at the end of a party I do not look nearly as nice as I did at the beginning. Should like to think that this applies to every woman, but am not sure—and anyway, this thought ungenerous—like so many others.

Robert says, Why don't I get into Bed? I say,

Because I am writing my Diary. Robert replies, kindly, but quite definitely, that In his opinion, That is Waste of Time.

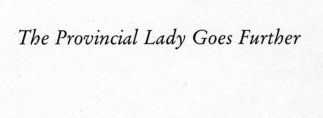

The Provincial Lady Goes Further

June 9th.—Life takes on entirely new aspect, owing to astonishing and unprecedented success of minute and unpretentious literary effort, published last December, and—incredibly—written by myself. Reactions of family and friends to this unforeseen state of affairs most interesting and varied.

Dear Vicky and Robin more than appreciative although not allowed to read book, and compare me variously to Shakespeare, Dickens, author of the *Dr. Dolittle* books, and writer referred to by Vicky as Lambs' Tails.

Mademoiselle—who has read book—only says *Ah, je m'en doutais bien!* which makes me uneasy, although cannot exactly say why.

Robert says very little indeed, but sits with copy of book for several evenings, and turns over a page quite often. Eventually he shuts it and says Yes. I ask what he thinks of it, and after a long silence he says that It is Funny—but does not look amused. Later he refers to financial situation—as well he may, since it has been exceedingly grave for some time past—and we agree that this ought to Make a Difference.

Conversation is then diverted to merits or demerits of the Dole—about which Robert feels strongly, and I try to be intelligent but do not bring it off—and difficulty of obtaining satisfactory raspberries from old and inferior canes.

June 12th.—Letter from Aunt Gertrude, who says that she has not read my book and does not as a rule care about modern fiction, as *nothing* is left to the imagination. Personally, am of opinion that this, in Aunt Gertrude's case, is fortunate—but do not, of course, write back and say so.

Cissie Crabbe, on postcard picturing San Francisco—but bearing Norwich postmark as usual—says that a friend has lent her copy of book and she is looking forward to reading it. Most unlike dear Rose, who unhesitatingly spends seven-and-sixpence on acquiring it, in spite of free copy presented to her by myself on day of publication.

Customary communication from Bank, drawing my attention to a state of affairs which is only too well known to me already, enables me to write back in quite unwonted strain of optimism, assuring them that large cheque from publishers is hourly expected. Follow this letter up by much less confidently worded epistle to gentleman who has recently become privileged to act as my Literary Agent, enquiring when I may expect money from publishers, and how much.

Cook sends in a message to say that there has been a misfortune with the chops, and shall she make do with a tin of sardines? Am obliged to agree to this, as only alternative is eggs, which will be required for breakfast. (*Mem.*: Enquire into nature of alleged misfortune in the morning.)

(*Second, and more straightforward, Mem.*: Try not to

lie awake cold with apprehension at having to make this enquiry, but remind myself that it is well known that all servants despise mistresses who are afraid of them, and therefore it is better policy to be firm.)

June 14th.—Note curious and rather disturbing tendency of everybody in the neighbourhood to suspect me of Putting Them into a Book. Our Vicar's Wife particularly eloquent about this, and assures me that she recognised every single character in previous literary effort. She adds that she has never had time to write a book herself, but has often thought that she would like to do so. Little things, she says—one here, another there—quaint sayings such as she hears every day of her life as she pops round the parish—*Cranford,* she adds in conclusion. I say Yes indeed, being unable to think of anything else, and we part.

Later on, Our Vicar tells me that he, likewise, has never had time to write a book, but that if he did so, and put down some of his personal experiences, no one would ever believe them to be true. Truth, says Our Vicar, is stranger than fiction.

Very singular speculations thus given rise to, as to nature of incredible experiences undergone by Our Vicar. Can he have been involved in long-ago *crime passionnel*, or taken part in a duel in distant student days when sent to acquire German at Heidelberg? Imagination, always so far in advance of reason, or even propriety, carries me to farther lengths, and obliges me to go upstairs and count laundry in order to change current of ideas.

Vicky meets me on the stairs and says with no

preliminary Please can she go to school. Am unable to say either Yes or No at this short notice, and merely look at her in silence.

June 15th.—Cheque arrives from publishers, via Literary Agent, who says that further instalment will follow in December. Wildest hopes exceeded, and I write acknowledgment to Literary Agent in terms of hysterical gratification that I am subsequently obliged to modify, as being undignified. Robert and I spend pleasant evening discussing relative merits of Rolls-Royce, electric light, and journey to the South of Spain—this last suggestion not favoured by Robert—but eventually decide to pay bills and Do Something about the Mortgage. Robert handsomely adds that I had better spend some of the money on myself, and what about a pearl necklace? I say Yes, to show that I am touched by his thoughtfulness, but do not commit myself to pearl necklace. Should like to suggest very small flat in London, but violent and inexplicable inhibition intervenes, and find myself quite unable to utter the words. Go to bed with flat still unmentioned, but register cast-iron resolution, whilst brushing my hair, to make early appointment in London for new permanent wave.

Also think over question of school for Vicky very seriously, and find myself coming to at least three definite conclusions, all diametrically opposed to one another.

June 16th.—Singular letter from entire stranger enquires whether I am aware that the doors of every decent home will henceforward be shut to me? Publications such as mine, he says, are harmful to art and morality alike. Should like to have this elucidated farther, but signature illegible, and address highly improbable, so nothing can be done. Have recourse to waste-paper basket in absence of fires, but afterwards feel that servants or children may decipher fragments, so remove them again and ignite small private bonfire, with great difficulty, on garden path.

(*N.B.* Marked difference between real life and fiction again exemplified here. Quite massive documents, in books, invariably catch fire on slightest provocation, and are instantly reduced to ashes.)

Question of school for Vicky recrudesces with immense violence, and Mademoiselle weeps on the sofa and says that she will neither eat nor drink until this is decided. I say that I think this resolution unreasonable, and suggest Horlick's Malted Milk, to which Mademoiselle replies *Ah, ça, jamais!* and we get no farther. Vicky remains unmoved throughout, and spends much time with Cook and Helen Wills. I appeal to Robert, who eventually—after long silence—says, Do as I think best.

Write and put case before Rose, as being Vicky's godmother and person of impartial views. Extreme tension meanwhile prevails in the house, and Mademoiselle continues to refuse food. Cook says darkly that it's well known as foreigners have no powers of resistance, and go to pieces-like all in a moment. Mademoiselle does not, however, go to pieces, but instead writes phenomenal number of letters, all in purple ink, which runs all over the paper whenever she cries.

I walk to the village for no other purpose than to get

out of the house, which now appears to me intolerable, and am asked at the Post Office if it's really true that Miss Vicky is to be sent away, she seems such a baby. Make evasive and unhappy reply, and buy stamps. Take the longest way home, and meet three people, one of whom asks compassionately how the foreign lady is. Both the other two content themselves with being sorry to hear that we're losing Miss Vicky.

Crawl indoors, enveloped in guilt, and am severely startled by seeing Vicky, whom I have been thinking of as a moribund exile, looking blooming, lying flat on her back in the hall eating peppermints. She says in a detached way that she needs a new sponge, and we separate without further conversation.

June 17th. — Mademoiselle shows signs of recovery, and drinks cup of tea at eleven o'clock, but relapses again later, and has *une crise de nerfs.* I suggest bed, and escort her there. Just as I think she can safely be left, swathed in little shawls and eiderdown quilt, she recalls me and enquires feebly if I think her health would stand life in a convent. Refuse—though I hope kindly—to discuss the question, and leave the room.

Second post brings letter from secretary of Literary Club, met once in London, informing me that I am now a member, and thoughtfully enclosing Banker's Order in order to facilitate payment of subscription, also information concerning International Congress to be held shortly in Brussels, and which she feels certain that I shall wish to attend. Decide that I *would* like to attend it, but am in some doubt as to whether Robert can be persuaded that my presence is essential to welfare of Literature.

June 18th.—Dear Rose, always so definite, writes advocating school for Vicky. Co-educational, she says firmly, and Dalcroze Eurhythmics. Robert, on being told this, says violently that no child of his shall be brought up amongst natives of any description. Am quite unable either to move him from this attitude, or to make him see that it is irrelevant to educational scheme at present under discussion.

Post also brings officious communication from old Mrs. Blenkinsop's Cousin Maud, saying that if I'm looking for a school for my brat, she could put in a word at dear old Roedean. Shall take no notice of this whatever.

June 20th.—Take bold step of writing to secretary of Literary Society to say that I will accompany its members to Brussels, and assist at Conference. Am so well aware that I shall regret this letter within an hour of writing it, that I send Vicky to village with instructions to post it instead of leaving it in box in hall as usual.

(*Query*: Does this denote extreme strength of mind or the reverse? *Answer* immediately presents itself, but see no reason for committing it to paper.)

Mademoiselle reappears in family circle, and has apparently decided that half-mourning is suitable to present crisis, as she wears black dress from which original green accessories have been removed, and fragments of mauve tulle wound round head and neck. Robert, meeting her on stairs, says kindly Mew, mam'zelle? which Mademoiselle receives with very long and involved reply, to which Robert merely returns Oh wee, and leaves her. Mademoiselle, later, tells Vicky, who repeats it to me, that it is not always education, nor even intelligence, that makes a gentleman.

Go through the linen in the afternoon, and find entirely unaccountable deficit of face-towels, but table-napkins, on the other hand, as numerous as they ever were. Blankets, as usual, require washing, but cannot be spared for the purpose, and new sheets are urgently required. Add this item to rapidly lengthening list for London. Just as I am going downstairs again, heavily speckled with fluff off blankets and reeking of camphor, enormous motor-car draws up in perfect silence at open front-door, and completely unknown woman—wearing brand-new hat about the size of a saucer with little plume over one eye—descends from it. I go forward with graceful cordiality and say, Come in, come in, which she does, and we sit and look at one another in drawing-room for ten minutes, and talk about wireless, the neighbourhood—which she evidently doesn't know—the situation in Germany, and old furniture. She turns out to be Mrs. Callington-Clay, recently come to live in house at least twenty miles away.

(Cannot imagine what can ever have induced me to call upon her, but can distinctly remember doing so, and immense relief at finding her out when I did.)

An old friend of mine, says Mrs. Callington-Clay, is a neighbour of hers. Do I remember Pamela Pringle? Am obliged to say that I do not. Then perhaps I knew her as Pamela Templer-Tate? I say No again, and repress inclination to add rather tartly that I have never heard of her in my life. Mrs. C.-C. is undefeated and brazenly suggests Pamela Stevenson—whom I once more repudiate. Then, Mrs. C.-C. declares, I *must* recollect Pamela Warburton. Am by this time dazed, but admit that I did once, about twenty-three years ago, meet extraordinary pretty girl called Pamela Warburton, at a picnic on the river. Very well then, says Mrs. C.-C., there I am! Pamela Warburton married man called Stevenson, ran away from him with man called Templer-Tate, but this, says Mrs. C.-C., a failure, and divorce ensued. She is now married to Pringle—very rich. Something in the City—Templer-Tate children live with them, but *not* Stevenson child. Beautiful old place near Somersetshire border, and Mrs. C.-C. hopes that I will call. Am still too much stunned at extraordinary activity of my contemporary to do more than say Yes, I will, and express feeble and quite insincere hope that she is as pretty as she used to be at eighteen—which is a manifest absurdity.

Finally, Mrs. C.-C. says that she enjoyed my book, and I say that that was very kind, and she asks if it takes long to write a book, and I reply Oh no, and then think it sounds conceited and wish that I had said Oh yes instead, and she departs.

Write to Rose, and say that I will come and stay with her next week and inspect possible schools for Vicky, but cannot promise to patronise any of them.

June 21st.—Post agreeably diversified by most unusual preponderance of receipts over bills.

I pack for London, and explain to Robert that I am

going on to Brussels for Literary Conference of international importance. He does not seem to take it in, and I explain all over again. Am sorry to realise that explanation gradually degenerates into something resembling rather a whining apology than a straightforward statement of rational intentions.

Mademoiselle appears soon after breakfast and says, coldly and elaborately, that she would Like to Speak to me when I can spare ten minutes. I say that I can spare them at once, but she replies No, no, it is not her intention to *déranger la matinée*, and she would prefer to wait, and in consequence I spend extremely unpleasant morning anticipating interview, and am quite unable to give my mind to anything at all.

(*Mem.*: This attitude positively childish, but cannot rid myself of overwhelming sensation of guilt.)

Interview with Mademoiselle takes place after lunch, and is fully as unpleasant as I anticipated.

(*Mem.*: Generalisation, so frequently heard, to the effect that things are never as bad as one expects them to be, once more proved untrue up to the hilt.)

Main conclusions to emerge from this highly distressing conference are: (*a*) That Mademoiselle is *pas du tout susceptible, tout au contraire*; (*b*) that she is profoundly *blessée*, and *froissée*, and *agacée*, and (*c*) that she could endure every humiliation and privation heaped upon her, if at least her supper might be brought up punctually.

This sudden introduction of entirely new element in the whole situation overcomes me completely, and we both weep.

June 23rd.—Find myself in London with greatest possible relief. Rose takes one look at me and then enquires if we have had a death in the house. I explain atmospheric conditions recently prevailing there, and she assures me that she quite understands, and the sooner I get my new permanent wave the better. Following this advice, I make early appointment.

June 24th.—Rose takes me to visit school, which she says she is pretty certain I shall not like. Then why, I ask, go there? She replies that it is better to leave no stone unturned, and anyhow it will give me some idea of the kind of thing.

(On thinking over this reply, it seems wholly inadequate, but at the time am taken in by it.)

We go by train to large and airy red-brick establishment standing on a hill and surrounded by yellow-ochre gravel which I do not like. The Principal—colouring runs to puce and canary, and cannot avoid drawing inward parallel between her and the house—receives us in large and icy drawing-room, and is bright. I catch Rose's eye and perceive that she is unfavourably impressed, as I am myself, and that we both know that This will Never Do—nevertheless we are obliged to waste entire morning inspecting classrooms—very light and cold—dormitories—hideously tidy, and red blankets like an institution—and gymnasium with dangerous-looking apparatus.

Children all look healthy, except one with a bandage on leg, which Principal dismisses lightly, when I enquire, as boils—and adds that child was born in India.

(This event must have taken place at least ten years ago, and cannot possibly have any bearing on the case.)

Rose, behind Principal's back, forms long sentence silently with her lips, of which I do not understand one word, and then shakes her head violently. I shake mine in reply, and we are shown Chapel—chilly and unpleasant building—and Sick-room, where forlorn-looking child with inadequate little red cardigan on over school uniform is sitting in a depressed way over deadly-looking jigsaw puzzle of extreme antiquity.

The Principal says Hallo, darling, unconvincingly, and darling replies with a petrified stare, and we go out again.

I say Poor little thing! and Principal replies, more brightly than ever, that Our children love the sick-room, they have such a good time there. (This obviously untrue—and if not, reflects extremely poorly on degree of enjoyment prevalent out of the sick-room.)

Principal, who has referred to Vicky throughout as "your daughter" in highly impersonal manner, now presses on us terrific collection of documents, which she calls All Particulars, I say that I Will Write, and we return to station.

I tell Rose that really, if that is her idea of the kind of place I want—but she is apologetic, and says the next one will be quite different, and she *does*, really, know exactly what I want. I accept this statement, and we entertain ourselves on journey back to London by telling one another how much we disliked the Principal, her establishment, and everything connected with it.

I even go so far as to suggest writing to parents of

bandaged child with boils, but as I do not know either her name or theirs, this goes no farther.

(Am occasionally made uneasy at recollection of pious axiom dating back to early childhood, to the effect that every idle word spoken will one day have to be accounted for. If this is indeed fact, can foresee a thoroughly well-filled Eternity for a good many of us.)

June 25th.—Undergo permanent wave, with customary interludes of feeling that nothing on earth can be worth it, and eventual conviction that it *was.*

I go back to Rose's flat, and display waves, and am told that I look fifteen years younger—which leaves me wondering what on earth I could have looked like before, and how long I have been looking it.

Rose and I go shopping, and look in every shop to see if my recent publication is in window, which it never is except once. Rose suggests that whenever we do not see book, we ought to go in and ask for it, with expressions of astonishment, and I agree that certainly we ought. We leave it at that.

June 26th.—Inspect another school, and think well of Headmistress, also of delightful old house and grounds. Education, however, appears to be altogether given over to Handicrafts—green raffia mats and mauve paper boxes—and Self-expression—table manners of some of the pupils far from satisfactory. Decide, once more, that this does not meet requirements, and go away again.

Rose takes me to a party, and introduces me to several writers, one male and eight females. I wear new mauve frock, purchased that afternoon, and, thanks to that and permanent wave, look nice, but must remember to have evening shoes re-covered, as worn gold brocade quite unsuitable.

June 28th.—Letter reaches me forwarded from home, written by contemporary of twenty-three years ago, then Pamela Warburton and now Pamela Pringle. She has heard so much of me from Mrs. Callington-Clay (who has only met me once herself and cannot possibly have anything whatever to say about me, except that I exist) and would so much like to meet me again. Do I remember picnic on the river in dear old days now so long ago? Much, writes Pamela Pringle—as well she may—has happened since then, and perhaps I have heard that after many troubles, she has at last found Peace, she trusts lasting. (Uncharitable reflection crosses my mind that P. P., judging from outline of her career given by Mrs. Callington-Clay, had better not count too much upon this, if by Peace she means matrimonial stability.)

Will I, pathetically adds Pamela, come and see her soon, for the sake of old times?

Write and reply that I will do so on my return—though less for the sake of old times than from lively curiosity, but naturally say nothing about this (extremely inferior) motive.

Go to large establishment which is having a Sale, in order to buy sheets. Find, to my horror, that I return having not only bought sheets, but blue lace tea-gown, six pads of writing-paper, ruled, small hair-slide, remnant of red brocade, and reversible black-and-white bath-mat, with slight flaw in it.

Cannot imagine how any of it happened.

Rose and I go to French film called *Le Million*, and are much amused. Coming out we meet Canadian, evidently old friend of Rose's, who asks us both to dine and go to theatre on following night, and says he will bring another man. We accept, I again congratulate myself on new and successful permanent wave.

After lunch—cutlets excellent, and quite unlike very uninspiring dish bearing similar name which appears at frequent intervals at home—go by Green Line bus to Mickleham, near Leatherhead. Perfect school is discovered, Principal instantly enquires Vicky's name and refers to her by it afterwards, house, garden and children alike charming, no bandages to be seen anywhere, and Handicrafts evidently occupy only rational amount of attention. Favourite periodical *Time and Tide* lies on table, and Rose, at an early stage, nods at me with extreme vehemence behind Principal's back. I nod in return, but feel they will think better of me if I go away without committing myself. This I succeed in doing, and after short conversation concerning fees, which are not unreasonable, we take our departure. Rose enthusiastic, I say that I must consult Robert—but this is mostly *pour la forme*, and we feel that Vicky's fate is decided.

June 29th.—Colossal success of evening's entertainment offered by Rose's Canadian. He brings with him delightful American friend, we dine at exotic and expensive restaurant, filled with literary and theatrical celebrities, and go to a revue. American friend says that he understands I have written a book, but does not seem to think any the worse of me for this, and later asks to be told name of book, which he writes down in a business-like way on programme, and puts into his pocket.

They take us to the Berkeley, where we remain until two o'clock in the morning, and are finally escorted to Rose's flat. Have I, asks the American, also got a flat? I say No, unfortunately I have not, and we all agree that this is a frightful state of things and should be remedied immediately. Quite earnest discussion ensues on the pavement, with taxi waiting at great expense.

At last we separate, and I tell Rose that this has been the most wonderful evening I have known for years, and she says that champagne often does that, and we go to our respective rooms.

Query presents itself here: Are the effects of alcohol always wholly to be regretted, or do they not sometimes serve useful purpose of promoting self-confidence? *Answer*, to-night, undoubtedly Yes, but am not prepared to make prediction as to to-morrow's reactions.

June 30th.—Realise with astonishment that Literary Conference in Brussels is practically due to begin, and that much has yet to be done with regard to packing, passport, taking of tickets and changing money. Much of this accomplished, with help of Rose, and I write long letter to Robert telling him where to telegraph in case anything happens to either of the children.

Decide to travel in grey-and-white check silk if day hot.

July 2nd.—Cannot decide whether it is going to be hot or cold, but finally decide Hot, and put on grey-and-white check silk in which I think I look nice, with small black hat. Sky immediately clouds over and everything becomes chilly. Finish packing, weather now definitely cold, and am constrained to unpack blue coat and skirt, with Shetland jumper, and put it on in place of grey-and-white check; which I reluctantly deposit in suitcase, where it will get crushed. Black hat now becomes unsuitable, and I spend much time trying on remaining hats in wardrobe, to the total of three.

Suddenly discover that it is late—boat-train starts in an hour—and take taxi to station. Frightful conviction that I shall miss it causes me to sit on extreme edge of seat in taxi, leaning well forward, in extraordinarily uncomfortable position that subsequently leads to acute muscular discomfort. However, either this, or other cause unspecified, leads to Victoria being reached with rather more than twenty minutes to spare.

Embarkation safely accomplished. Crossing more successful than usual. Reach Brussels, and am at Hotel Britannia by eight o'clock. All is red plush, irrelevant gilt mouldings, and Literary Club members. I look at them, and they at me, with horror and distrust. (*Query*: Is not this reaction peculiar to the English, and does patriotism forbid conviction that it is by no means to be admired? Americans totally different, and, am inclined to think, much nicer in consequence.)

Find myself at last face to face with dear old friend, Emma Hay, author of many successful plays. Dear old friend is wearing emerald green, which would be trying to almost anyone, and astonishing quantity of rings, brooches and necklaces. She says, Fancy seeing me here!

and have I broken away at last? I say, No, certainly not, and suggest dinner. Am introduced by Emma to any number of literary lights, most of whom seem to be delegates from the Balkans.

(*N.B.* Should be very, very sorry, if suddenly called upon to give details as to situation, and component parts, of the Balkans.)

Perceive, without surprise, that the Balkans are as ignorant of my claims to distinction as I of theirs, and we exchange amiable conversation about Belgium, and ask one another if we know Mr. Galsworthy, which none of us do.

July 3rd.—Literary Conference takes place in the morning. The Balkans very eloquent. They speak in French, and are translated by inferior interpreters into English. Am sorry to find attention wandering on several occasions to entirely unrelated topics, such as Companionate Marriage, absence of radiators in Church at home, and difficulty in procuring ice. Make notes on back of visiting-card, in order to try and feel presence at Conference in any way justified. Find these again later, and discover that they refer to purchase of picture-postcards for Robin and Vicky, memorandum that blue evening dress requires a stitch before it can be worn again, and necessity for finding out whereabouts of Messrs. Thos. Cook & Son, in case I run short of money—which I am certain to do.

Emma introduces Italian delegate, who bows and kisses my hand. Feel certain that Robert would not care for this Continental custom. Conference continues. I sit next to (moderately) celebrated poet, who pays no attention to me, or anybody else. Dear Emma, always so energetic, takes advantage of break in Conference to introduce more Balkans, both to me and to adjacent poet. The latter remains torpid throughout, and elderly Balkan, who has mistakenly endeavoured to rouse him to conversation, retires with embittered ejaculation: *Ne vous réveillez pas, monsieur.*

Close of Conference, and general conversation, Emma performing many introductions, including me and Italian delegate once more. Italian delegate remains apparently unaware that he has ever set eyes on me before, and can only conclude that appearance and personality alike have failed to make slightest impression.

Find myself wondering why I came to Belgium at all. Should like to feel that it was in the interests of literature, but am doubtful, and entirely disinclined to probe farther. Feminine human nature sometimes very discouraging subject for speculation.

Afternoon devoted to sight-seeing. We visit admirable Town Hall, are received by Mayor, who makes speech, first in English, and then all over again in French, other speeches are made in return, and energetic Belgian gentleman takes us all over Brussels on foot. Find myself sympathising with small and heated delegate—country unknown, but accent very odd—who says to me dejectedly, as we pace the cobbles: *C'est un tour de la Belgique à pied, hein?*

July 5th.—Extreme exhaustion overwhelms me, consequent on excessive sight-seeing. I ask Emma if she would think it unsporting if I evaded charabanc expedition to Malines this afternoon, and she looks pained and astonished and says Shall she be quite honest? I lack courage to say how much I should prefer her not to be honest at all, and Emma assures me that it is my duty, in the interests of literature and internationalism alike, to go to Malines. She adds that there will be tea in the Town Hall—which I know means more speeches—and that afterwards we shall hear a Carillon Concert.

Shall she, Emma adds, wear her green velvet, which will be too hot, or her Rumanian peasant costume, which is too tight, but may please our Rumanian delegates? I advocate sacrificing our Rumanian delegates without hesitation.

Large motor-bus is a great relief after so much walking, and I take my seat beside an unknown French lady with golden hair and a bust, but am beckoned away by Emma, who explains in agitation that the French lady has come to Belgium entirely in order to see something of a Polish friend, because otherwise she never gets away from her husband. Am conscious of being distinctly shocked by this, but do not say so in case Emma should think me provincial. Yield my place to the Polish friend, who seems to me to be in need of soap and water and a shave, but perhaps this mere insular prejudice, and go and sit next to an American young gentleman, who remains indifferent to my presence.

(*Query*: Does this complaisancy on my part amount to countenancing very singular relation which obviously obtains between my fellow-littérateurs? If so, have not the moral courage to do anything about it.)

Nothing of moment passes during drive, except that the French lady takes off her hat and lays her head on her neighbour's shoulder, and that I hear Belgian delegate enquiring of extremely young and pretty Englishwoman: What is the English for Autobus, to which she naïvely returns that: It is Charabanc.

Arrival at Town Hall, reception, speeches and tea take place exactly as anticipated, and we proceed in groups, and on foot, to the Carillon Concert. American neighbour deserts me—have felt certain all along that he always meant to do so at earliest possible opportunity —and I accommodate my pace to that of extremely elderly Belgian, who says that it is certainly not for us to emulate *les jeunes* on a hot day like this, and do I realise that for *nous autres* there is always danger of an apoplexy? Make no reply to this whatever, but inwardly indulge in cynical reflections about extremely poor reward afforded in this life to attempted acts of good-nature.

July 6th.—Final Conference in the morning, at which much of importance is doubtless settled, but cannot follow owing to reading letters from home, which have just arrived. Robert says that he hopes I am enjoying myself, and we have had one and a quarter inches of rain since Thursday, and bill for roof-repairs has come in and is even more than he expected. Robin and Vicky write briefly, but affectionately, information in each case being mainly concerned with food, and— in Robin's case—progress of Stamp Collection, which now, he says, must be worth 10*d.* or 11*d.* altogether.

Inspection of Antwerp Harbour by motor-launch takes place in the afternoon, and the majority of us sit with our backs to the rails and look at one another. Conversation in my immediate vicinity concerns President

Hoover, the novels of J. B. Priestley and *Lady Chatterley's Lover*, which everyone except myself seems to have read and admired. I ask unknown lady on my right if it can be got from the Times Book Club, and she says No, only in Paris, and advises me to go there before I return home. Cannot, however, feel that grave additional expense thus incurred would be justified, and in any case could not possibly explain *détour* satisfactorily to Robert.

Disembark from motor-launch chilled and exhausted, and with conviction that my face has turned pale-green. Inspection in pocket-mirror more than confirms this intuition. Just as I am powdering with energy, rather than success, Emma—vitality evidently unimpaired either by society of fellow-writers or by motor-launch —approaches with Italian delegate, and again introduces us.

All is brought to a close by State Banquet this evening, for which everyone—rather strangely—has to pay quite a large number of francs. Incredible number of speeches delivered: ingenious system prevails by which bulb of crimson light is flashed on as soon as any speech has exceeded two and a half minutes. Unfortunately this has no effect whatever on many of our speakers, who disregard it completely. Dear Emma not amongst these, and makes admirably concise remarks which are met with much applause. I sit next to unknown Dutchman—who asks if I prefer to speak English, French, Dutch or German—and very small and dusty Oriental, who complains of the heat.

We rise at eleven o'clock, and dancing is suggested. Just as I move quietly away in search of cloak, taxi and bed, Emma appears and says This will never do, and I must come and dance. I refuse weakly, and she says Why not? to which the only rational reply would be that I have splitting headache, and am not interested in my colleagues nor they in me. Do not, needless to say, indulge in any such candour, and result is that I am thrust by Emma upon American young gentleman for a foxtrot. I say that I dance very badly, and he says that no one can ever keep step with him. Both statements turn out to be perfectly true, and I go back to Hotel dejected, and remind myself that It is Useless to struggle against Middle-age.

July 8th.—Embark for England, not without thankfulness. Am surprised to discover that I have a sore throat, undoubted result of persistent endeavour to out-screech fellow-members of Literary Club for about a week on end.

Emma travels with me, and says that she is camping in Wales all next month, and will I join her? Nothing but a tent, and she lives on bananas and milk chocolate. Associations with the last words lead me to reply absently that the children would like it, at which Emma seems hurt and enquires whether I intend to spend my life between the nursery and the kitchen. The only possible answer to this is that I *like* it, and discussion becomes animated and rather painful. Emma, on board, avoids me, and I am thrown into society of insufferable male novelist, who is interested in Sex. He has an immense amount to say about it, and we sit on deck for what seems like hours and hours. He says at last that he hopes he is not boring me, and I hear myself, to my incredulous horror, saying pleasantly No, not at all—at which he naturally goes on.

Become gradually paralysed, and unable to think of anything in the world except how I can get away, but nothing presents itself. At last I mutter something about being cold—which I am—and he at once suggests walking round and round the deck, while he tells me about extraordinarily distressing marriage customs prevalent amongst obscure tribes of another hemisphere. Find myself wondering feebly whether, if I suddenly jumped overboard, he would stop talking. Am almost on the verge of trying this experiment when Emma surges up out of deck-chair and enveloping rugs, and says Oh, there I am, she has been looking for me everywhere.

Sink down beside her with profound gratitude, and male novelist departs, assuring me that he will remember to send me list of books on return to London. Can remember nothing whatever of any books discussed between us, but am absolutely convinced that they will be quite unsuitable for inclusion in respectable bookshelves.

Emma is kind, says that she didn't mean a single word she said—(have quite forgotten by this time what she did say, but do not tell her so)—and assures me that what I need is a good night's rest. She then tells me all about a new Trilogy that she is planning to write and also about her views on Bertrand Russell, the works of Stravinsky and Relativity. At one o'clock in the morning we seek our cabin, last thing I hear being Emma's positive assurance that I need not be afraid of America's influence on the English stage. . . .

July 9th.—London regained, though not before I have endured further spate of conversation from several lights of literature.

(*Query*: Does not very intimate connection exist between literary ability and quite inordinate powers of talk? And if so, is it not the duty of public-spirited persons to make this clear, once for all? *Further Query*: How?)

Part from everybody with immeasurable relief, and wholly disingenuous expressions of regret.

Find Rose in great excitement, saying that she has found the Very Thing. I reply firmly If Bertrand Russell for Vicky, then *No*, to which Rose rejoins that she does not know what I am talking about, but she has found me a flat. Logical and straightforward reply to this would be that I am not looking for a flat, and cannot afford one. This, however, eludes me altogether, and I accompany Rose, via bus No. 19, to Doughty Street, where Rose informs me that Charles Dickens once lived. She adds impressively that she *thinks*, but is not sure, that Someone-or-other was born at a house in Theobald's Road, close by. Brisk discussion as to relative merits of pronouncing this as "Theobald" or "Tibbald" brings us to the door of the flat, where ground-floor tenant hands us keys. Entirely admirable first-floor flat is revealed, unfurnished, and including a bedroom, sitting-room, bathroom and kitchen. To the last, I say that I would rather go out for all my meals than do any cooking at all. Then, Rose replies with presence of mind, use it as a box-room. We make intelligent notes of questions to be referred to agents—Rose scores highest for sound common-sense enquiries as to

Power being Laid On and Rates included in Rent—and find soon afterwards that I am committed to a three-year tenancy, with power to sub-let, and a choice of wall-papers, cost not to exceed two shillings a yard. From September quarter, says the agent, and suggests a deposit of say two pounds, which Rose and I muster with great difficulty, mostly in florins.

Go away feeling completely dazed, and quite unable to imagine how I shall explain any of it to Robert. This feeling recrudesces violently in the middle of the night, and in fact keeps me awake for nearly an hour, and is coupled with extremely agitating medley of quite unanswerable questions, such as What I am to Do about a Telephone, and who will look after the flat when I am not in it, and what about having the windows cleaned? After this painful interlude I go to sleep again, and eventually wake up calm, and only slightly apprehensive. This, however, may be the result of mental exhaustion.

July 11th.—Return home, and am greeted with customary accumulation of unexpected happenings, such as mysterious stain on ceiling of spare bedroom, enormous bruise received by Vicky in unspecified activity connected with gardener's bicycle, and letters which ought to have been answered days ago and were never forwarded. Am struck by the fact that tea is very nasty, with inferior bought cake bearing mauve decorations, and no jam. Realisation that I shall have to speak to Cook about this in the morning shatters me completely, and by the time I go to bed, Rose, Belgium and Doughty Street have receded into practically forgotten past.

Robert comes to bed soon after one—am perfectly aware that he has been asleep downstairs—and I begin to tell him about the flat. He says that it is very late, and that he supposes the washerwoman puts his pyjamas through the mangle, as the buttons are always broken. I brush this aside and revert to the flat, but without success. I then ask in desperation if Robert would like to hear about Vicky's school; he replies Not now, and we subside into silence.

July 12th.—Cook gives notice.

July 14th.—Pamela Warburton—now Pamela Pringle—and I meet once again, since I take the trouble to motor into the next county in response to an invitation to tea.

Enormous house, with enormous gardens—which I trust not to be asked to inspect—and am shown into room with blue ceiling and quantities of little dogs, all barking. Pamela surges up in a pair of blue satin pyjamas and an immense cigarette-holder, and astonishes me by looking extremely young and handsome. Am particularly struck by becoming effect of brilliant coral lip-stick, and insane thoughts flit through my mind of appearing in Church next Sunday similarly adorned, and watching the effect upon our Vicar. This flight of fancy routed by Pamela's greetings, and introduction to what seems like a small regiment of men, oldest and baldest of whom turns out to be Pringle. Pamela then tells them that she and I were at school together—which is entirely untrue—and that I haven't changed in the least—which I should like to believe, and can't—and offers me a cocktail, which I recklessly accept in order to show how modern I am. Do not, however, enjoy it in the least, and cannot see that it increases my conversational powers. Am moreover thrown on my beam-ends at the very start by unknown young man who asks if I am not the Colonel's wife? Repudiate this on the spot with startled negative, and then wonder if I have not laid foundations of a scandal, and try to put it right by feeble addition to the effect that I do not even know the Colonel, and am married to somebody quite different. Unknown young man looks incredulous, and at once begins to talk about interior decoration, the Spanish Royal Family, and modern lighting. I respond faintly, and try to remember if Pamela P. always had auburn hair. Should moreover very much like to know how she has collected her men, and totally eliminated customary accompanying wives.

Later on, have an opportunity of enquiring into these phenomena, as P. P. takes me to see children. Do not like to ask much about them, for fear of becoming involved in very, very intricate questions concerning P.'s matrimonial extravagances.

Nurseries are entirely decorated in white, and furnished exactly like illustrated articles in *Good Housekeeping*, even to coloured frieze all round the walls. Express admiration, but am inwardly depressed, at contrast with extraordinarily inferior school-room at home. Hear myself agreeing quite firmly with P. P. that it is most important to Train the Eye from the very beginning—and try not to remember large screen covered with scraps from illustrated papers, extremely hideous Brussels carpet descended from dear Grandmamma, and still more hideous oil-painting of quite unidentified peasant carrying improbable-looking jar—all of which form habitual surroundings of Robin and Vicky.

P. P. calls children, and they appear, looking, if possible, even more expensive and hygienic than their nursery. Should be sorry to think that I pounce with satisfaction on the fact that all of them wear spectacles, and one a plate, but cannot quite escape suspicion that this is so. All have dark hair, perfectly straight, and am more doubtful than ever about P.'s auburn waves.

Pamela, on the way downstairs, is gushing, and hopes that she is going to see a great deal of me, now that we are neighbours. Forty-one miles does not, in my opinion, constitute being neighbours, but I make appropriate response, and Pamela says that some day we must have a long, long talk. Cannot help hoping this means that she is going to tell me the story of former husbands Stevenson, Templer-Tate and Co.

(*N.B.* Singular and regrettable fact that I should not care twopence about the confidences of P. P. except for the fact that they are obviously bound to contain references to scandalous and deplorable occurrences, which would surely be better left in oblivion.)

July 17th.—Am obliged to take high line with Robert and compel him to listen to me whilst I tell him about the flat. He eventually gives me his attention, and I pour out torrents of eloquence, which grow more and more feeble as I perceive their effect upon Robert. Finally he says, kindly but gloomily, that he does not know what can have possessed me—neither do I, by this time—but that he supposes I had to do *something,* and there is a good deal too much furniture here, so some of it can go to Doughty Street.

At this I revive, and we go into furniture in detail, and eventually discover that the only things we can possibly do without are large green glass vase from drawing-room, small maple-wood table with one leg missing, framed engraving of the Prince Consort from bathroom landing, and strip of carpet believed—without certainty—to be put away in attic. This necessitates complete readjustment of furniture question on entirely new basis. I become excited, and Robert says Well, it's my own money, after all, and Why not leave it alone for the present, and we can talk about it again later? Am obliged to conform to this last suggestion, as he follows it up by immediately leaving the room.

July 19th.—Question of Vicky's school recrudesces, demanding and receiving definite decisions. Am confronted with the horrid necessity of breaking this to Mademoiselle. Decide to do so immediately after breakfast, but find myself inventing urgent errands in quite other parts of the house, which occupy me until Mademoiselle safely started for walk with Vicky.

(*Query*: Does not moral cowardice often lead to very marked degree of self-deception? *Answer*: Most undoubtedly yes.)

Decide to speak to Mademoiselle after lunch. At lunch, however, she seems depressed, and says that the weather *lui porte sur les nerfs,* and I feel better perhaps leave it till after tea. Cannot decide if this is true consideration, or merely further cowardice. Weather gets steadily worse as day goes on, and is probably going to *porter sur les nerfs* of Mademoiselle worse than ever, but register cast-iron resolution not to let this interfere with speaking to her after Vicky has gone to bed.

Robin's Headmaster's wife writes that boys are all being sent home a week earlier, owing to case of jaundice, which is—she adds—*not* catching. Can see neither sense nor logic in this, but am delighted at having Robin home almost at once. This satisfaction, most regrettably, quite unshared by Robert. Vicky, however, makes up for it by noisy and prolonged display of enthusiasm. Mademoiselle, as usual, is touched by this, exclaims *Ah, quel bon petit cœur!* and reduces me once more to despair at thought of the blow in store for her. Find myself desperately delaying Vicky's bed-time, and prolonging game of Ludo to quite inordinate lengths.

Robert, after dinner, is unwontedly talkative—about hay—and do not like to discourage him, so bed-time is reached with Mademoiselle still unaware of impending doom.

July 21st.—Interview two cooks, results wholly unfavourable. Return home in deep depression, and Mademoiselle offers to make me a *tisane*—but substitutes tea at my urgent request—and shows so much kindness that I once more postpone painful task of enlightening her as to immediate future.

July 22nd.—Return of Robin, who is facetious about jaundice case—supposed to be a friend of his—and looks well. He eats enormous tea and complains of starvation at school. Mademoiselle says *Le pauvre gosse!* and produces packet of Menier chocolate, which Robin accepts with gratitude—but am only too well aware that his alliance is of highly ephemeral character.

I tell Robin about Doughty Street flat and he is most interested and sympathetic, and offers to make me a box for shoes, or a hanging bookshelf, whichever I prefer. We then adjourn to garden and all play cricket. Mademoiselle's plea for *une balle de caoutchouc* being, rightly, ignored by all. Robin kindly allows me to keep wicket, as being post which I regard as least dangerous, and Vicky is left to bowl, which she does very slowly, and with many wides. Cat Helen Wills puts in customary appearance, but abandons us on receiving cricket-ball on front paws. After what feels like several hours of this, Robert appears, and game at once takes on entirely different—and much brisker—aspect. Mademoiselle immediately says firmly *Moi, je ne joue plus* and walks indoors. Cannot feel that this is altogether a sporting spirit, but have private inner conviction that nothing but moral cowardice prevents my following her example. However, I remain at my post—analogy with Casabianca indicated here—and go so far as to stop a couple of balls and miss one or two catches, after which I am told to bat, and succeed in scoring two before Robin bowls me.

Cricket decidedly not my game, but this reflection closely followed by unavoidable enquiry: What is? Answer comes there none.

July 23rd.—Take the bull by the horns, although belatedly, and seek Mademoiselle at two o'clock in the afternoon—Vicky resting, and Robin reading *Sherlock Holmes* on front stairs, which he prefers to more orthodox sitting-rooms—May I, say I feebly, sit down for a moment?

Mademoiselle at once advances her own armchair and says *Ah, ça me fait du bien de recevoir Madame dans mon petit domaine*—which makes me feel worse than ever.

Extremely painful half-hour follows. We go over ground that we have traversed many times before, and reach conclusions only to unreach them again, and the whole ends, as usual, in floods of tears and mutual professions of esteem. Emerge from it all with only two solid facts to hold on to—that Mademoiselle is to return to her native land at an early date, and that Vicky goes to school at Mickleham in September.

Spend a great deal of time writing to Principal of Vicky's school, to dentist for appointments, and to Army and Navy Stores for groceries. Am quite unable to say why this should leave me entirely exhausted in mind and body—but it does.

July 25th.—Go to Exeter in order to interview yet another cook, and spend exactly two hours and twenty minutes in Registry Office waiting for her to turn up—which she never does. At intervals, I ask offensive-looking woman in orange beret, who sits at desk, What she thinks can have Happened, and she replies that she couldn't say, she's sure, and such a thing has never happened in the office before, never—which makes me feel that it is all my fault.

Harassed-looking lady in transparent pink mackintosh trails in, and asks for a cook-general, but is curtly dismissed by orange beret with assurance that cooks-general for the country are not to be found. If they were, adds the orange beret cynically, her fortune would have been made long ago. The pink mackintosh, like Queen Victoria, is not amused, and goes out again. She is succeeded by a long interval, during which the orange beret leaves the room and returns with a cup of tea, and I look—for the fourteenth time—at only available literature, which consists of ridiculous little periodical called "Do the Dead Speak?" and disembowelled copy of the *Sphere* for February two years ago.

Orange beret drinks tea, and has long and entirely mysterious conversation conducted in whispers with client who looks like a charwoman.

Paralysis gradually invades me, and feel that I shall never move again—but eventually, of course, do so, and find that I have very nearly missed bus home again. Evolve scheme for selling house and going to live in hotel, preferably in South of France, and thus disposing for ever of servant question. Am aware that this is not wholly practicable idea, and would almost certainly lead to very serious trouble with Robert.

(*Query*: Is not theory mistaken, which attributes idle and profitless day-dreaming to youth? Should be much more inclined to add it to many other unsuitable and unprofitable weaknesses of middle-age.)

July 26th—Spirited discussion at breakfast concerning annual problem of a summer holiday. I hold out for Brittany, and produce little leaflet obtained from Exeter

Travel Agency, recklessly promising unlimited sunshine, bathing and extreme cheapness of living. Am supported by Robin—who adds a stipulation that he is not to be asked to eat frogs. Mademoiselle groans, and says that the crossing will assuredly be fatal to us all and this year is one notable for *naufrages*. At this stage Vicky confuses the issue by urging travel by air, and further assures us that in France all the little boys have their hair cut exactly like convicts. Mademoiselle becomes *froissée*, and says *Ah, non, par exemple, je ne m' offense pas, moi, mais ça tout de même*—and makes a long speech, the outcome of which is that Vicky has neither heart nor common sense, at which Vicky howls, and Robert says My God and cuts ham.

Would it not, I urge, be an excellent plan to shut up the house for a month, and have thorough change, beneficial to mind and body alike? (Should also, in this way, gain additional time in which to install new cook, but do not put forward this rather prosaic consideration.)

Just as I think my eloquence is making headway, Robert pushes back his chair and says Well, all this is great waste of time, and he wants to get the calf off to market—which he proceeds to do.

Mademoiselle then begs for ten minutes' Serious Conversation—which I accord with outward calm and inward trepidation. The upshot of the ten minutes—which expand to seventy by the time we have done with them—is that the entire situation is more than Mademoiselle's nerves can endure, and unless she has a complete change of environment immediately, she will *succomber*.

I agree that this must at all costs be avoided, and beg her to make whatever arrangements suit her best. Mademoiselle weeps, and is still weeping when Gladys comes in to clear the breakfast things. (Cannot refrain from gloomy wonder as to nature of comments that this prolonged *tête-à-tête* will give rise to in kitchen.)

Entire morning seems to pass in these painful activities, without any definite result, except that Mademoiselle does not appear at lunch, and both children behave extraordinarily badly.

(*Mem.*: A mother's influence, if any, almost always entirely disastrous. Children invariably far worse under maternal supervision than any other.)

Resume Brittany theme with Robert once more in the evening, and suggest—stimulated by unsuccessful lunch this morning—that a Holiday Tutor might be engaged.

July 29th.—Brittany practically settled, small place near Dinard selected, passports frantically looked for, discovered in improbable places, such as linen cupboard, and—in Robert's case—acting as wedge to insecurely poised chest-of-drawers in dressing-room—and brought up to date at considerable expense.

I hold long conversation with Travel Agency regarding hotel accommodation and registration of luggage, and also interview two holiday tutors, between whom and myself instant and violent antipathy springs up at first sight.

July 30th.—Wholly frightful day, entirely given up to saying good-bye to Mademoiselle. She gives us all presents, small frame composed entirely of mussel shells covered with gilt paint falling to Robert's share, and pink wool bed-socks, with four-leaved clover worked on each, to mine. We present her in return with blue leather hand-bag—into inner pocket of which I have inserted cheque—travelling-clock, and small rolled-gold brooch representing crossed tennis racquets, with artificial pearl for ball—(individual effort of Robin and Vicky). All ends in emotional crescendo, culminating in floods of tears from Mademoiselle, who says nothing except *Mais voyons! Il faut se calmer*, and then weeps harder than ever. Should like to see some of this feeling displayed by children, but they remain stolid, and I explain to Mademoiselle that the reserve of the British is well known, and denotes no lack of heart, but rather the contrary.

(On thinking this over, am pretty sure that it is not in the least true—but am absolutely clear that if occasion arose again, should deliberately say the same thing.)

August 4th.—Travel to Salisbury, for express purpose of interviewing Holiday Tutor, who has himself journeyed from Reading. Terrific expenditure of time and money involved in all this makes me feel that he must at all costs be engaged—but am aware that this is irrational, and make many resolutions against foolish impetuosity.

We meet in uninspiring waiting-room, untenanted by anybody else.

Tutor looks about eighteen, but assures me that he is

nearly thirty, and has been master at Prep. School in Huntingdonshire for years and years.

(*N.B.* Huntingdon most improbable-sounding, but am nearly sure that it does exist. *Mem.*: Look it up in Vicky's atlas on return home.)

Conversation leads to mutual esteem, and we part cordially, with graceful assurances on my part that "I will write". Just as he departs I remember that small, but embarrassing issue still has to be faced, and recall him in order to enquire what I owe him for to-day's expenses. He says Oh, nothing worth talking about, and then mentions a sum which appals me. Pay it, however, without blenching, although well aware it will mean that I shall have to forgo tea in the train, owing to customary miscalculation as to amount of cash required for the day.

Consult Robert on my return; he says Do as I think best, and adds irrelevant statement about grass needing cutting, and I write to Huntingdonshire forthwith, and engage tutor to accompany us to Brittany.

August 6th.—Mademoiselle departs, with one large trunk and eight pieces of hand luggage, including depressed-looking bouquet of marigolds spontaneously offered by Robin. We exchange embraces; she promises to come and stay with us next summer, and says *Allons, du courage, n'est-ce pas?* and weeps again. Robert says that she will miss her train, and they depart for the station, Mademoiselle waving her handkerchief to the last, and hanging across the door at distinctly dangerous angle.

Vicky says cheerfully, How soon will the Tutor

arrive? and Robin picks up Helen Wills and offers to take her to see if there are any greengages—(which there cannot possibly be, as he ate the last ones, totally unripe, yesterday).

Second post brings me letter from Emma Hay, recalling Belgium—where, says Emma, I was the greatest success, underlined—which statement is not only untrue, but actually an insult to such intelligence as I may possess. She hears that I have taken a flat in London—(How?)—and is more than delighted, and there are many, many admirers of my work who will want to meet me the moment I arrive.

Am distressed at realising that although I know every word of dear Emma's letter to be entirely untrue, yet nevertheless cannot help being slightly gratified by it. Vagaries of human vanity very, very curious. Cannot make up my mind in what strain to reply to Emma, so decide to postpone doing so at all for the present.

Children unusually hilarious all the evening, and am forced to conclude that loss of Mademoiselle leaves them entirely indifferent.

August 7th.—Holiday Tutor arrives, and I immediately turn over both children to him, and immerse myself in preparations for journey, now imminent, to Brittany. At the same time, view of garden from behind bedroom window curtains permits me to ascertain that all three are amicably playing tip-and-run on lawn. This looks like auspicious beginning, and am relieved.

August 8th.—Final, and exhaustive, preparations for journey. Eleventh-hour salvation descends in shape of temporary cook. Maids dismissed on holiday, gardener and wife solemnly adjured to Keep an Eye on the house and feed cat, and I ask tutor to sit on Robin's suit-case so that I can shut it, then forget having done so and go to store-cupboard for soap—French trains and hotels equally deficient in this commodity—and return hours later to find him still sitting there exactly like Casabianca. Apologise profusely, am told that it does not matter, and suit-case is successfully dealt with.

Weather gets worse and worse, Shipping Forecast reduces us all to despair—(except Vicky, who says she does so hope we shall be wrecked)—and gale rises hourly. I tell Casabianca that I hope he's a good sailor; he says No, very bad indeed, and Robert suddenly announces that he can see no sense whatever in leaving home at all.

August 10th.—St. Briac achieved, at immense cost of nervous wear and tear. Casabianca invaluable in every respect, but am—rather unjustly—indignant when he informs me that he has slept all night long. History of my own night very different to this, and have further had to cope with Vicky, who does not close an eye after four A.M. and is brisk and conversational, and Robin, who becomes extremely ill from five onwards.

Land at St. Malo, in severe gale and torrents of rain, and Vicky and Robin express astonishment at hearing French spoken all round them, and Robert says that the climate reminds him of England. Casabianca says nothing, but gives valuable help with luggage and later on tells us, very nicely, that we have lost one suit-case. This causes delay, also a great deal of conversation between taxi-driver who is to take us to St. Briac, porter and unidentified friend of taxi-driver's who enters passionately into the whole affair and says fervently *Ah, grâce à Dieu!* when suit-case eventually reappears.

We pass through several villages, and I say This must be it, to each, and nobody takes any notice except Casabianca, who is polite and simulates interest, until we finally whisk into a little *place* and stop in front of cheerful-looking hotel with awning and little green tables outside—all dripping wet. Am concerned to notice no sign of sea anywhere, but shelve this question temporarily, in order to deal with luggage, allotment of bedrooms—(mistake has occurred here, and Madame shows cast-iron determination to treat Casabianca and myself as husband and wife)—and immediate *cafés complets* for all. These arrive, and we consume them in the hall under close and unwavering inspection of about fifteen other visitors, all British and all objectionable-looking.

Inspection of rooms ensues; Robin says When can we bathe—at which, in view of temperature, I feel myself growing rigid with apprehension—and general process of unpacking and settling in follows. Robert, during this, disappears completely, and is only recovered hours later, when he announces that The Sea is about Twenty Minutes' Walk.

General feeling prevails that I am to blame about this, but nothing can be done, and Casabianca, after thoughtful silence, remarks that Anyway the walk will warm us. Subsequent experience, however, proves that it is totally untrue, as we all—excepting children—arrive at large and windy beach in varying degrees of chilliness.

(*N.B.* Never select blue bathing-cap again. This may be all right when circulation normal, but otherwise, effect repellent in the extreme.)

Children dash in boldly, closely followed by Holiday Tutor—to whom I mentally assign high marks for this proof of devotion to duty, as he is pea-green with cold, and obviously shivering—Robert remains on edge of sea, looking entirely superior, and I crawl with excessive reluctance into several inches of water and there become completely paralysed. Shrieks from children, who say that It is Glorious, put an end to this state of affairs, and eventually we all swim about, and tell one another that really it isn't so very cold *in* the water, but better not stay in too long on the first day.

Regain bathing-huts thankfully and am further cheered by arrival of ancient man with *eau chaude pour les pieds.*

Remainder of day devoted to excellent meals, exploring of St. Briac between terrific downpours of rain, and purchase of biscuits, stamps, writing-pad, peaches —(very inexpensive and excellent)—and Tauchnitz volume of *Sherlock Holmes* for Robin, and *Robinson Crusoe* for Vicky.

August 13th.—Opinion that St. Briac is doing us all good, definitely gaining ground. Bathing becomes less agonising, and children talk French freely with hotel chambermaids, who are all charming. Continental breakfast unhappily not a success with Robert, who refers daily to bacon in rather embittered way, but has nothing but praise for *langoustes* and *entrecôtes* which constitute customary luncheon menu.

August 15th.—I enter into conversation with two of fellow-guests at hotel, one of whom is invariably referred to by Robert as "the retired Rag-picker" owing to unfortunate appearance, suggestive of general decay. He tells me about his wife, dead years ago—(am not surprised at this)—who was, he says, a genius in her own way. Cannot find out what way was. He also adds that he himself has written books. I ask what about, and he says Psychology, but adds no more. We talk about weather—bad here, but worse in England—Wolverhampton, which he once went through and where I have never been at all—and humane slaughter, of which both of us declare ourselves to be in favour. Conversation then becomes languid, and shows a tendency to revert to weather, but am rescued by Casabianca, who says he thinks I am wanted—which sounds like the police, but is not.

Look for Vicky in *place*, where she habitually spends much time, playing with mongrel French dogs in gutter. Elderly English spinster—sandy-haired, and name probably Vi—tells me excitedly that some of the dogs have not been behaving quite decently, and it isn't very nice for my little girl to be with them. I reply curtly that Dogs will be Dogs, and think—too late—of many much better answers. Dogs all seem to me to be entirely respectable and well-conducted and see no reason whatever for interfering with any of them. Instead, go with Robin to grocery across the street, where we buy peaches, biscuits and bunches of small black grapes. It pours with rain, Vicky and dogs disperse, and we return indoors to play General Information in obscure corner of dining-room.

Casabianca proves distressingly competent at this, and defeats everybody, Robert included, with enquiry: "What is Wallace's Line?" which eventually turns out to be connected with distinction—entirely unintelligible to me—between one form of animal life and another. Should like to send him to explain it to Vi, and see what she says—but do not, naturally, suggest this.

Children ask excessively ancient riddles, and supply the answers themselves, and Robert concentrates on arithmetical problems. Receive these in silence, and try and think of any field of knowledge in which I can hope to distinguish myself—but without success. Finally, Robin challenges me with what are Seven times Nine? to which I return brisk, but, as it turns out, incorrect, reply.

Bathing takes place as usual, but additional excitement is provided by sudden dramatic appearance of unknown French youth who asks us all in turns if we are doctors, as a German gentleman is having a fit in a bathing-hut. Casabianca immediately dashes into the sea—which—he declares—an English doctor has just entered. (*Query*: Is this second sight, or what?) Robin and Vicky enquire with one voice if they can go and *see* the German gentleman having a fit, and are with great difficulty withheld from making one dash for his bathing-cabin, already surrounded by large and excited collection.

Opinions fly about to the effect that the German gentleman is unconscious—that he has come round—that he is already dead—that he has been murdered. At this, several people scream, and a French lady says *Il ne manquait que cela!* which makes me wonder what the rest of her stay at St. Briac can possibly have been like.

Ask Robert if he does not think he ought to go and help, but he says What for? and walks away.

Casabianca returns, dripping, from the sea, followed by equally dripping stranger, presumably the doctor, and I hastily remove children from spectacle probably to be seen when bathing-hut opens; the last thing I hear being assurance from total stranger to Casabianca that he is *tout à fait aimable*.

Entire episode ends in anti-climax when Casabianca shortly afterwards returns, and informs us that The Doctor Said it was Indigestion, and the German gentleman is now walking home with his wife—who is, he adds impressively, a Norwegian. This, for reasons which continue to defy analysis, seems to add weight and respectability to whole affair.

We return to hotel, again caught in heavy shower, are besought by Robin and Vicky to stop and eat ices at revolting English tea-shop, which they patriotically prefer to infinitely superior French establishments, and weakly yield. Wind whistles through cotton frock— already wet through—that I have mistakenly put on.

On reaching hotel, defy question of expense, and take hot bath, at cost of four francs, *prix spécial*.

Children, with much slamming of doors, and a great deal of conversation, eventually get to bed, and I say to Robert that we *might* look in at the local dance after dinner—which seems easier than saying that I should like to go to it.

Robert's reply much what I expected.

Eventually find myself crawling into dance-room,

sideways, and sitting in severe draught, watching *le tango*, which nobody dances at all well. Casabianca, evidently feeling it his duty, reluctantly suggests that we should dance the next foxtrot—which we do, and it turns out to be Lucky Spot dance and we very nearly—but not quite—win bottle of champagne. This, though cannot say why, has extraordinarily encouraging effect, and we thereupon dance quite gaily until midnight.

August 18th.—Discover that Robin is wearing last available pair of shorts, and that these are badly torn, which necessitates visit to Dinard to take white shorts to cleaners and buy material with which to patch grey ones. No one shows any eagerness to escort me on this expedition and I finally depart alone.

French gentleman with moustache occupies one side of bus and I the other, and we look at one another. Extraordinary and quite unheralded idea springs into my mind to the effect that it is definitely agreeable to find myself travelling anywhere, for any purpose, without dear Robert or either of the children. Am extremely aghast at this unnatural outbreak and try to ignore it.

(*Query*: Does not modern psychology teach that definite danger attaches to deliberate stifling of any impulse, however unhallowed? Answer probably Yes. Cannot, however, ignore the fact that even more definite danger probably attached to encouragement of unhallowed impulse. Can only conclude that peril lies in more or less every direction.)

The moustache and I look out of our respective windows, but from time to time turn round. This exercise not without a certain fascination. Should be very sorry indeed to recall in any detail peculiar fantasies that pass through my mind before Dinard is reached.

Bus stops opposite Casino, the moustache and I rise simultaneously—unfortunately bus gives a last jerk and I sit violently down again—and all is over. Final death-blow to non-existent romance is given when Robin's white shorts, now in last stages of dirt and disreputability, slide out of inadequate paper wrappings and are collected from floor by bus-conductor and returned to me.

Dinard extremely cold, and full of very unengaging trippers, most of whom have undoubtedly come from Lancashire. I deal with cleaners, packet of Lux, chocolate for children, and purchase rose-coloured bathing-cloak for myself, less because I think it suitable or becoming than because I hope it may conduce to slight degree of warmth.

Am moved by obscure feelings of remorse—(what about, in Heaven's name?)—to buy Robert a present, but can see nothing that he would not dislike immeasurably. Finally in desperation select small lump of lead, roughly shaped to resemble Napoleonic outline, and which I try to think may pass as rather unusual antique.

Drink chocolate in crowded *pâtisserie*, all by myself, and surrounded by screeching strangers; am sure that French cakes used to be nicer in far-away youthful days, and feel melancholy and middle-aged. Sight of myself in glass when I powder my nose does nothing whatever to dispel any of it.

August 19th.—Robert asks if Napoleonic figure is meant for a paper-weight? I am inwardly surprised and relieved at this extremely ingenious idea, and at once say Yes, certainly. Can see by Robert's expression that he feels doubtful, but firmly change subject immediately.

Day unmarked by any particularly sensational development except that waves are even larger than usual, and twice succeed in knocking me off my feet, the last time just as I am assuring Vicky that she is perfectly safe with *me*. Robert retrieves us both from extremest depths of the ocean, and Vicky roars. Two small artificial curls—Scylla and Charybdis—always worn under bathing-cap in order that my own hair may be kept dry—are unfortunately swept away, together with bathing-cap, in this disaster, and seen no more.

August 21st.—End of stay at St. Briac approaches, and I begin to feel sentimental, but this weakness unshared by anybody else.

Loss of Scylla and Charybdis very inconvenient indeed.

August 23rd.—Robert shows marked tendency to say that Decent English Food again will come as a great relief, and is more cheerful than I have seen him since we left home. Take advantage of this to suggest that he and I should visit Casino at Dinard and play roulette, which may improve immediate finances, now very low.

Casino agreed upon, and we put on best clothes— which have hitherto remained folded in suit-case and extremely inadequate shelves of small wardrobe which always refuses to open.

Bus takes us to Dinard at breakneck speed, and

deposits us at Casino. All is electric light, advertisement—(*Byrrh*)—and vacancy, and bar-tender tells us that no one will think of arriving before eleven o'clock. We have a drink each, for want of anything better to do, and sit on green velvet sofa and read advertisements. Robert asks What is *Gala des Toutous*? and seems disappointed when I say that I think it is little dogs. Should like—or perhaps not—to know what he thought it was.

We continue to sit on green velvet sofa, and bar-tender looks sorry for us, and turns on more electric light. This obliges us, morally, to have another drink each, which we do. I develop severe pain behind the eyes—(*Query*: Wood-alcohol, or excess of electric light?)—and feel slightly sick. Also *Byrrh* now wavering rather oddly on wall.

Robert says Well, as though he were going to make a suggestion, but evidently thinks better of it again, and nothing transpires. After what seems like several hours of this, three men with black faces and musical instruments come in, and small, shrouded heap in far corner of *salle* reveals itself as a piano.

Bar-tender, surprisingly, has yet further resources at his command in regard to electric light, and we are flooded with still greater illumination. Scene still further enlivened by arrival of very old gentleman in crumpled dress-clothes, stout woman in a green beaded dress that suggests Kensington High Street, and very young girl with cropped hair and scarlet arms. They stand in the very middle of the *salle* and look bewildered, and I feel that Robert and I are old *habitués*.

Robert says dashingly What About Another Drink? and I say No, better not, and then have one, and feel worse than ever. Look at Robert to see if he has noticed anything, and am struck by curious air about him, as of having been boiled and glazed. Cannot make up my mind whether this is, or is not, illusion produced by my own state, and feel better not to enquire, but devote entire attention to focusing *Byrrh* in spot where first sighted, instead of pursuing it all over walls and ceiling.

By the time this more or less accomplished, quite a number of people arrived, though all presenting slightly lost and *dégommé* appearance.

Robert stares at unpleasant-looking elderly man with red hair, and says Good Heavens, if that isn't old Pinkie Morrison, whom he last met in Shanghai Bar in nineteen-hundred-and-twelve. I say, Is he a friend? and Robert replies No, he never could stand the fellow, and old Pinkie Morrison is allowed to lapse once more.

Am feeling extremely ill, and obliged to say so, and Robert suggests tour of the rooms, which we accomplish in silence. Decide, by mutual consent, that we do not want to play roulette, or anything else, but would prefer to go back to bed, and Robert says he thought at the time that those drinks had something fishy about them.

I am reminded, by no means for the first time, of Edgeworthian classic, *Rosamond and the Party of Pleasure*—but literary allusions never a great success with Robert at any time, and feel sure that this is no moment for taking undue risks.

We return to St. Briac and make no further reference to evening's outing, except that Robert enquires, just as I am dropping off to sleep, whether it seems quite worth while having spent seventy francs or so just for the sake of being poisoned and seeing a foul sight like old Pinkie Morrison. This question entirely rhetorical, and make no attempt to reply to it.

August 27th.—Last Day now definitely upon us, and much discussion as to how we are to spend it. Robert suggests Packing—but this is not intended to be taken seriously—and Casabianca assures us that extremely interesting and instructive Ruins lie at a distance of less than forty kilometres, should we care to visit them. Am sorry to say that none of us *do* care to visit them, though I endeavour to palliate this by feeble and unconvincing reference to unfavourable weather.

I say what about Saint Cast, which is reputed to have admirable water-chute? or swimming-baths at Dinard? Children become uncontrollably agitated here, and say Oh, *please* can we bathe in the morning, and then come back to hotel for lunch, and bathe again in the afternoon and have tea at English Tea-Rooms? As this programme is precisely the one that we have been following daily ever since we arrived, nothing could be easier, and we agree. I make mental note to the effect that the young are definitely dependent on routine, and have dim idea of evolving interesting little article on the question, to be handsomely paid for by daily Press—but nothing comes of it.

We go to bathe as usual, and I am accosted by strange woman in yellow pyjamas—cannot imagine how she can survive the cold—who says she met me in South Audley Street some years ago, don't I remember? Have no association whatever with South Audley Street, except choosing dinner-service there with Robert in distant days of wedding presents—(dinner-service now no longer with us, and replaced by vastly inferior copy of Wedgwood). However, I say Yes, yes, of course, and yellow pyjamas at once introduces My boy at Dartmouth—very lank and mottled, and does not look me in the eye—My Sister who Has a Villa Out Here, and My Sister's Youngest Girl—Cheltenham College. Feel that I ought to do something on my side, but look round in vain, family all having departed, with superhuman rapidity, to extremely distant rock.

The sister with the villa says that she has read my book—ha-ha-ha—and how *do* I think of it all? I look blankly at her and say that I don't know, and feel that I am being inadequate. Everybody else evidently thinks so too, and rather distressing silence ensues, ice-cold wind—cannot say why, or from whence—suddenly rising with great violence and blowing us all to pieces.

I say Well, more feebly than ever, and yellow pyjamas says Oh dear, this weather, really—and supposes that we shall all meet down here to-morrow, and I say Yes, of course, before I remember that we cross to-night—but feel quite unable to reopen discussion, and retire to bathing-cabin.

Robert enquires later who that woman was, and I say that I cannot remember, but think her name was something like Busvine. After some thought, Robert says Was it Morton? to which I reply No, more like Chamberlain.

Hours later, remember that it was Heywood.

August 28th.—Depart from St. Briac by bus at seven o'clock, amidst much agitation. Entire personnel of

hotel assembles to see us off, and Vicky kisses everybody. Robin confines himself to shaking hands quite
suddenly with elderly Englishman in plus-fours—with
whom he has never before exchanged a word—and
elderly Englishman says that *Now*, doors will no longer
slam on his landing every evening, he supposes. (*N.B.*
Disquieting thought: does this consideration perhaps
account for the enthusiasm with which we are all being
despatched on our way?)

Robert counts luggage, once in French and three
times in English. Bus removes us from St. Briac, and we
reach Dinard, and are there told that boat is *not* sailing
to-night, and that we can (*a*) Sleep at St. Malo, (*b*)
Remain at Dinard or (*c*) Return to St. Briac. All agree
that this last would be intolerable anti-climax and not
be thought of, and that accommodation must be sought
at Dinard.

Robert says that this is going to run us in for another
ten pounds at least—which it does.

September 1st.—Home once more, and customary
vicissitudes thick as leaves in Vallombrosa.

Temporary cook duly arrived, and is reasonably
amiable—though soup a disappointment and strong
tincture of Worcester Sauce bodes ill for general standard of cooking—but tells me that Everything was left in
sad muddle, saucepans not even clean, and before she
can do anything whatever will require three pudding
basins, new frying-pan, fish-kettle and colander, in
addition to egg-whisk, kitchen forks, and complete
restocking of store-cupboard.

St. Briac hundreds of miles away already, and feel

that twenty years have been added to my age and appearance since reaching home. Robert, on the other hand, looks happier.

Weather cold, and it rains in torrents.

September 3rd.—Ask Robert if he remembers my bridesmaid, Felicity Fairmead, and he says Was that the little one with fair hair? and I say No, the very tall one with dark hair, and he says Oh yes—which does not at all convince me. Upshot of this conversation, rather strangely, is that I ask Felicity to stay, as she has been ill, and is ordered rest in the country.

September 5th.—I go up to London—Robert says, rather unnecessarily, that he supposes money is no object nowadays—to see about the Flat. This comprises very exhausting, but interesting, sessions at furniture-shop, where I lose my head to the tune of about fifty pounds, and realise too late that dear Robert's attitude perhaps not altogether without justification.

Rose unfortunately out of town, so have to sleep at Club, and again feel guilty regarding expenditure, so dine on sausage-and-mash at Lyons establishment opposite to pallid young man who reads book mysteriously shrouded in holland cover. Feel that I must discover what this is at all costs, and conjectures waver between *The Well of Loneliness* and *The Colonel's Daughter*, until title can be spelt out upside down, when it turns out to be *Gulliver's Travels*. Distressing sidelight thrown here on human nature by undeniable fact that I am distinctly disappointed by this discovery, although cannot imagine why.

In street outside I meet Viscountess once known to me in South of France, but feel doubtful if she will remember me, so absorb myself passionately in shop-front, which I presently discover to be entirely filled with very peculiar appliances. Turn away again, and confront Viscountess, who remembers me perfectly, and is charming about small literary effort, which she definitely commits herself to having read. I walk with her to Ashley Gardens and tell her about the flat, which she says is the Very Thing—but does not add what for.

I say it is too late for me to come up with her, and she says Oh no, and we find lift out of order—which morally compels me to accept her invitation, as other-wise it would look as if I didn't think her worth five flights of stairs.

Am shown into beautiful flat—first-floor Doughty Street would easily fit, lock, stock and barrel, into dining-room—and Viscountess says that the house-keeper is out, but would I like anything? I say a glass of water, please, and she is enthusiastic about the excellence of this idea, and goes out, returning, after prolonged absence, with large jug containing about an inch of water, and two odd tumblers, on a tray. I medi-tate writing a short article on How the Rich Live, but naturally say nothing of this aloud, and Viscountess explains that she does not know where drinking-water in the flat is obtainable, so took what was left from dinner. I make civil pretence of thinking this entirely admirable arrangement, and drink about five drops— which is all that either of us can get after equitable division of supplies. We talk about the South of France, and I add a few words about Belgium, but lay no stress on literary society encountered there.

Finally go, at eleven o'clock, and man outside Victoria Station says Good-night, girlie, but cannot view this as tribute to lingering remnant of youthful attractions as (*a*) it is practically pitch-dark, (*b*) he sounds as though he were drunk.

Return to Club bedroom and drink entire contents of water-bottle.

September 6th. — Housekeeper from flat above mine in Doughty Street comes to my rescue, offers to obtain charwoman, stain floors, receive furniture and do everything else. Accept all gratefully, and take my departure with keys of flat — which makes me feel, quite unreasonably, exactly like a burglar. Should like to analyse this rather curious complex, and consider doing so in train, but all eludes me, and read *Grand Hotel* instead.

September 7th — Felicity arrives, looking ill. (*Query:* Why is this by no means unbecoming to her, whereas my own afflictions invariably entail mud-coloured complexion, immense accumulation of already only-too-visible lines on face, and complete limpness of hair?) She is, as usual, charming to the children — does not tell them they have grown, or ask Robin how he likes school, and scores immediate success with both.

I ask what she likes for dinner — (should be indeed out of countenance if she suggested anything except chicken, sardines or tinned corn, which so far as I know is all we have in the house) — and she says An Egg.

And what about breakfast to-morrow morning? She says An Egg again, and adds in a desperate way that an egg is all she wants for any meal, ever.

Send Vicky to the farm with a message about quantity of eggs, to be supplied daily for the present.

Felicity lies down to rest, and I sit on window-sill and talk to her. We remind one another of extraordinary, and now practically incredible, incidents in bygone schooldays, and laugh a good deal, and I feel temporarily younger and better-looking.

Remember with relief that Felicity is amongst the few of my friends that Robert *does* like, and evening passes agreeably with wireless and conversation. Suggest a picnic for to-morrow—at which Robert says firmly that he is obliged to spend entire day in Plymouth—and tie knot in handkerchief to remind myself that Cook must be told jam sandwiches, not cucumber. Take Felicity to her room, and hope that she has enough blankets—if not, nothing can be easier than to produce others without any trouble whatever—Well, in that case, says Felicity, perhaps—Go to linen-cupboard and can find nothing there whatever except immense quantities of embroidered tea-cloths, unhealthy-looking pillow oozing feathers, and torn roller towel. Go to Robin's bed, but find him wide-awake, and quite impervious to suggestion that he does not *really* want more than one blanket on his bed, so have recourse to Vicky, who is asleep. Remove blanket, find it is the only one and replace it, and finally take blanket off my own bed, and put it on Felicity's, where it does not fit, and has to be tucked in till mattress resembles a valley between two hills. Express hope—which sounds ironical—that she may sleep well, and leave her.

September 8th.—Our Vicar's Wife calls in the middle of the morning, in deep distress because no one can be found to act as producer in forthcoming Drama Competition. Will I be an angel? I say firmly No, not on this occasion, and am not sure that Our Vicar's Wife does not, on the whole, look faintly relieved. But what, I ask, about herself? No—Our Vicar has put his foot down. Mothers' Union, Women's Institute, G.F.S. and Choir Outings by all means—but one evening in the week must and shall be kept clear. Our Vicar's Wife, says Our Vicar, is destroying herself, and this he cannot allow. Quite feel that the case, put like this, is unanswerable.

Our Vicar's Wife then says that she knows the very person—excellent actress, experienced producer, willing to come without fee. Unfortunately, is now living at Melbourne, Australia. Later on she also remembers other, equally talented, acquaintances, one of whom can now never leave home on account of invalid husband, the other of whom died just eleven months ago.

I feel that we are getting no farther, but Our Vicar's Wife says that it has been a great relief to talk it all over, and perhaps after all she can persuade Our Vicar to let her take it on, and we thereupon part affectionately.

September 10th.—Picnic, put off on several occasions owing to weather, now takes place, but is—like so many entertainments—rather qualified success, partly owing to extremely mountainous character of spot selected.

Felicity shows gallant determination to make the best of this, and only begs to be allowed to take her own time, to which we all agree, and divide rugs, baskets, cushions, Thermos flasks and cameras amongst ourselves. Ascent appears to me to take hours, moreover am agitated about Felicity, who seems to be turning a rather sinister pale blue colour. Children full of zeal and activity, and dash on ahead, leaving trail of things dropped on the way.

Question as to whether we shall sit in the sun or out of the sun arises, and gives rise to much amiable unselfishness, but is finally settled by abrupt disappearance of sun behind heavy clouds, where it remains. Felicity sits down and pants, but is less blue. I point out scenery, which constitutes only possible excuse for having brought her to such heights, and she is appreciative. Discover that sugar has been left behind. Children suggest having tea at once, but are told that it is only four o'clock, and they had better explore first. This results in Robin's climbing a tree, and taking *Pickwick Papers* out of his pocket to read, and Vicky lying flat on her back in the path, and chewing blades of grass. Customary caution as to unhygienic properties peculiar to blades of grass ensues, and I wonder—not for the first time—why parents continue to repeat admonitions to which children never have paid, and never will pay, slightest attention. Am inspired by this reflection to observe suddenly to Felicity that, anyway, I'm glad my children aren't *prigs*—at which she looks startled, and says, Certainly not—far from it—but perceive that she has not in any way followed my train of thought—which is in no way surprising.

We talk about Italy, the Book Society, and how can Mr. Hugh Walpole find time for all that reading, and write his own books as well—and then again revert to far-distant schooldays, and ask one another what became of that girl with the eyes, who had a father in Patagonia, and if anybody ever heard any more of the black satin woman who taught dancing the last year we were there?

Robin returns, followed by unknown black-and-white dog, between whom and Vicky boisterous and ecstatic friendship instantly springs into being—and I unpack baskets, main contents of which appear to be bottles of lemonade—at which Felicity again reverts to pale-blueness—and pink sugar-biscuits. Can only hope that children enjoy their meal.

Customary feelings of chill, cramp and general discomfort invade me—feel certain that they have long ago invaded Felicity, although she makes no complaint—and picnic is declared to be at an end. Black-and-white dog remains glued to Vicky's heels, is sternly dealt with, and finally disappears into the bracken, but at intervals during descent of hill, makes dramatic reappearances, leaping up in attitudes reminiscent of ballet-dancing. Owners of dog discovered at foot of hill, large gentleman in brown boots, and very thin woman with spats and eye-glasses.

Vicky is demonstrative with dog, the large gentleman looks touched, and the eye-glasses beg my pardon, but if my little girl has really taken a fancy to the doggie, why, they are looking for a home for him—just off to Zanzibar—otherwise, he will have to be destroyed. I say Thank you, thank you, we really couldn't think of such a thing, and Vicky screams and ejaculates.

The upshot of it all is that we *do* think of such a thing—the large gentleman says Dog may not be one of these pedigree animals—which I can see for myself he isn't—but has no vice, and thoroughly good-natured and affectionate—and Felicity, at whom I look, nods twice—am reminded of Lord Burleigh, but do not know why—and mutters *Oui, oui, pourquoi pas?*— which she appears to think will be unintelligible to anyone except herself and me.

Final result is that Vicky, Robin and dog occupy most of the car on the way home, and I try and make up my mind how dog can best be introduced to Robert and Cook.

September 11th.—Decision reached—but cannot say how—that dog is to be kept, and that his name is to be Kolynos.

September 12th.—All is overshadowed by National Crisis, and terrific pronouncements regarding income-tax and need for economy. Our Vicar goes so far as to talk about the Pound from the pulpit, and Robert is asked by Felicity to explain the whole thing to her after dinner—which he very wisely refuses to do.

We lunch with the Frobishers, who are depressed, and say that the wages of everyone on the Estate will have to be reduced by ten per cent. (*Query*: Why are they to be sympathised with on this account? Am much sorrier for their employés.)

Young Frobisher, who is down from Oxford, says

that he has seen it coming for a long while now. (Should like to know why, in that case, he did not warn the neighbourhood.) He undertakes to make all clear—this, once more, at Felicity's request—and involved monologue follows, in which the Pound, as usual, figures extensively. Am absolutely no wiser at the end of it all than I was at the beginning and feel rather inclined to say so, but Lady F. offers me coffee, and asks after children—whom she refers to as "the boy and that dear little Virginia"—and we sink into domesticities and leave the Pound to others. Result is that it overshadows the entire evening and is talked about by Felicity and Robert all the way home in very learned but despondent strain.

(*N.B.* A very long while since I have heard Robert so eloquent, and am impressed by the fact that it takes a National Crisis to rouse him, and begin to wish that own conversational energies had not been dissipated for years on such utterly unworthy topics as usually call them forth. Can see dim outline of rather powerful article here, or possibly *vers libres* more suitable form—but nothing can be done to-night.) Suggest hot milk to Felicity, who looks cold, take infinite trouble to procure this, but saucepan boils over and all is wasted.

September 13th.—Curious and regrettable conviction comes over me that Sunday in the country is entirely intolerable. Cannot, however, do anything about it.

Kolynos chases Helen Wills up small oak-tree, and eats arm and one ear off teddy-bear owned by Vicky. This not a success, and Robert says tersely that if the dog is going to do *that* kind of thing—and then leaves the sentence unfinished, which alarms us all much more than anything he could have said.

Am absent-minded in Church, but recalled by Robin singing hymn, entirely out of tune, and half a bar in advance of everybody else.

Return to roast beef—underdone—and plates not hot. I say boldly that I think roast beef every Sunday is a mistake—why not chicken, or even mutton? but at this everyone looks aghast, and Robert asks What next, in Heaven's name? so feel it better to abandon subject, and talk about the Pound, now familiar topic in every circle.

General stupor descends upon Robert soon after lunch, and he retires to study with *Blackwood's Magazine*. Robin reads *Punch*; Vicky, amidst customary protests, disappears for customary rest.

I tell Felicity that I *must* write some letters, and she rejoins that so must she, and we talk until twenty minutes to four, and then say that it doesn't really matter, as letters wouldn't have gone till Monday anyhow.

Chilly supper—only redeeming feature, baked potatoes—concludes evening, together with more talk of the Pound, about which Robert and Casabianca become, later on, technical and masculine, and Felicity and I prove unable to stay the course, and have recourse to piano instead.

Final peak of desolation is attained when Felicity, going to bed, wishes to know why I have so completely given up my music, and whether it isn't a Great Pity?

Point out to her that all wives and mothers always *do* give up their music, to which she agrees sadly, and we part without enthusiasm.

Should be very sorry to put on record train of thought aroused in me by proceedings of entire day.

September 15th.—End of holidays, as usual, suddenly reveal themselves as being much nearer than anyone had supposed, and Cash's Initials assume extraordinary prominence in scheme of daily life, together with School Lists, new boots for Robin, new everything for Vicky, and tooth-paste for both.

This all dealt with, more or less, after driving Felicity to station, where we all part from her with regret. Train moves out of station just as I realise that egg sandwiches promised her for journey have been forgotten. Am overcome with utterly futile shame and despair, but can do nothing. Children sympathetic, until distracted by man on wheels—Stop me and Buy One—which they do, to the extent of fourpence. Should be prepared to take my oath that far more than fourpenny-worth of icecream will subsequently be found in car and on their clothes.

Extraordinarily crowded morning concluded with visit to dentist, who says that Vicky is Coming Along Nicely, and that Robin can be Polished Off Now, and offers, on behalf of myself, to have a look round, to which I agree, with unsatisfactory results. Look at this! says dentist unreasonably. *Look* at it! Waving in the Wind! Object strongly to this expression, which I consider gross exaggeration, but cannot deny that tooth in question is not all it should be. Much probing and tapping follows, and operator finally puts it to me—on the whole very kindly and with consideration—that this is a Question of Extraction. I resign myself to extraction accordingly, and appoint a date after the children have gone to school.

(Have often wondered to what extent mothers, if left to themselves, would carry universal instinct for putting off everything in the world until after children have gone to school? Feel certain that this law would, if it were possible, embrace everything in life, death itself included.)

It is too late to go home to lunch, and we eat fried fish, chipped potatoes, galantine and banana splits in familiar café.

September 20th.—Suggest to Robert that the moment has now come for making use of Doughty Street flat. I can take Vicky to London, escort her from thence to Mickleham, and then settle down in flat. Settle down what to? says Robert. Writing, I suggest weakly, and seeing Literary Agent. Robert looks unconvinced, but resigned. I make arrangements accordingly.

Aunt Gertrude writes to say that sending a little thing of Vicky's age right away from home is not only unnatural, but absolutely wrong. Have I, she wants to know, any idea of what a childless home will be like? Decide to leave this letter unanswered, but am disgusted to find that I mentally compose at least twelve different replies in the course of the day, each one more sarcastic than the last. Do not commit any of them to paper, but am just as much distracted by them as if I had— and have moments, moreover, of regretting that Aunt Gertrude will never know all the things I *might* have said.

Vicky, whom I observe anxiously, remains unmoved

and cheerful, and refers constantly and pleasantly to this being her Last Evening at home. Moreover, pillow remains bone-dry, and she goes peacefully to sleep rather earlier than usual.

September 22nd.—Robin is taken away by car, and Casabianca escorts Vicky and myself to London, and parts from us at Paddington. I make graceful speech, which I have prepared beforehand, about our gratitude, and hope that he will return to us at Christmas. (Am half inclined to add, if state of the Pound permits—but do not like to.) He says, Not at all, to the first part, and Nothing that he would like better, to the second, and makes a speech on his own account. Vicky embraces him with ardour and at some length, and he departs, and Vicky immediately says Now am I going to school? Nothing is left but to drive with her to Waterloo and thence to Mickleham. Fearful inclination to tears comes over me, but Principal is tact personified, and provides tea at exactly right moment.

September 25th.—*Doughty Street.*—Quite incredibly, find myself more or less established, and startlingly independent. Flat—once I have bought electric fire, and had it installed by talkative young man with red hair—very comfortable; except for absence of really restful armchair, and unfamiliarity of geyser-bath, of which I am terrified. Bathroom is situated on stairs, which are in continual use, and am therefore unable to take bath with door wide open, as I should like to do. Compromise with open window, through which blacks come in, and smell of gas and immense quantities of steam go out. Remainder of steam has strange property of gathering itself on to the ceiling and there collecting, whence it descends upon my head and shoulders in extraordinarily cold drops. Feel sure that there is scientific, and doubtless interesting, explanation of this minor chemical phenomenon, but cannot at the moment work it out. (*N.B.* Keep discussion of this problem for suitable occasion, preferably when seated next to distinguished scientist at dinner-party. In the meantime, cower beneath bath-towel in farthest corner of bathroom—which is saying very little—but am quite unable to dodge unwanted shower-bath.)

Excellent reports reach me of Vicky at Mickleham—Robin writes—as usual—about unknown boy called Felton who has brought back a new pencil-box this term, and other, equally unknown, boy whose parents have become possessed of house in the New Forest —and Robert sends laconic, but cheerful, account of preparations for Harvest Home supper. Less satisfactory communication arrives from Bank, rather ungenerously pointing out extremely small and recent overdraft.

Rose telephones to ask if I would like to come to literary evening party, to be given by distinguished novelist whose books are well known to me, and who lives in Bloomsbury. I say Yes, if she is sure it will be All Right. Rose replies Why not, and then adds— distinct afterthought—that I am myself a Literary Asset to society nowadays. Pause that ensues in conversation makes it painfully evident that both of us know the last statement to be untrue, and I shortly afterwards ring off.

I consider the question of what to wear, and decide that black is dowdy, but green brocade with Ciro pearls will be more or less all right, and shall have to have old white satin shoes recovered to match.

September 28th.—Literary party, to which Rose takes me as promised. Take endless trouble with appearance, and am convinced, before leaving flat, that this has reached very high level indeed, thanks to expensive shampoo-and-set, and moderate use of cosmetics. Am obliged to add, however, that on reaching party and seeing everybody else, at once realise that I am older, less well dressed, and immeasurably plainer than any other woman in the room. (Have frequently observed similar reactions in myself before.)

Rose introduces me to hostess—she looks much as I expected, but photographs which have appeared in Press evidently, and naturally, slightly idealised. Hostess says how glad she is that I was able to come—(*Query*: Why?)—and is then claimed by other arrivals, to whom she says exactly the same thing, with precisely similar intonation. (*Note*: Society of fellow-creatures promotes cynicism. Should it be avoided on this account? If so, what becomes of Doughty Street flat?)

Rose says Do I see that man over there? Yes, I do. He has written a book that will, says Rose impressively, undoubtedly be seized before publication and burnt. I enquire how she knows, but she is claimed by an acquaintance and I am left to gaze at the man in silent astonishment and awe. Just as I reach the conclusion that he cannot possibly be more than eighteen years old, I hear a scream—this method of attracting attention absolutely unavoidable, owing to number of people all talking at once—and am confronted by Emma Hay in rose-coloured fish-net, gold lace, jewelled turban and necklace of large barbaric pebbles.

Who, shrieks Emma, would have dreamt of this? and do I see that man over there? He has just finished a book that is to be seized and burnt before publication. A genius, of course, she adds casually, but far in advance of his time. I say Yes, I suppose so, and ask to be told who else is here, and Emma gives me rapid outline of many rather lurid careers, leading me to conclusion that literary ability and domestic success not usually compatible. (*Query*: Will this invalidate my chances?)

Dear Emma then exclaims that It is Too Bad I should be so utterly Out of It—which I think might have been better worded—and introduces a man to me, who in his turn introduces his wife, very fair and pretty. (Have unworthy spasm of resentment at sight of so much attractiveness, but stifle instantly.) Man offers to get me a drink, I accept, he offers to get his wife one, she agrees, and he struggles away through dense crowd. Wife points out to me young gentleman who has written a book that is to be seized, etc., etc. Am disgusted to hear myself saying in reply Oh really, in tone of intelligent astonishment.

Man returns with two glasses of yellow liquid—mine tastes very nasty, and wife leaves hers unfinished after one sip—and we talk about Income Tax, the Pound, France, and John van Druten, of whom we think well. Rose emerges temporarily from press of distinguished talkers, asks Am I all right? and is submerged again before I can do more than nod. (Implied lie here.) Man and his wife, who do not know anyone present, remain firmly glued to my side, and I to theirs for precisely similar reason. Conversation flags, and my throat feels extremely sore. Impossibility of keeping the Pound out of the conversation more and more apparent, and character of the observations that we make about it distinguished neither for originality nor for sound constructive quality.

Emma recrudesces later, in order to tell me that James—(totally unknown to me)—has at last chucked Sylvia—(of whom I have never heard)—and is definitely living with Naomi—(again a complete blank)—who will have to earn enough for both, and for her three children—but James' children by Susan are being looked after by dear Arthur. I say, without conviction, that this at least is a comfort, and Emma—turban now definitely over right eyebrow—vanishes again.

Original couple introduced by Emma still my sole hope of companionship, and am morally certain that I am theirs. Nevertheless am quite unable to contemplate resuming analysis of the Pound, which I see looming ahead, and am seriously thinking of saying that there is a man here whose book is to be seized prior to publication, when Rose intervenes, and proposes departure. Our hostess quite undiscoverable, Emma offers officious and extremely scandalous explanation of this disappearance, and Rose and I are put into taxi by elderly man, unknown to me, but whom I take to be friend of Rose's, until she tells me subsequently that she has never set eyes on him in her life before. I suggest that he may be man-servant hired for the occasion, but

Rose says No, more likely a distinguished dramatist from the suburbs.

October 1st.—Direct result of literary party is that I am rung up on telephone by Emma, who says that she did not see anything like enough of me and we must have a long talk, what about dinner together next week in Soho where she knows of a cheap place? (This, surely, rather odd form of invitation?) Am also rung up by Viscountess's secretary, which makes me feel important, and asked to lunch at extremely expensive and fashionable French restaurant. Accept graciously, and spend some time wondering whether circumstances would justify purchase of new hat for the occasion. Effect of new hat on morale very beneficial, as a rule.

Also receive letter—mauve envelope with silver cipher staggers me from the start—which turns out to be from Pamela Pringle, who is mine affectionately as ever, and is so delighted to think of my being in London, and *must* talk over dear old days, so will I ring her up immediately and suggest something? I do ring her up—although not immediately—and am told that she can just fit me in between massage at four and Bridge at six, if I will come round to her flat in Sloane Street like an angel. This I am willing to do, but make mental reservation to the effect that dear old days had better remain in oblivion until P. P. herself introduces them into conversation, which I feel certain she will do sooner or later.

Proceed in due course to flat in Sloane Street— entrance impressive, with platoons of hall-porters, one of whom takes me up in lift and leaves me in front of bright purple door with antique knocker representing mermaid, which I think unsuitable for London, although perhaps applicable to Pamela's career. Interior of flat entirely furnished with looking-glass tables, black pouffes, and acutely angular blocks of green wood. Am overawed, and wonder what Our Vicar's Wife would feel about it all—but imagination jibs.

Pamela receives me in small room—more looking-glass, but fewer pouffes, and angular blocks are red with blue zigzags—and startles me by kissing me with utmost effusion. This very kind, and only wish I had been expecting it, as could then have responded better and with less appearance of astonishment amounting to alarm. She invites me to sit on a pouffe and smoke a Russian cigarette, and I do both, and ask after her children. Oh, says Pamela, the *children*! and begins to cry, but leaves off before I have had time to feel sorry for her, and bursts into long and complicated speech. Life, declares Pamela, is very, *very* difficult, and she is perfectly certain that I feel, as she does, that nothing in the world matters except Love. Stifle strong inclination to reply that banking account, sound teeth and adequate servants matter a great deal more, and say Yes Yes, and look as intelligently sympathetic as possible.

Pamela then rushes into impassioned speech, and says that It is not her fault that men have always gone mad about her, and no doubt I remember that it has always been the same, ever since she was a mere tot— (do not remember anything of the kind, and if I did, should certainly not say so)—and that after all, divorce is not looked upon as it used to be, and it's always the woman that has to pay the penalty, don't I agree? Feel it unnecessary to make any very definite reply to this, and am in any case not clear as to whether I do agree or not, so again have recourse to air of intelligent understanding, and inarticulate, but I hope expressive, sound. Pamela apparently completely satisfied with this, as she goes on to further revelations to which I listen with eyes nearly dropping out of my head with excitement. Feel I ought to say something, so enquire tentatively if her first marriage was a happy one—which sounds better than asking if *any* of her marriages were happy ones. *Happy?* says Pamela. Good Heavens, what am I talking about? Conclude from this that it was *not* a happy one. Then what, I suggest, about Templer-Tate? That, Pamela replies sombrely, was Hell. (Should like to enquire for whom, but do not, naturally, do so.) Next branch of the subject is Pringle. Waddell—such is his Christian name, which rouses in me interesting train of speculative thought as to mentality of his parents— Waddell does not understand his wife. Never has understood her, never possibly could understand her. She is sensitive, affectionate, intelligent in her own way though of course not *clever*, says Pamela—and really, although she says so herself, remarkably easy to get on with. A Strong Man could have done anything in the world with her. She is like that. The ivy type. Clinging. I nod, to show agreement. Further conversation reveals that she has clung in the wrong directions, and that this has been, and is being, resented by Pringle. Painful domestic imbroglio is unfolded. I say weakly that I am sorry to hear this—which is not true, as I am thoroughly enjoying myself.

Telephone-calls five times interrupt us, when Pamela

is effusive and excitable to five unknown conversation-alists and undertakes to meet someone on Friday at three, to go and see someone else who is being too, too ill in a Nursing Home, and to help somebody else to meet a woman who knows someone who is connected with films.

Finally, take my leave, after being once more em-braced by Pamela, and am shot down in lift—full of looking-glass, and am much struck with the inadequacy of my appearance in these surroundings, and feel certain that lift-attendant is also struck by it, although aware that his opinion ought to be matter of complete indif-ference to me.

Temperature of Sloane Street seems icy after interior of flat, and cold wind causes my nose to turn scarlet and my eyes to water. Fate selects this moment for the emergence of Lady B.—sable furs up to her eyebrows and paint and powder unimpaired—from hat-shop, to waiting car and chauffeur. She sees me and screams—at which passers-by look at us, astonished—and says Good gracious her, what next? She would as soon have expected to see the geraniums from the garden uproot-ing themselves from the soil and coming to London. (Can this be subtle allusion to effect of the wind upon my complexion?) I say stiffly that I am staying at My Flat for a week or two. Where? demands Lady B. sceptically—to which I reply, Doughty Street, and she shakes her head and says that conveys *nothing*. Should like to refer her sharply to *Life of Charles Dickens*, but before I have time to do so she asks what on earth I am doing in Sloane Street, of all places, and offers to give me a lift to Brondesbury or wherever-it-is, as her chauffeur is quite brilliant at knowing his way *any-where*. Thank her curtly and refuse.

October 3rd.—Observe in myself tendency to go farther and farther in search of suitable cheap restaurants for meals—this not so much from economic considerations, as on extremely unworthy grounds that walking in the streets amuses me. (Cannot for one instant contemplate even remote possibility of Lady B.'s ever coming to hear of this, and do not even feel disposed to discuss it with Robert. Am, moreover, perfectly well aware that I have come to London to Write, and not to amuse myself.)

Determination to curb this spirit causes me to lunch at small establishment in Theobald's Road, completely filled by hatless young women with cigarettes, one old lady with revolting little dog that growls at everyone, and small, pale youth who eats custard, and reads mysterious periodical entitled *Helping Hands*.

Solitary waitress looks harassed, and tells me—unsolicited—that she has only a *small* portion of The Cold left. I say Very Well, and The Cold, after long interval, appears, and turns out to be pork. Should like to ask for a potato, but waitress avoids me, and I go without.

Hatless young women all drink coffee in immense quantities, and I feel this is literary, and should like to do the same, but for cast-iron conviction that coffee will be nasty. Am also quite unattracted by custard, and finally ask for A Bun, please, and waitress—more harassed than ever—enquires in return if I mind the one in the window. I recklessly say No, if it hasn't been there too long, and waitress says Oh, not very, and seems relieved.

Singular conversation between hatless young women engages my attention, and distracts me from rather severe struggle with the bun. My neighbours discuss Life, and the youngest of them remarks that Perversion has practically gone out altogether now. The others seem to view this as pessimistic, and assure her encouragingly that, so far, nothing else has been found to take its place. One of them adjures her to Look at Sprott and Nash—which sounds like suburban grocers, but is, I think, mutual friends. Everybody says Oh, of course, to Sprott and Nash, and seems relieved. Someone tells a story about a very old man, which I try without success to overhear, and someone else remarks disapprovingly that *he* can't know much about it, really, as he's well over seventy, and it only came into fashion a year or two ago. Conversation then becomes inconsequent, and veers about between *Cavalcade*, methods of hair-dressing, dog-breeding, and man called William—but with tendency to revert at intervals to Sprott and Nash.

Finish bun with great difficulty, pay tenpence for entire meal, leave twopence for waitress, and take my departure. Decide quite definitely that this, even in the cause of economy, wasn't worth it. Remember with immense satisfaction that I lunch to-morrow at Boulestin's with charming Viscountess, and indulge in reflections concerning strange contrasts offered by Life: cold pork and stale bun in Theobald's Road on Tuesday, and lobster and *poire Hélène*—(I hope)—at Boulestin's on Wednesday. Hope and believe with all my heart that similar startling dissimilarity will be observable in nature of company and conversation.

Decide to spend afternoon in writing and devote much time to sharpening pencils, looking for india-rubber—finally discovered inside small cavity of gramophone, intended for gramophone needles. This starts train of thought concerning whereabouts of gramophone needles, am impelled to search for them, and am eventually dumb-founded at finding them in a match-box, on shelf of kitchen cupboard. (Vague, but unpleasant, flight of fancy here, beginning with Vicky searching for biscuits in insufficient light, and ending in Coroner's Court and vote of severe censure passed—rightly—by Jury.)

(*Query*: Does not imagination, although in many ways a Blessing, sometimes carry its possessor too far? *Answer* emphatically Yes.)

Bell rings, and fails to leave off. I am filled with horror, and look up at it—inaccessible position, and nothing to be seen except two mysterious little jam-jars and some wires. Climb on a chair to investigate, then fear electrocu-tion and climb down again without having done anything. Housekeeper from upstairs rushes down, and unknown females from basement rush up, and we all look at the ceiling and say Better fetch a Man. This is eventually done, and I meditate ironical article on Feminism, while bell rings on madly. Man, however, arrives, says Ah, yes, he thought as much, and at once reduces bell to order, apparently by sheer power of masculinity.

Am annoyed, and cannot settle down to anything.

October 7th.—Extraordinary behaviour of dear Rose, with whom I am engaged—and have been for days past—to go and have supper to-night. Just as I am trying to decide whether bus to Portland Street or tube to Oxford Circus will be preferable, I am called up on telephone by Rose's married niece, who lives in Hertfordshire, and is young and modern, to say that speaker for her Women's Institute to-night has failed, and that Rose, on being appealed to, has at once suggested my name and expressed complete willingness to dispense with my society for the evening. Utter impossibility of pleading previous engagement is obvious; I contemplate for an instant saying that I have influenza, but remember in time that niece, very intelligently, started the conversation by asking how I was, and that I replied Splendid, thanks—and there is nothing for it but to agree.

(*Query*: Should much like to know if it was for this that I left Devonshire.)

Think out several short, but sharply worded, letters to Rose, but time fails; I can only put brush and comb, slippers, sponge, three books, pyjamas and hot-water bottle into case—discover later that I have forgotten powder-puff and am very angry, but to no avail—and repair by train to Hertfordshire.

Niece meets me—clothes immensely superior to anything that I ever have had, or shall have—is charming, expresses gratitude, and asks what I am going to speak about. I reply, Amateur Theatricals. Excellent of course, she says unconvincingly, and adds that the Institute has a large Dramatic Society already, that they are regularly produced by well-known professional actor, husband of Vice-President, and were very well placed in recent village-drama competition, open to all England.

At this I naturally wilt altogether, and say Then perhaps better talk about books or something—which sounds weak, even as I say it, and am convinced that niece feels the same, though she remains imperturbably charming. She conducts me into perfectly delightful, entirely modern, house, which I feel certain—rightly, I discover later—has every newest labour-saving device ever invented.

Niece shows me her children—charming small boy, angelic baby—both, needless to say, have curls. She asks civilly about Robin and Vicky, and I can think of nothing whatever to the credit of either, so merely reply that they are at school.

N.B. Victorian theory as to maternal pride now utterly discredited. Affection, yes. Pride, no.

We have dinner—niece has changed into blue frock which suits her and is, of course, exactly right for the occasion. I do the best I can with old red dress and small red cap that succeeds in being thoroughly unbecoming without looking in the least up to date, and endeavour to make wretched little compact from bag do duty for missing powder-puff. Results not good.

Evening at Institute reasonably successful—am much impressed by further display of efficiency from niece, as President—I speak about Books, and obtain laughs by introduction of three entirely irrelevant anecdotes.

Niece asks kindly if I am tired. I say No, not at all, which is a lie, and she presently takes me home and I go to bed. Spare-room admirable in every respect, but no waste-paper basket. This solitary flaw in general perfection a positive relief.

October 10th.—Am exercised over minor domestic problem, of peculiarly prosaic description, centring round collection of dust-bins in small, so-called back garden of Doughty Street flat. All these dust-bins invariably brim-full, and am convinced that contents of alien waste-paper baskets contribute constantly to mine, as have no recollection at all of banana-skin, broken blue-and-white saucer, torn fragments of *Police-Court Gazette*, or small, rusty tin kettle riddled with holes.

Contemplate these phenomena with great dislike, but cannot bring myself to remove them, so poke my contribution down with handle of feather-duster, and retire.

October 13th.—Call upon Rose, in rather unusual frame of mind which suddenly descends upon me after lunch—cannot at all say why—impelling me to demand explanation of strange behaviour last week.

Rose at home, and says How nice to see me, which takes the wind out of my sails, but I rally, and say firmly that That is All Very Well, but what about that evening at the Women's Institute? At this Rose, though holding her ground, blanches perceptibly, and tells me to sit down quietly and explain what I mean. Am very angry at *quietly*, which sounds as if I usually smashed up all the furniture, and reply—rather scathingly—that I will do my best not to rouse the neighbourhood. Unfortunately, rather unguarded movement of annoyance results in upsetting of small table, idiotically loaded with weighty books, insecurely fastened box of cigarettes, and two ash-trays. We collect them again in silence—cigarettes particularly elusive, and roll to immense distances underneath sofa and behind electric fire—and finally achieve an arm-chair apiece, and glare at one another across expanse of Persian rug.

Am astonished that Rose is able to look me in the face at all, and say so, and long and painful conversation ensues, revealing curious inability on both our parts to keep to main issue. Should be sorry to recall in any detail exact number and nature of utterly irrelevant observations exchanged, but have distinct recollection that Rose asserts at various times that: (*a*) If I had been properly psycho-analysed years ago, I should realise that my mind has never really come to maturity at all. (*b*) It is perfectly ridiculous to wear shoes with such high heels. (*c*) Robert is a perfect *saint* and has a lot to put up with. (*d*) No one in the world can be readier than Rose is to admit that I can Write, but to talk about The Piano is absurd.

Cannot deny that in return I inform her in the course of the evening that: (*a*) Her best friend could never call Rose tidy—look at the room now! (*b*) There is a great difference between being merely impulsive, and being utterly and grossly inconsiderate. (*c*) Having been to America does not, in itself, constitute any claim to infallibility on every question under the sun. (*d*) Naturally, what's past is past, and I don't want to remind her about the time she lost her temper over those idiotic iris-roots.

Cannot say at what stage I am reduced to tears, but this unfortunately happens, and I explain that it is entirely due to rage, and nothing else. Rose suddenly says there is nothing like coffee, and rings the bell.

Retire to the bathroom in great disorder, mop myself up—tears highly unbecoming, and should much like to know how film-stars do it, usual explanation of Glycerine seems to me quite inadequate. Return to sitting-room and find that Rose, with extraordinary presence of mind, has put on the gramophone. Listen in silence to Rhapsody in Blue, and feel better.

Admirable coffee is brought in, drink some, and feel better still. Am once more enabled to meet Rose's eye, which now indicates contrition, and we simultaneously say that this is Perfectly Impossible, and Don't let's quarrel, whatever we do. All is harmony in a moment, and I kiss Rose, and she says that the whole thing was her fault, from start to finish, and I say No, it was mine *absolutely*, and we both say that we didn't really mean anything we said.

(Cold-blooded and slightly cynical idea crosses my mind later that entire evening has been complete waste of nervous energy, if neither of us meant any of the things we said—but refuse to dwell on this aspect of the case.)

Eventually go home feeling extraordinarily tired. Find letter from Vicky, with small drawing of an elephant, that I think distinctly clever and modernistic, until I read letter and learn that it is A Table, laid for Dinner, also communication from Literary Agent saying how much he looks forward to seeing my new manuscript. (Can only hope that he enjoys the pleasures of anticipation as much as he says, since they are, at present rate of progress, likely to be prolonged.)

Am also confronted by purple envelope and silver cipher, now becoming familiar, and scrawled invitation from Pamela Pringle to lunch at her flat and meet half a dozen dear friends who simply adore my writing. Am sceptical about this, but shall accept, from degraded motives of curiosity to see the dear friends, and still more degraded motives of economy, leading me to accept a free meal from whatever quarter offered.

October 16th. — Find myself in very singular position as regards the Bank, where distinctly unsympathetic attitude prevails in regard to quite small overdraft. Am interviewed by the Manager, who says he very much regrets that my account at present appears to be absolutely *Stationary*. I say with some warmth that he cannot regret it nearly as much as I do myself, and deadlock appears to have been reached. Manager — cannot imagine why he thinks it a good idea — suddenly opens a large file, and reads me out extract from correspondence with very unendearing personality referred to as his Director, instructing him to bring pressure to bear upon this client — (me). I say Well, that's all right, he *has* brought pressure to bear, so he needn't worry — but perfect understanding fails to establish itself, and we part in gloom.

October 18th. — Determine to stifle impending cold, if only till after Pamela's luncheon-party to-morrow, and take infinite trouble to collect jug, boiling water, small bottle of Friar's Balsam and large bath-towel. All is ruined by one careless movement, which tips jug, Friar's Balsam and hot water down front of my pyjamas. Am definitely scalded — skin breaks in one place and turns scarlet over area of at least six inches — try to show presence of mind and remember that Butter is The Thing, remember that there is no butter in the flat—frantic and irrelevant quotation here, *It was the Best butter*—remember vaseline, use it recklessly, and retire to bed in considerable pain and with cold unalleviated.

October 19th.—Vagaries of Fate very curious and inexplicable. Why should severe cold in the head assail me exactly when due to lunch with Pamela Pringle in character of reasonably successful authoress, in order to meet unknown gathering of smart Society Women? Answer remains impenetrably mysterious.

Take endless trouble with appearance, decide to wear my Blue, then take it all off again and revert to my Check, but find that this makes me look like a Swiss nursery governess, and return once more to Blue. Regret, not for the first time, that Fur Coat, which constitutes my highest claim to distinction of appearance, will necessarily have to be discarded in hall.

Sloane Street achieved, as usual, via bus No. 19, and I again confront splendours of Pamela's purple front door. Am shown into empty drawing-room, where I meditate in silence on unpleasant, but all-too-applicable, maxim that It is Provincial to Arrive too Early. Presently strange woman in black, with colossal emerald brooch pinned in expensive-looking frills of lace, is shown in, and says How d'y do, very amiably, and we talk about the weather, Gandhi and French poodles. (Why? There are none in the room, and can trace no association of ideas whatsoever.)

Two more strange women in black appear, and I feel that my Blue is becoming conspicuous. All appear to know one another well, and to have met last week at lunch, yesterday evening at Bridge, and this morning at an Art Exhibition. No one makes any reference to Pamela, and grave and unreasonable panic suddenly assails me that I am in wrong flat altogether. Look madly round to see if I can recognise any of the furniture, and woman with osprey and ropes of pearl enquires if I am missing that *precious* horse. I say No, not really—which is purest truth—and wonder if she has gone off her head. Subsequent conversation reveals that horse was made of soapstone.

More and more anxious about non-appearance of Pamela P., especially when three more guests arrive— black two-piece, black coat-and-skirt, and black crêpe-de-chine with orange-varnished nails. (My Blue now definitely revealed as inferior imitation of Joseph's coat, no less, and of very nearly equal antiquity.)

They all call one another by Christian names, and have much to say about mutual friends, none of whom I have ever heard of before.

Door flies open and Pamela Pringle, of whom I have now given up all hope, rushes in, kisses everybody, falls over little dog—which has mysteriously appeared out of the blue and vanishes again after being fallen over— and says Oh, do we all know one another, and isn't she a *fearfully* bad hostess but she simply could *not* get away from Amédé, who really is a Pet. (Just as I have decided that Amédé is another little dog, it turns out that he is a Hairdresser.)

Lunch is announced, and we all show customary reluctance to walking out of the room in simple and straightforward fashion, and cluster round the threshold with self-depreciating expressions until herded out by Pamela. I find myself sitting next to her—quite undeserved position of distinction, and probably intended for somebody else—with extraordinarily elegant black crêpe-de-chine on other side.

Black crêpe-de-chine says that she adored my book, and so did her husband, and her sister-in-law, who is Clever and never says *Anything* unless she really Means It, thought it quite marvellous. Having got this off her chest, she immediately begins to talk about recent visit of her own to Paris, and am forced to the conclusion that her standards of sincerity must fall definitely below those of unknown sister-in-law.

Try to pretend that I know Paris as well as she does, but can see that she is not in the least taken in by this.

Conversation veers about between Paris, weight-reduction—(quite unnecessary, none of them can possibly weigh more than seven stone, if that)—and annexation by someone called Diana of second husband of someone else called Tetsie, which everyone agrees was *utterly* justified, but no reason definitely given for this, except that Tetsie is a perfect *darling*, we all know, but no one on earth could possibly call her smartly turned-out.

(Feel that Tetsie and I would have at least one thing in common, which is more than I can say about anybody else in the room—but this frame of mind verging on the sardonic, and not to be encouraged.)

Pamela turns to me just as we embark on entirely admirable *coupe Jacques*, and talks about books, none published for more than five minutes and none of which, in consequence, I have as yet read—but feel that

I am expected to be on my own ground here, and must—like Mrs. Dombey—make an effort, which I do by the help of remembering Literary Criticisms in *Time and Tide's* issue of yesterday.

Interesting little problem hovers on threshold of consciousness here: How on earth do Pamela and her friends achieve conversation about books which I am perfectly certain they have none of them read? Answer, at the moment, baffles me completely.

Return to drawing-room ensues. Am definitely relieved when emerald-brooch owner says that It is too, too sad, but she must fly, as she really is responsible for the whole thing, and it can't begin without her—which might mean a new Permanent Wave, or a command performance at Buckingham Palace, but shall never know now which, as she departs without further explanation.

Make very inferior exit of my own, being quite unable to think of any reason for going except that I have been wanting to almost ever since I arrived—which cannot, naturally, be produced. Pamela declares that having me has been Quite Wonderful, and we part.

October 23rd.—Telephone bell rings at extraordinary hour of eleven-eighteen P.M., and extremely agitated voice says Oh is that me, to which I return affirmative answer and rather curt rider to the effect that I have been in bed for some little while. Voice then reveals itself as belonging to Pamela P.—which doesn't surprise me in the least—who is, she says, in great, great trouble, which she cannot possibly explain. (Should much like to ask whether it was worth while getting me out of bed in order to hear that no explanation is available.) But, Pamela asks, will I, whatever happens, *swear* that she has spent the evening with me, in my flat? If I will not do this, then it is—once more—perfectly impossible to say what will happen. But Pamela knows that I will—I always was a darling—and I couldn't refuse such a tiny, tiny thing, which is simply a question of life and death.

Am utterly stunned by all this, and try to gain time by enquiring weakly if Pamela can by any chance tell me where she really *has* spent the evening. Realise as soon as I have spoken that this is not a tactful question, and am not surprised when muffled scream vibrates down receiver into my ear. Well, never mind *that*, then, I say, but just give me some idea as to who is likely to ask me what Pamela's movements have been, and why. Oh, replies Pamela, she is the most absolutely misunderstood woman on earth, and don't I feel that men are simply brutes? There isn't one of them—not one—whom one can trust to be really tolerant and broad-minded and understanding. They only want One Thing.

Feel quite unable to cope with this over telephone wire, and am, moreover, getting cold, and find attention straying towards possibility of reaching switch of electric fire with one hand whilst holding receiver with the other. Flexibility of the human frame very remarkable, but cannot altogether achieve this and very nearly over-balance, but recover in time to hear Pamela saying that if I will do this one thing for her, she will never, never forget it. There isn't anyone else, she adds, whom she *could* ask. (Am not at all sure if this is any compliment.) Very well, I reply, if asked, I am prepared to say that

Pamela spent the evening with me here, but I hope that no one *will* ask and Pamela must distinctly understand that this is the first and last time I shall ever do anything of the kind. Pamela begins to be effusive, but austere voice from the unseen says that Three Minutes is Up, will we have another Three, to which we both say No simultaneously, and silence abruptly supervenes.

Crawl into bed again feeling exactly as if I had been lashed to an iceberg and then dragged at the cart's tail. Very singular and unpleasant sensation. Spend disturbed and uncomfortable night, evolving distressing chain of circumstances by which I may yet find myself at the Old Bailey committing perjury and—still worse—being found out—and, alternatively, imagining that I hear rings and knocks at front door, heralding arrival of Pamela P.'s husband bent on extracting information concerning his wife's whereabouts.

Wake up, after uneasy dozings, with bad headache, impaired complexion and strong sensation of guilt. Latter affects me to such a degree that am quite startled and conscience-stricken at receiving innocent and child-like letters from Robin and Vicky, and am inclined to write back and say that they ought not to associate with me—but breakfast restores balance, and I resolve to relegate entire episode to oblivion.

October 25th.—Am taken out to lunch by Literary Agent, which makes me feel important, and celebrated writers are pointed out to me—mostly very disappointing, but must on no account judge by appearances. Literary Agent says Oh, by the way, he has a small cheque for me at the office, shall he send it along? Try to emulate this casualness, and reply Yes, he may as well, and shortly afterwards rush home and write to inform Bank Manager that, reference our recent conversation, he may shortly expect to receive a Remittance— which I think sounds well, and commits me to nothing definite.

October 27th.—Am chilled by reply from Bank Manager, who has merely Received my letter and Noted Contents. This lack of *abandon* very discouraging, moreover very different degree of eloquence prevails when subject under discussion is deficit, instead of credit, and have serious thoughts of writing to point this out.

Receive curious and unexpected tribute from total stranger in the middle of Piccadilly Circus, where I have negotiated crossing with success, but pause on refuge, when voice says in my ear that owner has been following me ever since we left the pavement—which does, indeed, seem like hours ago—and would like to do so until Haymarket is safely reached. Look round at battered-looking lady carrying three parcels, two library books, small umbrella and one glove, and say Yes, yes, certainly, at the same time wondering if she realises extraordinarily insecure foundations on which she has built so much trust. Shortly afterwards I plunge, Look Right, Look Left, and execute other manœuvres, and find myself safe on opposite side. Battered-looking lady has, rather to my horror, disappeared completely, and I see her no more. Must add this to life's many other unsolved mysteries.

October 31st.—Letters again give me serious cause for reflection. Robert definitely commits himself to wishing that I would come home again, and says—rather touchingly—that he finds one can see the house from a hill near Plymouth, and he would like me to have a look at it. Shall never wholly understand advantages to be derived from seeing any place from immense distance instead of close at hand, as could so easily be done from the tennis lawn without any exertion at all—but quite realise that masculine point of view on this question, as on so many others, differs from my own, and am deeply gratified by dear Robert's thought of me.

Our Vicar's Wife sends postcard of Lincoln Cathedral, and hopes on the back of it that I have not forgotten our Monthly Meeting on Thursday week, and it seems a long time since I left home, but she hopes I am enjoying myself and has no time for more as post just going, and if I am anywhere near St. Paul's Churchyard, I might just pop into a little bookseller's at the corner of a little courtyard somewhere quite near the Cathedral, and see if they are doing anything about Our Vicar's little pamphlet, of which they had several copies in the summer. But I am not to take *any* trouble about this, on any account. Also, across the top of postcard, could I just look in at John Barker's, when I happen to be anywhere near, and ask the price of filet lace there? But *not* to put myself out, in any way. Robert, she adds across top of address, seems *very lonely*, underlined, also three exclamation marks, which presumably denote astonishment. Why?

November 2nd.—Regretfully observe in myself cynical absence of surprise when interesting invitations pour in on me just as I definitely decide to leave London and return home. Shall not, however, permit anything to interfere with date appointed and undertaking already given by Robert on half-sheet of note-paper, to meet 4.18 train at local station next Tuesday.

Buy two dust-sheets—yellow-and-white check, very cheap—with which to swathe furniture of flat during my absence. Shopman looks doubtful and says Will two be all I require? and I say Yes, I have plenty of others. Absolute and gratuitous lie, which covers me with shame when I think of it afterwards.

November 3rd.—Further telephone communication from Pamela P., but this time of a less sensational character, as she merely says that the fog makes her feel too, too suicidal, and she's had a fearful run of bad luck at Bridge and lost twenty-three pounds in two afternoons and don't I feel that when things have got to *that* stage there's nothing for it but a complete change? To this I return with great conviction Oh, absolutely *nothing*, and mentally frame witty addition to the effect that after finding myself unplaced in annual whist-drive in our village, I always make a point of dashing over the Somerset border. This quip, however, joins so many others in limbo of the unspoken.

Meanwhile, however, have I a free afternoon because Pamela has heard of a really marvellous clairvoyante, and she wants someone she can really *trust* to go there with her, only not one word about it to Waddell, ever. Should like to reply to this that I now take it for granted that any activity of Pamela's is subject to similar condition—but instead say that I should like to come to marvellous clairvoyante, and am prepared to consult her on my own account. All is accordingly arranged, including invitation from myself to Pamela to lunch with me at my Club beforehand, which she effusively agrees to do.

Spend the rest of the afternoon wishing that I hadn't asked her.

November 6th.—Altogether unprecedented afternoon, with Pamela Pringle. Lunch at my Club not an unmitigated success, as it turns out that Pamela is slimming and can eat nothing that is on menu and drink only orangeade, but she is amiable whilst I deal with chicken casserole and pineapple flan, and tells me about a really wonderful man—(who knows about wild beasts)—who has adored her for years and years, absolutely without a thought of self. Exactly like something in a book, says Pamela. She had a letter from him this morning, and do I think it's fair to go on writing to him? If there is one thing that Pamela never has been, never possibly could be, it is the kind of woman who Leads a Man On. Lead, kindly Light, I say absently, and then feel I have been profane as well as unsympathetic, but Pamela evidently not hurt by this as she pays no attention to it whatever and goes on to tell me about brilliant man-friend in the Diplomatic Service, who telephoned from The Hague this morning and is coming over next week by air apparently entirely in order that he may take Pamela out to dine and dance at the Berkeley.

Anti-climax supervenes here whilst I pay for lunch

and conduct Pamela to small and crowded dressing-room, where she applies orange lipstick and leaves her rings on wash-stand and has to go back for them after taxi has been called and is waiting outside.

Just as I think we are off page-boy dashes up and says Is it Mrs. Pringle, she is wanted on the telephone, and Pamela again rushes. Ten minutes later she returns and says Will I forgive her, she gave this number as a very great friend wanted to ring her up at lunch-time, and in Sloane Street flat the telephone is often so difficult, not that there's anything to conceal, but people get such queer ideas, and Pamela has a perfect horror of things being misunderstood. I say that I can quite believe it, then think this sounds unkind, but on the whole do not regret having said it.

Obscure street in Soho is reached, taxi dismissed after receiving vast sum from Pamela, who insists on paying, and we ascend extraordinarily dirty stairs to second floor, where strong smell of gas prevails. Pamela says Do I think it's all right? I reply, with more spirit than sincerity, that of course it is, and we enter and are received by anæmic-looking young man with curls, who takes one look at us and immediately vanishes behind green plush curtain, but reappears, and says that Madame Inez is quite ready but can only receive one client at a time. Am not surprised when Pamela compels me to go first, but give her a look which I hope she understands is not one of admiration.

Interview with unpleasant-looking sibyl follows. She gazes into large glass ball and says that I have known grief—(should like to ask her who hasn't)—and that I am a wife and a mother. Juxtaposition of these statements no doubt unintentional. Long and apparently inspired monologue follows, but little of practical value emerges except that: (*a*) There is trouble in the near future (If another change of cook, this is definitely unnerving.) (*b*) I have a child whose name will one day be famous. (Reference here almost certainly to dear Vicky.) (*c*) In three years' time I am to cut loose from my moorings, break new ground and throw my cap over the windmill.

None of it sounds to me probable, and I thank her and make way for Pamela. Lengthy wait ensues, and I distinctly hear Pamela scream at least three times from behind curtain. Finally she emerges in great agitation, throws pound notes about, and tells me to Come away quickly—which we both do, like murderers, and hurl ourselves into first available taxi quite breathless.

Pamela shows disposition to clutch me and weep, and says that Madame Inez has told her she is a re-incarnation of Helen of Troy and that there will never be peace in her life. (Could have told her the last part myself, without requiring fee for doing so.) She also adds that Madame Inez predicts that Love will shortly enter into her life on hitherto unprecedented scale, and alter it completely—at which I am aghast, and suggest that we should both go and have tea somewhere at once.

We do so, and it further transpires that Pamela did not like what Madame Inez told her about the past. This I can well believe.

We part in Sloane Street, and I go back to flat and spend much time packing.

November 7th.—Doughty Street left behind, yellow-and-white dust-sheets amply sufficing for entire flat, and Robert meets me at station. He seems pleased to see me, but says little until seated in drawing-room after dinner, when he suddenly remarks that He has Missed Me. Am astonished and delighted, and should like him to enlarge on theme, but this he does not do, and we revert to wireless and *The Times.*

April 13th.—Immense and inexplicable lapse of time since diary last received my attention, but on reviewing past five months, can trace no unusual activities, excepting arrears of calls—worked off between January and March on fine afternoons, when there appears to be reasonable chance of finding everybody out—and unsuccessful endeavour to learn cooking by correspondence in twelve lessons.

Financial situation definitely tense, and inopportune arrival of Rates casts a gloom, but Robert points out that they are not due until May 28th, and am unreasonably relieved. *Query*: Why? *Reply* suggests, not for the first time, analogy with Mr. Micawber.

April 15th.—Felicity Fairmead writes that she *could* come for a few days' visit, if we can have her, and may she let me know exact train later, and it will be either the 18th or the 19th, but, if inconvenient, she could make it the 27th, only in that case, she would have to come by Southern Railway and *not* G.W.R. I write back five pages to say that this would be delightful, only not the 27th, as Robert has to take the car to Crediton that day, and any train that suits her best, of course, but Southern easiest for us.

Have foreboding that this is only the beginning of lengthy correspondence and number of extremely involved arrangements. This fear confirmed by telegram received at midday from Felicity: Cancel letter posted yesterday could after all come on twenty-first if convenient writing suggestions tonight.

Say nothing to Robert about this, but unfortunately fresh telegram arrives over the telephone, and is taken down by him to the effect that Felicity is So sorry but plans altered Writing.

Robert makes no comment, but goes off at seven o'clock to a British Legion Meeting, and does not return till midnight. Casabianca and I have dinner *tête-à-tête*, and talk about dog-breeding, the novels of E. F. Benson, and the Church of England, about which he holds to my mind optimistic views. Just as we retire to the drawing-room and wireless, Robin appears in pyjamas, and says that he has distinctly heard a burglar outside his window.

I give him an orange and after short session by the fire, Robin departs and no more is heard about burglar. Drawing-room, in the most extraordinary way, smells of orange for the rest of the evening to uttermost corners of the room.

April 19th.—Felicity not yet here, but correspondence continues briskly, and have given up telling Robert anything about which train he will be required to meet.

Receive agreeable letter from well-known woman writer, personally unknown to me, who says that We have Many Friends in Common, and will I come over to lunch next week and bring anyone I like with me? Am flattered, and accept for self and Felicity. (*Mem.*: Notify Felicity on postcard of privilege in store for her, as this may help her to decide plans.) Further correspondence consists of Account Rendered from Messrs. Frippy and Coleman, very curtly worded, and far more elaborate epistle, which fears that it has escaped my memory, and ventures to draw my attention to enclosed, also typewritten notice concerning approaching Jumble Sale—(about which I know a good deal already, having contributed two hats, three suspender-belts, disintegrating fire-guard, and a foot-stool with Moth)—and request for reference of last cook but two.

Weather very cold and rainy, and daily discussion takes place between Casabianca and children as to desirability or otherwise of A Walk. Compromise finally reached with Robin and Vicky each wheeling a bicycle uphill, and riding it down, whilst Casabianca, shrouded in mackintosh to the eyebrows, walks gloomily in the rear, in unrelieved solitude. Am distressed at viewing this unnatural state of affairs from the window, and meditate appeal to Robin's better feelings, if any, but shall waste no eloquence upon Vicky.

Stray number of weekly Illustrated Paper appears in hall—cannot say why or how—and Robert asks where this rag came from? and then spends an hour after lunch glued to its pages. Paper subsequently reaches the hands of Vicky, who says Oh, look at that picture of a naked lady and screams with laughter. Ascertain later that this description, not wholly libellous, applies to full-page photograph of Pamela Pringle—wearing enormous feathered headdress, jewelled breast-plates, one garter, and a short gauze skirt—representing Chastity at recent Pageant of Virtue through the Ages organised by Society women for the benefit of Zenana Mission.

Ethel's afternoon out, and customary fatality of callers ensues, who are shown in by Cook with unsuitable formula: Someone to see you, 'm. Someone turns out to be unknown Mrs. Poppington, returning call with quite unholy promptitude, and newly grown-up daughter, referred to as My Girl. Mrs. Poppington sits on window-seat—from which I hastily remove Teddy-bear, plasticine, and two pieces of bitten chocolate—and My Girl leans back in arm-chair and reads *Punch* from start to finish of visit.

Mrs. P. and I talk about servants, cold East Winds and clipped yew hedges. She also says hopefully that she thinks I know Yorkshire, but to this I have to reply that I don't, which leads us nowhere. Am unfortunately inspired to add feebly—Except, of course, the Brontës—at which Mrs. P. looks alarmed, and at once takes her leave. My Girl throws *Punch* away disdainfully, and we exchange good-byes, Mrs. P. saying fondly that she is sure she does not know what I must think of My Girl's manners. Could easily inform her, and am much tempted to do so, but My Girl at once starts engine of car, and drives herself and parent away.

April 21st.—Final spate of letters, two postcards, and a telegram, herald arrival of Felicity—not, however, by train that she had indicated, and minus luggage, for which Robert is obliged to return to station later. Am gratified to observe that in spite of this, Robert appears pleased to see her, and make mental note of the effect that a Breath of Air from the Great World is of advantage to those living in the country.

April 22nd.—Singular reaction of Felicity to announcement that I am taking her to lunch with novelist famous in two continents for numerous and brilliant contributions to literature. It is very kind of me, says Felicity, in very unconvincing accents, but should I mind if she stayed at home with the children? I should, I reply, mind very much indeed. At this we glare at one another for some moments in silence, after which Felicity—spirit evidently quailing—mutters successively that: *(a)* She has no clothes. *(b)* She won't know what to talk about. *(c)* She doesn't want to be put into a book.

I treat *(a)* and *(b)* with silent contempt, and tell her that *(c)* is quite out of the question, to which she retorts sharply that she doesn't know what I mean.

Deadlock is again reached.

Discussion finally closed by my declaring that Casabianca and the children are going to Plymouth to see the dentist, and that Robert will be out, and I have told the maids that there will be no dining-room lunch. Felicity submits, I at once offer to relinquish expedition altogether, she protests violently, and we separate to go and dress.

Query, at this point, suggests itself: Why does my wardrobe never contain anything except heavy garments suitable for arctic regions, or else extraordinarily flimsy ones suggestive of the tropics? Golden mean apparently non-existent.

Am obliged to do the best I can with brown tweed

coat and skirt, yellow wool jumper—sleeves extremely uncomfortable underneath coat sleeves—yellow handkerchief tied in artistic sailor's knot at throat, and brown straw hat with ciré ribbon, that looks too summery for remainder of outfit. Felicity achieves better results with charming black-and-white check, short pony-skin jacket, and becoming black felt hat.

Car, which has been washed for the occasion, is obligingly brought to the door by Casabianca, who informs me that he does not think the self-starter is working, but she will probably go on a slope, only he doesn't advise me to try and wind her, as she kicked badly just now. General impression diffused by this speech is to the effect that we are dealing with a dangerous wild beast rather than a decrepit motor-car.

I say Thank you to Casabianca, Good-bye to the children, start the car, and immediately stop the engine. Not a very good beginning, is it? says Felicity, quite unnecessarily.

Casabianca, Robin and Vicky, with better feeling, push car vigorously, and eventually get it into the lane, when engine starts again. Quarter of a mile farther on, Felicity informs me that she thinks one of the children is hanging on to the back of the car. I stop, investigate, and discover Robin, to whom I speak severely. He looks abashed, I relent, and say, Well, never mind this time, at which he recovers immediately, and waves us off with many smiles from the top of a hedge.

Conversation is brisk for the first ten miles. Pause presently ensues, and Felicity—in totally different voice—wishes to know if we are nearly there. We are; I stop the car before the turning so that we can powder our noses, and we attain small and beautiful Queen Anne house in silence.

Am by this time almost as paralysed as Felicity, and cannot understand why I ever undertook expedition at all. Leave car in most remote corner of exquisite court-yard—where it presents peculiarly sordid and degraded appearance—and permit elegant parlourmaid—mauve-and-white dress and mob cap—to conduct us through panelled hall to sitting-room evidently designed and furnished entirely regardless of cost.

Madam is in the garden, says parlourmaid, and departs in search of her. Felicity says to me, in French —(Why not English?)—*Dites que je ne suis pas* literary *du tout*, and I nod violently just as celebrated hostess makes her appearance.

She is kind and voluble; Felicity and I gradually recover; someone in a blue dress and pince-nez appears, and is introduced as My Friend Miss Postman who Lives with Me; someone else materialises as My Cousin Miss Crump, and we all go into lunch. I sit next to hostess, who talks competently about modern poetry, and receives brief and evasive replies from myself. Felicity has My Friend Miss Postman, whom I hear opening the conversation rather unfortunately with amiable remark that she has so much enjoyed Felicity's book. Should like to hear with exactly what energetic turn of phrase Felicity disclaims having had anything to do with any book ever, but cannot achieve this, being under necessity of myself saying something reasonably convincing about Masefield, about whose work I can remember nothing at all.

Hostess then talks about her own books, My Friend

Miss Postman supplies intelligent and laudatory comments, seconded by myself, and Felicity and the cousin remain silent, but wear interested expressions.

This carries us on safely to coffee in the *loggia*, where Felicity suddenly blossoms into brilliancy owing to knowing names, both Latin and English, of every shrub and plant within sight.

She is then taken round the garden at great length by our hostess, with whom she talks gardening. Miss P. and I follow, but ignore flora, and Miss P. tells me that Carina—(reference, evidently, to hostess, whose name is Charlotte Volley)—is Perfectly Wonderful. Her Work is Wonderful, and so are her Methods, her Personality, her Vitality and her Charm.

I say Yes, a great many times, and feel that I can quite understand why Carina has Miss P. to live with her. (Am only too certain that neither Felicity nor dear Rose would dream of presenting me to visitors in similar light, should occasion for doing so ever arise.)

Carina and herself, continues Miss P., have been friends for many years now. She has nursed Carina through illness—Carina is not at all strong, and never, never rests. If only she would sometimes *spare* herself, says Miss P. despairingly—but, no, she has to be Giving Out all the time. People make demands upon her. If it isn't one, it's another.

At this, I feel guilty, and suggest departure. Miss P. protests, but faintly, and is evidently in favour of scheme. Carina is approached, but says, No, no, we must stay to tea, we are expected. Miss P. murmurs energetically, and is told, No, no, *that* doesn't matter, and Felicity and I feign absorption in small and unpleasant-looking yellow plant at our feet. Later, Miss P. admits to me that Carina ought to relax *absolutely* for at least an hour every afternoon, but that it is terribly, terribly difficult to get her to do it. To-day's failure evidently lies at our door, and Miss P. remains dejected, and faintly resentful, until we finally depart.

Carina is cordial to the last, sees us into car, has to be told that *that* door won't open, will she try the other side, does so, shuts it briskly, and says that we must come again *soon*. Final view of her is with her arm round Miss P.'s shoulder, waving vigorously. What, I immediately enquire, did Felicity think of her? to which Felicity replies with some bitterness that it is not a very good moment for her to give an opinion, as Carina has just energetically slammed door of the car upon her foot.

Condolences follow, and we discuss Carina, Miss P., cousin, house, garden, food and conversation, all the way home. Should be quite prepared to do so all over again for benefit of Robert in the evening, but he shows no interest, after enquiring whether there wasn't a man anywhere about the place, and being told Only the Gardener.

April 23rd.—Felicity and I fetch as many of Carina's works as we can collect from Boots', and read them industriously. Great excitement on discovering that one of them—the best-known—is dedicated to Carina's Beloved Friend, D. P., whom we immediately identify as Miss Postman, Felicity maintaining that D. stands for Daisy, whilst I hold out for Doris. Discussion closes with ribald reference to *Well of Loneliness.*

April 26th.—Felicity, after altering her mind three times, departs, to stay with married sister in Somersetshire. Robin and Vicky lament and I say that we shall all miss her, and she replies that she has loved being here, and it is the only house she knows where the bath-towels are really *large*. Am gratified by this compliment, and subsequently repeat it to Robert, adding that it proves I *can't* be such a bad housekeeper. Robert looks indulgent, but asks what about that time we ran out of flour just before a Bank Holiday weekend? To which I make no reply—being unable to think of a good one.

Telephone message from Lady Frobisher, inviting us to dinner on Saturday next, as the dear Blamingtons will be with her for the week-end. I say The Blamingtons? in enquiring tones, and she says Yes, yes, *he* knew me very well indeed eighteen years ago, and admired me tremendously. (This seems to me to constitute excellent reason why we should not meet again, merely in order to be confronted with deplorable alterations wrought by the passage of eighteen years.)

Lady F., however, says that she has promised to produce me—and Robert, too, of course, she adds hastily—and we *must* come. The Blamingtons are wildly excited. (Have idle and frivolous vision of the Blamingtons standing screaming and dancing at her elbow, waiting to hear decision.)

But, says Lady F., in *those* days—reference as to period preceding the Stone Age at least—in *those* days, I probably knew him as Bill Ransom? He has only this moment come into the title. I say Oh! *Bill Ransom*, and lapse into shattered silence, while Lady F. goes on to tell me what an extraordinarily pretty, intelligent, attractive and wealthy woman Bill has married, and how success-ful the marriage is. (Am by no means disposed to credit this offhand.)

Conversation closes with renewed assurances from Lady F. of the Blamingtons' and her own cast-iron determination that they shall not leave the neighbour-hood without scene of reunion between Bill and myself, and my own enfeebled assent to this preposterous scheme.

Tell Robert about invitation, and he says Good, the Frobishers have excellent claret, but remains totally un-moved at prospect of the Blamingtons. This—perhaps unjustly—annoys me, and I answer sharply that Bill Ransom once liked me very much indeed, to which Robert absently replies that he daresays, and turns on the wireless. I raise my voice, in order to dominate Happy Returns to Patricia Trabbs of Streatham, and screech that Bill several times asked me to marry him, and Robert nods, and walks out through the window into the garden.

Spend much time in arranging how I can best get in to hairdresser's for shampoo-and-set before Saturday, and also consider purchase of new frock, but am aware that financial situation offers no justification whatever for this.

Much later on, Robert enquires whether I am ill, and on receiving negative reply, urges that I should try and get to sleep. As I have been doing this, without success, for some time, answer appears to me to be unnecessary.

(*Mem.*: Self-control very, very desirable quality,

especially where imagination involved, and must certainly endeavour to cultivate.)

April 30th.—Incredible quantity of household requirements immediately springs into life on my announcing intention of going into Plymouth in order to visit hairdresser. Even Casabianca suddenly says Would it be troubling me too much to ask me to get a postal-order for three shillings and tenpence-halfpenny? Reply tartly that he will find an equally acceptable one at village Post Office, and then wish I hadn't when he meekly begs my pardon and says that, Yes, of course he can.

(*N.B.* This turning of the cheek has effect, as usual, of making me much crosser than before. Feel that doubt is being cast on Scriptural advice, and dismiss subject immediately.)

Bus takes me to Plymouth, where I struggle with Haberdashery—wholly uncongenial form of shopping, and extraordinarily exhausting—socks for Vicky, pants for Robin, short scrubbing-brush demanded by Cook, but cannot imagine what she means to do with it, or why it has to be short—also colossal list of obscure groceries declared to be unobtainable anywhere nearer than Plymouth. None of these are ever in stock at counters where I ask for them, and have to be procured either Upstairs or in the Basement, and am reminded of comic song prevalent in days of youth: The Other Department, If you please, Straight On and Up the Stairs. Quote it to grey-headed shopman, in whom I think it may rouse memories, but he only replies Just so, moddam, and we part without further advances on either side.

Collect number of small parcels—including particularly degraded-looking paper-bags containing Chips for which Robin and Vicky have implored—sling them from every available finger until I look like inferior Christmas-tree, thrust library-books under one arm— (they slip continually, and have to be pushed into safety from behind by means of ungraceful acrobatics)—and emerge into street. Unendearing glimpse of myself as I pass looking-glass reveals that my hat has apparently engulfed the whole of my head and half of my face as well. (Disquieting query here: Is this perhaps all for the best?) Also that blue coat with fur collar, reasonably becoming when I left home, has now assumed aspect of something out of a second-hand clothes-shop. Encourage myself with visions of unsurpassed brilliance that is to be mine after shampoo-and-set, careful dressing to-night, and liberal application of face-powder, and—if necessary—rouge.

Just as I have, mentally, seen exquisite Paris-model gown that exactly fits me, for sale in draper's window at improbable price of forty-nine shillings and sixpence, am recalled to reality by loud and cordial greetings of Our Vicar's Wife, who plunges through traffic at great risk to life in order to say what a coincidence this is, considering that we met yesterday, and are sure to be meeting to-morrow. She also invites me to come and help her choose white linen buttons for pillow-cases— but this evidently leading direct to Haberdashery once more, and I refuse—I hope with convincing appearance of regret.

Am subsequently dealt with by hairdresser—who says that I am the only lady he knows that still wears a bob—and once more achieve bus, where I meet Miss S. of the Post Office, who has also been shopping. We agree that a day's shopping is tiring—One's Feet, says Miss S.—and that the bus hours are inconvenient. Still, we can't hope for everything in this world, and Miss S. admits that she is looking forward to a Nice Cup of Tea and perhaps a Lay-Down, when she gets home. Reflect, not for the first time, that there are advantages in being a spinster. Should be sorry to say exactly how long it is since I last had a Lay-Down myself without being disturbed at least fourteen times in the course of it.

Spend much time, on reaching home, in unpacking and distributing household requirements, folding up and putting away paper and string, and condoling with Vicky, who alleges that Casabianca had made her walk miles and *miles*, and she has a pain in her wrist. Do not attempt to connect these two statements, but suggest the sofa and *Dr. Dolittle*, to which Vicky agrees with air of exhaustion, which is greatly intensified every time she catches my eye.

Later on, Casabianca turns up—looking pale-green with cold and making straight for the fire—and announces that he and the children have had a Splendid Walk and are all the better for it. Since I know, and Vicky knows, that this is being said for the express benefit of Vicky, we receive it rather tepidly, and conversation lapses while I pursue elusive sum of ten shillings and threepence through shopping accounts. Robin comes in by the window—I say, too late, Oh, your *boots*!—and Robert, unfortunately choosing this moment to appear, enquires whether there isn't a schoolroom in the house?

Atmosphere by this time is quite unfavourable to festivity, and I go up to dress for the Frobishers—or, more accurately, for the Blamingtons—feeling limp.

Hot bath restores me slightly—but relapse occurs when entirely vital shoulder-strap gives way and needle and thread become necessary.

Put on my Green, dislike it very much indeed, and once more survey contents of wardrobe, as though expecting to find miraculous addition to already perfectly well-known contents.

Needless to say, this does not happen, and after some contemplation of my Black—which looks rusty and entirely out of date—and my Blue—which is a candidate for the next Jumble-sale—I return to the looking-glass still in my Green, and gaze at myself earnestly.

(*Query*: Does this denote irrational hope of sudden and complete transformation in personal appearance? If so, can only wonder that so much faith should meet with so little reward.)

Jewel-case unfortunately rather low at present—(have every hope of restoring at least part of the contents next month, if American sales satisfactory)—but great-aunt's diamond ring fortunately still with us, and I put it on fourth finger of left hand, and hope that Bill will think Robert gave it to me. Exact motive governing this wish far too complicated to be analysed, but shelve entire question by saying to myself that Anyway, Robert certainly *would* have given it to me if he could have afforded it.

Evening cloak is smarter than musquash coat; put it on. Robert says Am I off my head and do I want to arrive frozen? Brief discussion follows, but I know he is right and I am wrong, and eventually compromise by putting on fur coat, and carrying cloak, to make decent appearance with on arrival in hall.

Fausse sortie ensues—as it so frequently does in domestic surroundings—and am twice recalled on the very verge of departure, once by Ethel, with superfluous observation that she supposes she had better not lock up at ten o'clock, and once by Robin, who takes me aside and says that he is very sorry, he has broken his bedroom window. It was, he says, entirely an accident, as he was only kicking his football about. I point out briefly, but kindly, that accidents of this nature are avoidable, and we part affectionately. Robert, at the wheel, looks patient, and I feel perfectly convinced that entire evening is going to be a failure.

Nobody in drawing-room when we arrive, and butler looks disapprovingly round, as though afraid that Lady F. or Sir William may be quietly hiding under some of the furniture, but this proving groundless, he says that he will Inform Her Ladyship, and leaves us. I immediately look in the glass, which turns out to be an ancient Italian treasure, and shows me a pale yellow reflection, with one eye much higher than the other. Before I have in any way recovered, Lady F. is in the room, so is Sir William, and so are the Blamingtons. Have not the slightest idea what happens next, but can see that Bill, except that he has grown bald, is unaltered, and has kept his figure, and that I do not like the look of his wife, who has lovely hair, a Paris frock, and is elaborately made-up.

We all talk a great deal about the weather, which is—as usual—cold, and I hear myself assuring Sir W.

that our rhododendrons are not yet showing a single bud. Sir W. expresses astonishment—which would be even greater if he realised that we only have one rhododendron in the world, and that I haven't set eyes on it for weeks owing to pressure of indoor occupations—and we go in to dinner. I am placed between Sir W. and Bill, and Bill looks at me and says Well, well, and we talk about Hampstead, and mutual friends, of whom Bill says Do you ever see anything of them nowadays? to which I am invariably obliged to reply No, we haven't met for years. Bill makes the best of this by observing civilly that I am lucky to live in such a lovely part of the world, and he supposes we have a very charming house, to which I reply captiously No, quite ordinary, and we both laugh.

Conversation after this much easier, and I learn that Bill has two children, a boy and girl. I say that I have the same, and before I can stop myself, have added that this is really a most extraordinary coincidence. Wish I hadn't been so emphatic about it, and hastily begin to talk about aviation to Sir William. He has a great deal to say about this, and I ejaculate Yes at intervals, and ascertain that Bill's wife is telling Robert that the policy of the Labour party is suicidal, to which he assents heartily, and that Lady F. and Bill are exchanging views about Norway.

Shortly after this, conversation becomes general, party-politics predominating—everyone except myself apparently holding Conservative views, and taking it for granted that none other exist in civilised circles—and I lapse into silence.

(*Query*: Would not a greater degree of moral courage

lead me to straightforward and open declaration of precise attitude held by myself in regard to the Conservative and other parties? *Answer*: Indubitably, yes—but results of such candour not improbably disastrous, and would assuredly add little to social amenities of present occasion.)

Entirely admirable dinner brought to a close with South African pears, and Lady F. says Shall we have coffee in the drawing-room?—entirely rhetorical question, as decision naturally rests with herself.

Customary quarter of an hour follows, during which I look at Bill's wife, and like her less than ever, especially when she and Lady F. discuss hairdressers, and topic of Permanent Waves being introduced—(probably on purpose)—by Bill's wife, she says that her own is Perfectly Natural, which I feel certain, to my disgust, is the truth.

Bridge follows—I play with Sir William, and do well, but as Robert loses heavily, exchequer will not materially benefit—and evening draws to a close.

Experience extraordinary medley of sensations as we drive away, and journey is accomplished practically in silence.

May 1st.—I ask Robert if he thought Lady Blamington good-looking, and he replies that he wouldn't say *that* exactly. What would he say, then? Well, he would say striking, perhaps. He adds that he'll eat his hat if they have a penny less than twenty thousand a year between them, and old Frobisher says that their place in Kent is a show place. I ask what he thought of Bill, and Robert says Oh, he seemed all right. Make final enquiry as to what *I* looked like last night, and whether Robert thinks that eighteen years makes much difference in one's appearance.

Robert, perhaps rightly, ignores the last half of this, and replies to the former—after some thought—that I looked just as usual, but he doesn't care much about that green dress. Am sufficiently unwise to press for further information, at which Robert looks worried, but finally admits that, to his mind, the green dress makes me look Tawdry.

Am completely disintegrated by this adjective, which recurs to me in the midst of whatever I am doing, for the whole of the remainder of the day.

Second post brings unexpected and most surprising letter from Mademoiselle, announcing that she is in England and cannot wait to embrace us once again— may she have one sight of Vicky—*ce petit ange*—and Robin—*ce gentil gosse*—before they return to school? She will willingly, in order to obtain this privilege, *courir nu-pieds* from Essex to Devonshire. Despatch immediate telegram inviting her for two nights, and debate desirability of adding that proposed barefooted Marathon wholly unnecessary—but difficulty of including this in twelve words deters me, moreover French sense of humour always incalculable to a degree. Announce impending visit to children, who receive it much as I expected. Robin says Oh, and continues to decipher "John Brown's Body" very slowly on the piano with one finger—which he has done almost hourly every day these holidays—and Vicky looks blank and eats unholy-looking mauve lozenge alleged to be a present from Cook.

(*Mem.*: Speak to Cook, tactfully and at the same time decisively. Must think this well out beforehand.)

Robert's reaction to approaching union with devoted friend and guardian of Vicky's infancy lacking in any enthusiasm whatever.

May 3rd.—Mademoiselle arrives by earlier train than was expected, and is deposited at front door, in the middle of lunch, by taxi, together with rattan basket, secured by cord, small attaché-case, large leather hat-box, plaid travelling rug, parcel wrapped in American oilcloth, and two hand-bags.

We all rush out (excepting Helen Wills, who is subsequently found to have eaten the butter off dish on sideboard) and much excitement follows. If Mademoiselle says *Ah, mais ce qu'ils ont grandis!* once, she says it thirty-five times. To me she exclaims that I have *bonne mine*, and do not look a day over twenty, which is manifestly absurd. Robert shakes hands with her— at which she cries *Ah! quelle bonne poignée de main anglaise!* and introduction of Casabianca is effected, but this less successful, and rather distant bows are exchanged, and I suggest adjournment to dining-room.

Lunch resumed—roast lamb and mint sauce recalled for Mademoiselle's benefit, and am relieved at respectable appearance they still present, which could never have been the case with either cottage pie or Irish stew —and news is exchanged. Mademoiselle has, it appears, accepted another post—doctor's household in *les environs de Londres*, which I think means Putney—but has touchingly stipulated for two days in which to visit us before embarking on new duties.

I say how glad I am, and she says, once more, that the children have grown, and throws up both hands towards the ceiling and tosses her head.

Suggestion, from Robert, that Robin and Vicky should take their oranges into the garden, is adopted, and Casabianca escorts them from the room.

Mademoiselle immediately enquires *Qu'est-ce que c'est que ce petit jeune homme?* in tones perfectly, and I think designedly, audible from the hall where Vicky and Casabianca can be heard in brisk dispute over a question of goloshes. I reply, in rebukefully lowered voice, with short outline of Casabianca's position in household—which is, to my certain knowledge, perfectly well known to Mademoiselle already. She slightingly replies *Tiens, c'est drôle*—words and intonation both, in my opinion, entirely unnecessary. The whole of this dialogue rouses in me grave apprehension as to success or otherwise of next forty-eight hours.

Mademoiselle goes to unpack, escorted by Vicky —should like to think this move wholly inspired by grateful affection, but am more than doubtful— Casabianca walks Robin up and down the lawn, obviously for purpose of admonishment—probably justifiable, but faint feeling of indignation assails me at the sight—and I stand idle just outside hall-door until Robert goes past me with a wheelbarrow and looks astonished, when I remember that I must (*a*) Write letters, (*b*) Telephone to the Bread, which ought to be here and isn't, (*c*) Go on sorting school clothes, (*d*) Put

Cash's initials on Vicky's new stockings, (*e*) See about sending schoolroom chintzes to the cleaners.

May 5th.—Fears relating to perfect harmony between Mademoiselle and Casabianca appear to have been well founded, and am relieved that entire party disperses to-morrow. Children, as usual on last day of holidays, extremely exuberant, but am aware, from previous experience, that fearful reaction will set in at eleventh hour.

Decide on picnic, said to be in Mademoiselle's honour, and Robert tells me privately that he thinks Casabianca had better be left behind. Am entirely of opinion that he is right, and spend some time in evolving graceful and kind-hearted little formula with which to announce this arrangement, but all ends in failure.

Casabianca says Oh no, it is very kind of me, but he would quite enjoy a picnic, and does not want an afternoon to himself. He has no letters to write—very kind of me to think of such a thing. Nor does he care about a quiet day in the garden, kind though it is of me. Final desperate suggestion that he would perhaps appreciate vague and general asset of A Free Day, he receives with renewed reference to my extreme kindness, and incontrovertible statement that he wouldn't know what to do with a free day if he had it.

Retire defeated, and tell Robert that Casabianca *wants* to come to the picnic—which Robert appears to think unnatural in the extreme. Towards three o'clock it leaves off raining, and we start, customary collection of rugs, mackintoshes, baskets and Thermos flasks in the back of car.

Mademoiselle says *Ah, combien ça me rappelle le passé que nous ne reverrons plus!* and rolls her eyes in the direction of Casabianca, and I remember with some thankfulness that his knowledge of French is definitely limited. Something tells me, however, that he has correctly interpreted meaning of Mademoiselle's glance.

Rain begins again, and by the time we reach appointed beauty-spot is falling very briskly indeed. Robert, who has left home under strong compulsion from Vicky, is now determined to see the thing through, and announces that he will walk the dog to the top of the hill, and that the children had better come too. Mademoiselle, shrouded in large plaid cape, exerts herself in quite unprecedented manner, and offers to go with them, which shames me into doing likewise, sorely against my inclination. We all get very wet indeed, and Vicky falls into mysterious gap in a hedge and comes out dripping and with black smears that turn out to be tar all over her.

Rain comes down in torrents, and I suggest tea in the car, but this is abandoned when it becomes evident that we are too tightly packed to be able to open baskets, let alone spread out their contents. Why not tea in the dining-room at home? is Robert's contribution towards solving difficulty, backed quietly, but persistently, by Casabianca. This has immediately effect of causing Mademoiselle to advocate *un goûter en plein air*, as though we were at Fontainebleau, or any other improbable spot, in blazing sunshine.

Robin suddenly and brilliantly announces that we are quite near Bull Alley Manor, which is empty, and that the gardener will allow us to have a picnic in the hen-house. Everybody says The Hen-house? except Vicky, who screams and looks enchanted, and Mademoiselle, who also screams, and refers to *punaises*, which she declares will abound. Robin explains that he means a summer-house on the Bull Alley tennis-ground, which has a wire-netting and *looks* like a hen-house, but he doesn't think it really is. He adds triumphantly that it has a bench that we can sit on. Robert puts in a final plea for the dining-room at home, but without conviction, and we drive ten miles to Bull Alley Manor, where picnic takes place under Robin's auspices, all of us sitting in a row on long wooden seat, exactly like old-fashioned school feast. I say that it reminds me of *The Daisy Chain*, but nobody knows what I mean, and reference is allowed to drop while we eat sandwiches and drink lemonade, which is full of pips.

Return home at half-past six, feeling extraordinarily exhausted. Find letter from Literary Agent, suggesting that the moment has now come when fresh masterpiece from my pen may definitely be expected, and may he hope to receive my new manuscript quite shortly? Idle fancy, probably born of extreme fatigue, crosses my mind as to results of a perfectly candid reply—to the effect that literary projects entirely swamped by hourly activities concerned with children, house-keeping, sewing, letter-writing, Women's Institute meetings, and necessity of getting eight hours' sleep every night.

Decide that another visit to Doughty Street is imperative, and say to Robert, feebly and untruthfully, that I am sure he would not mind my spending a week or two in London, to get some writing done. To this Mademoiselle, officiously and unnecessarily, adds that, naturally, *madame désire se distraire de temps en temps* —which is not in the least what I want to convey.

Robert says nothing, but raises one eyebrow.

May 6th. —Customary heart-rending half-hour in which Robin and Vicky appear to realise for the first time since last holidays that they must return to school. Robin says nothing whatever, but turns gradually *eau-de-nil*, and Vicky proclaims that she feels almost certain she will not be able to survive the first night away from home. I tell myself firmly that, as a modern mother, I must be Bracing, but very inconvenient lump in my throat renders this difficult, and I suggest instead that they should go and say good-bye to the gardener.

Mademoiselle without warning bursts into tears, kisses children and myself, says *On se reverra au Paradis, au moins*—which is on the whole optimistic—and is driven by Robert to the station.

Hired car removes Casabianca, after customary exchange of compliments between us, and extraordinarily candid display of utter indifference from both Robin and Vicky, and I take them to the Junction, when unknown parent of unknown schoolfellow of Robin's takes charge of him with six other boys, who all look to me exactly alike.

Vicky weeps, and I give her an ice and then escort her to station all over again, and put her in charge of the guard, to whom she immediately says Can she go in the Van with him? He agrees, and they disappear hand-in-hand.

Drive home again, and avoid schoolroom for the rest of the day.

May 10th. — Decide that a return to Doughty Street flat is imperative, and try to make clear to Robert that this course really represents Economy in the Long Run. Mentally assemble superb array of evidence to this effect, but it unfortunately eludes me when trying to put it into words and all becomes feeble and incoherent. Also observe in myself tendency to repeat over and over again rather unmeaning formula: It Isn't as if It was going to be For Long, although perfectly well aware that Robert heard me the first time, and was unimpressed.

May 17th. — Return to Doughty Street flat, and experience immense and unreasonable astonishment at finding it almost exactly as I left it, yellow-and-white check dust-sheets and all. Am completely entranced, and spend entire afternoon and evening arranging two vases of flowers, unpacking suit-case and buying tea and biscuits in Gray's Inn Road, where I narrowly escape extinction under a tram.

Ring up Rose, who says Oh, am I back? — which I obviously must be — and charmingly suggests dinner next week — two friends whom she wants me to meet — and a luncheon party at which I must come and help her. Am flattered, and say Yes, yes, how? to which Rose strangely replies, By leaving rather early, if I don't mind, as this may break up the party.

Note: Extraordinary revelations undoubtedly hidden below much so-called hospitality, if inner thoughts of many hostesses were to be revealed. This thought remains persistently with me, in spite of explanation from Rose that she has appointment miles away at three o'clock, on day of luncheon, and is afraid of not getting there punctually. Agree, but without enthusiasm, to leave at half-past two in the hopes of inducing fellow-guests to do likewise.

Pamela Pringle rings up, alleging that she "had a feeling" I should be in London again. Agree to go to cocktail party at her flat.

Pamela rings up again just before midnight, and hopes so, so much she hasn't disturbed me or anything like that, but she forgot to say—she knows so well that I shan't misunderstand—there's nothing in it at all—only if a letter comes for her addressed to my flat, will I just keep it till we meet? Quite likely it won't come at all, but *if* it does, will I just do that and not say anything about it, as people are so terribly apt to misunderstand the simplest thing? Am I sure I don't mind? As by this time I mind nothing at all except being kept out of my bed any longer, I agree to everything, say that I understand absolutely, and am effusively thanked by Pamela and rung off.

May 21st.—Attend Pamela Pringle's cocktail party after much heart-searching as to suitable clothes for the occasion. Consult Felicity—on a postcard—who replies—on a postcard—that she hasn't the least idea, also Emma Hay (this solely because I happen to meet her in King's Road, Chelsea, not because I have remotest intention of taking her advice). Emma says lightly Oh, pyjamas are the thing, she supposes, and I look at her and am filled with horror at implied suggestion that she herself ever appears anywhere in anything of the kind. But, says Emma, waving aside question which she evidently considers insignificant, Will I come with her next week to really delightful evening party in Blooms-bury, where every single Worthwhile Person in London is to be assembled? Suggest in reply, with humorous intention, that the British Museum has, no doubt, been reserved to accommodate them all, but Emma not in the least amused, and merely replies No, a basement flat in Little James Street, if I know where that is. As it is within two minutes' walk of my own door, I do, and agree to be picked up by Emma and go on with her to the party.

Question of clothes remains unsolved until eleventh hour, when I decide on black crêpe-de-chine and new hat that I think becoming.

Bus No. 19, as usual, takes me to Sloane Street, and I reach flat door at half-past six, and am taken up in lift, hall-porter—one of many—informing me on the way that I am the First. At this I beg to be taken down again and allowed to wait in the hall, but he replies, not unreasonably, that *Someone* has got to be first, Miss. Revive at being called Miss, and allow myself to be put down in front of P. P.'s door, where porter rings the bell as if he didn't altogether trust me to do it for myself—in which he is right—and I subsequently crawl, rather than walk, into Pamela's drawing-room. Severe shock ensues when Pamela—wearing pale pink flowered chiffon—reveals herself in perfectly brand-new incarnation as purest platinum blonde. Recover from this with what I consider well-bred presence of mind, but am shattered anew by passionate enquiry from Pamela as to whether I like it. Reply, quite truthfully, that she looks lovely, and all is harmony. I apologise for arriving early, and Pamela assures me that she is only too glad, and adds that she wouldn't have been here herself as early as this if her bedroom clock hadn't been an hour fast, and she wants to hear all my news. She then tells me all hers, which is mainly concerned with utterly unaccountable attitude of Waddell, who goes into a fit if any man under ninety so much as *looks* at Pamela. (Am appalled at cataclysmic nature of Waddell's entire existence, if this is indeed the case.)

Previous experience of Pamela's parties leads me to enquire if Waddell is to be present this afternoon, at which she looks astonished and says Oh Yes, she supposes so, he is quite a good host in his own way, and anyway she is sure he would adore to see me.

(Waddell and I have met exactly once before, on which occasion we did not speak, and am morally certain that he would not know me again if he saw me.)

Bells rings, and influx of very young gentlemen supervenes, and are all greeted by Pamela and introduced to me as Tim and Nicky and the Twins. I remain anonymous throughout, but Pamela lavishly announces that I am very, very clever and literary—with customary result of sending all the very young gentlemen into the farthermost corner of the room, from whence they occasionally look over their shoulders at me with expressions of acute horror.

They are followed by Waddell—escorting, to my immense relief, Rose's Viscountess, whom I greet as an old friend, at which she seems faintly surprised, although in quite a kind way—and elderly American with a bald head. He sits next me, and wants to know about Flag days, and—after drinking something out of a little glass handed me in a detached way by one of the very young gentlemen—I suddenly find myself extraordinarily eloquent and informative on the subject.

Elderly American encourages me by looking at me thoughtfully and attentively while I speak—(difference in this respect between Americans and ourselves is marked, and greatly to the advantage of the former)—and saying at intervals that what I am telling him Means Quite a Lot to him—which is more than it does to me. Long before I think I have exhausted the subject, Pamela removes the American by perfectly simple and direct method of telling him to come and talk to her, which he obediently does—but bows at me rather apologetically first.

Room is by this time entirely filled with men, cigarette smoke and conversation. Have twice said No, really, not any more, thank you, to Waddell, and he has twice ignored it altogether, and continued to pour things into my glass, and I to drink them. Result is a very strange mixture of exhilaration, utter recklessness and rather sentimental melancholy. Am also definitely giddy and aware that this will be much worse as soon as I attempt to stand up.

Unknown man, very attractive, sitting near me, tells me of very singular misfortune that has that day befallen him. He has, to his infinite distress, dealt severe blow with a walking-stick to strange woman, totally unknown to him, outside the Athenæum. I say Really, in concerned tones, Was that just an accident? Oh yes, purest accident. He was showing a friend how to play a stroke at golf, and failed to perceive woman immediately behind him. This unhappily resulted in the breaking of her spectacles, and gathering of a large crowd, and moral obligation on his own part to drive her immense distance in a taxi to see (a) a doctor, (b) an oculist, (c) her husband, who turned out to live at Richmond. I sympathise passionately, and suggest that he will probably have to keep both woman and her husband for the rest of their lives, which, he says, had already occurred to him.

This dismays us both almost equally, and we each drink another cocktail.

Pamela—had already wondered why she had left attractive unknown to me so long—now breaks up this agreeable conversation, by saying that Waddell will never, never, forgive anybody else for monopolising me, and I simply must do my best to put him into a really *good* mood, as Pamela has got to tell him about her dressmaker's bill presently, so will I be an angel—? She then removes delightful stranger, and I am left in a dazed condition. Have dim idea that Waddell is reluctantly compelled by Pamela to join me, and that we repeatedly assure one another that there are No Good Plays Running Nowadays. Effect of this eclectic pronouncement rather neutralised later, when it turns out that Waddell never patronises anything except films, and that I haven't set foot inside a London theatre for eight and a half months.

Later still it dawns on me that I am almost the last person left at the party, except for Waddell, who has turned on the wireless and is listening to Vaudeville, and Pamela, who is on the sofa having her palm read by one young man, while two others hang over the back of it and listen attentively.

I murmur a very general and unobtrusive good-bye, and go away. Am not certain, but think that hall-porter eyes me compassionately, but we content ourselves with exchange of rather grave smiles—no words.

Am obliged to return to Doughty Street in a taxi, owing to very serious fear that I no longer have perfect control over my legs.

Go instantly to bed on reaching flat, and room whirls round and round in distressing fashion for some time before I go to sleep.

May 25th.—Life one round of gaiety, and feel extremely guilty on receiving a letter from Our Vicar's Wife, saying that she is certain I am working hard at a New Book, and she should so like to hear what it's all about and what its name is. If I will tell her this, she will speak to the girl at Boots', as every little helps. She herself is extremely busy, and the garden is looking nice, but everything very late this year. *P.S.* Have I heard that old Mrs. Blenkinsop is going to Bournemouth?

Make up my mind to write really long and interesting reply to this, but when I sit down to do so find that I am quite unable to write anything at all, except items that would appear either indiscreet, boastful or scandalous. Decide to wait until after Emma Hay's party in Little James Street, as this will give me something to write about.

(*Mem.*: Self-deception almost certainly involved here, as reflection makes it perfectly evident that Our

Vicar's Wife is unlikely in the extreme to be either amused or edified by the antics of any acquaintances brought to my notice via Emma.)

May 26th. — Emma — in green sacque that looks exactly like *démodé* window-curtain, sandals and varnished toe-nails — calls for me at flat, and we go across to Little James Street. I ask whom I am going to meet and Emma replies, with customary spaciousness, Everyone, absolutely Everyone, but does not commit herself to names, or even numbers.

Exterior of Little James Street makes me wonder as to its capacities for dealing with Everyone, and this lack of confidence increases as Emma conducts me into extremely small house and down narrow flight of stone stairs, the whole culminating in long, thin room with black walls and yellow ceiling, apparently no furniture whatever, and curious, but no doubt interesting, collection of people all standing screaming at one another.

Emma looks delighted and says Didn't she tell me it would be a crush, that man over there is living with a negress now, and if she gets a chance she will bring him up to me.

(Should very much like to know with what object, since it will obviously be impossible for me to ask him the only thing I shall really be thinking about.)

Abstracted-looking man with a beard catches sight of Emma, and says Darling, in an absent-minded manner, and then immediately moves away, followed, with some determination, by Emma.

Am struck by presence of many pairs of horn-rimmed spectacles, and marked absence of evening dress, also by very odd fact that almost everybody in the room has either abnormally straight or abnormally frizzy hair. Conversation in my vicinity is mainly concerned with astonishing picture on the wall, which I think represents Adam and Eve at very early stage indeed, but am by no means certain, and comments overheard do not enlighten me in the least. Am moreover seriously exercised in my mind as to exact meaning of *tempo*, *brio*, *appassionata* and *coloratura* as applied to art.

Strange man enters into conversation with me, but gives it up in disgust when I mention Adam and Eve, and am left with the impression—do not exactly know why—that picture in reality represents Sappho on the Isle of Lesbos.

(*Query*: Who was Sappho, and what was Isle of Lesbos?)

Emma presently reappears, leading reluctant-looking lady with red hair, and informs her in my presence that I am a country mouse—which infuriates me—and adds that we ought to get on well together, as have identical inferiority complexes. Red-haired lady and I look at one another with mutual hatred, and separate as soon as possible, having merely exchanged brief comment on Adam and Eve picture which she seems to think has something to do with the 'nineties and the *Yellow Book*.

Make one or two abortive efforts to find out if we have a host or hostess, and if so what they look like, and other more vigorous efforts to discover a chair, but all to no avail, and finally decide that as I am not enjoying myself, and am also becoming exhausted, I had better leave. Emma makes attempt that we both know to be half-hearted to dissuade me, and I rightly disregard it altogether and prepare to walk out, Emma at the last moment shattering my nerve finally by asking what I think of that wonderful satirical study on the wall, epitomising the whole of the modern attitude towards Sex?

June 1st.—Life full of contrasts, as usual, and after recent orgy of Society, spend most of the day in washing white gloves and silk stockings, and drying them in front of electric fire. Effect of this on gloves not good, and remember too late that writer of Woman's Page in illustrated daily paper has always deprecated this practice.

Pay a call on Robert's Aunt Mary, who lives near Battersea Bridge, and we talk about relations. She says How do I think William and Angela are getting on? which sounds like preliminary to a scandal and excites me pleasurably, but it turns out to refer to recent venture in Bee-keeping, no reference whatever to domestic situation, and William and Angela evidently giving no grounds for agitation at present.

Aunt Mary asks about children, says that school is a great mistake for girls, and that she does so hope Robin is good at games—which he isn't—and do I find that it answers to have A Man in the house? Misunderstanding occurs here, as I take this to mean Robert, but presently realise that it is Casabianca.

Tea and seed-cake appear, we partake, and Aunt Mary hopes that my writing does not interfere with home life and its many duties, and I hope so too, but in spite of this joint aspiration, impression prevails that we are mutually dissatisfied with one another. We part, and I go away feeling that I have been a failure. Wish I could believe that Aunt Mary was similarly downcast on her own account, but have noticed that this is seldom the case with older generation.

Find extraordinary little envelope waiting for me at flat, containing printed assurance that I shall certainly be interested in recent curiosities of literature acquired by total stranger living in Northern manufacturing town, all or any of which he is prepared to send me under plain sealed cover. Details follow, and range from illustrated History of Flagellation to Unexpurgated Erotica.

Toy for some time with idea that it is my duty to communicate with Scotland Yard, but officials there probably overworked already, and would be far more grateful for being left in peace, so take no action beyond consigning envelope and contents to the dust-bin.

June 18th. — Heat-wave continues, and everybody says How lovely it must be in the country, but personally think it is lovely in London, and am more than content.

Write eloquent letter to Robert suggesting that he should come up too, and go with me to Robin's School Sports on June 25th and that we should take Vicky. Have hardly any hope that he will agree to any of this.

June 23rd. — Am pleased and astonished at being taken at my word by Robert, who appears at the flat, and undertakes to conduct me, and Vicky, to half-term Sports at Robin's school. In the meantime, he wants a hair-cut. I say that there is a place quite near Southampton Row, at which Robert looks appalled, and informs me that there is *No* place nearer than Bond Street. He accordingly departs to Bond Street, after telling me to meet him at twelve at his Club in St. James's. Am secretly much impressed by nonchalance with which Robert resumes these urban habits, although to my certain knowledge he has not been near Club in St. James's for years.

Reflection here on curious dissimilarity between the sexes as exemplified by self and Robert: in his place, should be definitely afraid of not being recognised by hall-porter of Club, and quite possibly challenged as to my right to be there at all. Robert, am perfectly well aware, will on the contrary ignore hall-porter from start to finish with probable result that h.-p. will crawl before him, metaphorically if not literally.

This rather interesting abstract speculation recurs to me with some violence when I actually do go to Club, and enter imposing-looking hall, presided over by still more imposing porter in uniform, to whom I am led up by compassionate-looking page, who evidently realises my state of inferiority. Am made no better by two elderly gentlemen talking together in a corner, both of whom look at me with deeply suspicious faces and evidently think I have designs on something or other—either the Club statuary, which is looming above me, or perhaps themselves. Page is despatched to look for Robert—feel as if my only friend had been taken from me—and I wait, in state of completely suspended animation, for what seems like a long week-end. This comes to an end at last, and am moved to greet Robert by extraordinary and totally unsuitable quotation: *Time and the hour runs through the roughest day*—which I hear myself delivering, in an inward voice, exactly as if I were talking in my sleep. Robert—on the whole wisely—takes not the faintest notice, beyond looking at me with rather an astonished expression, and receives his hat and coat, which page-boy presents as if they were Coronation robes and sceptre at the very least. We walk out of Club, and I resume customary control of my senses.

Day is one of blazing sunlight, streets thronged with people, and we walk along Piccadilly and Robert says Let's lunch at Simpson's in the Strand, to which I agree, and add Wouldn't it be heavenly if we were rich? Conversation then ensues on more or less accustomed lines, and we talk about school-bills, inelastic spirit shown by the Bank, probabilities that new house-parlour-maid will be giving notice within the next few weeks, and unlikelihood of our having any strawberries worth mentioning in the garden this year. Robert's contribution mostly consists of ejaculations about the traffic—he doesn't know what the streets are coming to, but it can't go *on* like this—and a curt assurance to the effect that we shall all be in the workhouse together before so very long. After that we reach Simpson's in the Strand, and Robert says that we may as well have a drink—which we do, and feel better.

Robert says there is to be a concert in the Village next month for most deserving local object, and he has been asked to promise my services as performer, which he has done. Definite conviction here that reference ought to be made to Married Women's Property Act or something like that, but exact phraseology eludes me, and Robert seems so confident that heart fails me, and I weakly agree to do what I can. (This, if taken literally, will amount to extraordinarily little, as have long ceased to play piano seriously, have never at any time been able to sing, and have completely forgotten few and amateurish recitations that have occasionally been forced upon me on local platforms.)

Plans for the afternoon discussed: Robert wishes to visit Royal Academy, and adds that he need not go and see his Aunt Mary as I went there the other day—which seems to me illogical, and altogether unjust—and that we will get stalls for to-night if I will say what play I want to see. After some thought, select *Musical Chairs*, mainly because James Agate has written well of it in the Press, and Robert says Good, he likes a musical show, and I have to explain that I don't think it *is* a musical show at all, and we begin all over again, and finally select a revue. Debate question of Royal Academy, but have no inclination whatever to go there, and have just said so, as nicely as I can, when Pamela Pringle appears beside us, puts her hand on Robert's shoulder —at which he looks startled and winces slightly—and announces that we *must* come to Hipps' picture-show this afternoon—it is in the Cygnet Galleries in Fitzroy Square, and if no one turns up it will break the poor pet's heart, and as far as she can see, no one but herself has ever heard of it, and we simply must go there, and help her out. She will meet us there at five.

Before we have recovered ourselves in any way, we are more or less committed to the Cygnet Galleries at five, Pamela has told us that she adores us both—but looks exclusively at Robert as she says it—and has left us again.

Robert again makes use of expletives, and we leave Simpson's and go our several ways, but with tacit agreement to obey Pamela's behest. I fill in the interval with prosaic purchases of soap, which I see in mountainous heaps at much reduced prices, filling an entire shop-window, sweets to take down to Robin on Saturday, and quarter-pound of tea in order that Robert may have usual early-morning cup before coming out—unwillingly—to breakfast at Lyons'.

Am obliged to return to Doughty Street, and get small jug in which to collect milk from dairy in Gray's Inn Road, pack suit-case now in order to save time in the morning, and finally proceed to Fitzroy Square, where Cygnet Galleries are discovered, after some search, in small adjoining street which is not in Fitzroy Square at all.

Robert and Hipps are already together, in what I think really frightful juxtaposition, and very, very wild collection of pictures hangs against the walls. Robert and I walk round and round, resentfully watched by Hipps, who never stirs, and Pamela Pringle fails to materialise.

Robert at last says in a strange voice that he must have a drink, and we accordingly go in search of it.

June 25th.—Vicky arrives by green bus from Mickleham, carrying circular hat-box of astonishing size and weight, with defective handle, so that every time I pick it up it falls down again, which necessitates a taxi. She is in great excitement, and has to be calmed with milk and two buns before we proceed to station, and take train to Robin's school.

Arrival, lunch at Hotel, and walk up to School follow normal lines, and in due course Robin appears and is received by Vicky with terrific demonstrations of affection and enthusiasm, to which he responds handsomely. (Reflect, as often before, that Fashion in this respect has greatly altered. Brothers and sisters now almost universally deeply attached to one another, and quite prepared to admit it. *O tempora! O mores!*) We are conducted to the playing-fields, where hurdles and other appliances of sports are ready, and where rows and rows of chairs await us.

Parents, most of whom I have seen before and have no particular wish ever to see again, are all over the place, and am once more struck by tendency displayed by all Englishwomen to cling to most unbecoming outfit of limp coat and skirt and felt hat even when blazing summer day demands cooler, and infinitely more becoming, *ensemble* of silk frock and shady hat.

Crowds of little boys all look angelic in running shorts and singlets, and am able to reflect that even if Robin's hair *is* perfectly straight, at least he doesn't wear spectacles.

Headmaster speaks a few words to me—mostly about the weather, and new wing that he proposes, as usual, to put up very shortly—I accost Robin's Form-master and demand to be told How the Boy is Getting On, and Form-master looks highly astonished at my audacity, and replies in a very off-hand way that Robin will never be a cricketer, but his football is coming on, and he has the makings of a swimmer. He then turns his back on me, but I persist, and go so far as to say that I should like to hear something about Robin's work.

Form-master appears to be altogether overcome by this unreasonable requirement, and there is a perceptible silence, during which he evidently meditates flight. Do my best to hold him by the Power of the Human Eye, about which I have read much, not altogether believingly. However, on this occasion, it does its job, and Form-master grudgingly utters five words or so, to the effect that we needn't worry about Robin's Common-entrance exam, in two years' time. Having so far committed himself he pretends to see a small boy in imminent danger on a hurdle and dashes across the grass at uttermost speed to save him, and for the remainder of the day, whenever he finds himself within yards of me, moves rapidly in opposite direction.

Sports take place, and are a great success. Robin murmurs to me that he thinks, he isn't at all sure, but he *thinks*, he may have a chance in the High Jump. I reply, with complete untruth, that I shan't mind a bit if he doesn't win and he mustn't be disappointed—and then suffer agonies when event actually takes place and he and another boy out-jump everybody else and are at last declared to have tied. (Vicky has to be rebuked by Robert for saying that this is Unjust and Robin jumped by far the best—which is not only an unsporting attitude, but entirely unsupported by fact.) Later in the afternoon Robin comes in a good second in Hurdling, and Vicky is invited to take part in a three-legged race, which she does with boundless enthusiasm and no skill at all.

Tea and ices follow—boys disappear, and are said to be changing—and I exchange remarks with various parents, mostly about the weather being glorious, the sports well organised, and the boys a healthy-looking lot.

Trophies are distributed—inclination to tears, of which I am violently ashamed, assails me when Robin goes up to receive two little silver cups—various people cheer various other people, and we depart for the Hotel, with Robin. Evening entirely satisfactory, and comes to an end at nine o'clock, with bed for Vicky and Robin's return to School.

June 27th.—Return to London, departure of Vicky by green bus and under care of the conductor, and of Robert from Paddington. I have assured him that I shall be home in a very few days now, and he has again reminded me about the concert, and we part. Am rung up by Pamela in the afternoon, to ask if I can bring Robert to tea, and have great satisfaction in informing her that he has returned to Devonshire. Pamela then completely takes the wind out of my sails by saying that she will be motoring through Devonshire quite soon, and would simply love to look us up. A really very interesting man who Rows will be with her, and she thinks that we should like to know him. Social exigencies compel me to reply that of course we should, and I hope she will bring her rowing friend to lunch or tea whenever she is in the neighbourhood.

After this, permit myself to enquire why P. P. never turned up at Cygnet Galleries on recent painful occasion; to which she answers, in voice of extreme distress, that I simply can't imagine how complicated life is, and men give one no peace at all, and it's so difficult when one friend hates another friend and threatens to shoot him if Pamela goes out with him again.

Am obliged to admit that attitude of this kind does probably lead to very involved situations, and Pamela says that I am so sweet and understanding, always, and I must give that angel Robert her love—and rings off.

June 29th.—Am filled with frantic desire to make the most of few remaining days in London, and recklessly buy two pairs of silk stockings, for no other reason than that they catch my eye when on my way to purchase sponge-bag and tooth-paste for Vicky.

(*Query*: Does sponge-bag exist anywhere in civilised world which is positively water-proof and will not sooner or later exude large, damp patches from sponge that apparently went into it perfectly dry? Secondary, but still important, *Query*: Is it possible to reconcile hostile attitude invariably exhibited by all children towards process of teeth-cleaning with phenomenal rapidity with which they demolish tube after tube of tooth-paste?)

Proceed later to small and newly established Registry Office, which has been recommended to me by Felicity, and am interviewed by lady in white satin blouse, who tells me that maids for the country are almost impossible to find—which I know very well already—but that she will do what she can for me, and I mustn't mind if it's only an inexperienced girl. She finally dismisses me, with pessimistic hopes that I may hear from her in the next few days, and demand for a booking-fee, which I pay.

Return to Doughty Street, where I am rung up by quite important daily paper and asked If I would care to write an Article about Modern Freedom in Marriage. First impulse is to reply that they must have made a mistake, and think me more celebrated than I am—but curb this, and ask how long article would have to be—really meaning what is the shortest they will take—and how much they are prepared to pay? They—represented by brisk and rather unpleasant voice—suggest fifteen hundred words, and a surprisingly handsome fee. Very well then, I will do it—how soon do they want it? Voice replies that early next week will be quite all right, and we exchange good-byes. Am highly exhilarated, decide to give a dinner-party, pay several bills, get presents for the children, take them abroad in the summer holidays, send Robert a cheque towards pacifying the Bank, and buy myself a hat. Realise, however, that article is not yet written, far less paid for, and that the sooner I collect my ideas about Modern Freedom in Marriage, the better.

Just as I have got ready to do so, interruption comes in the person of Housekeeper from upstairs, who Thinks that I would like to see the laundry-book. I do see it, realise with slight shock that it has been going on briskly for some weeks unperceived by myself, and produce the necessary sum. Almost immediately afterwards a Man comes to the door, and tells me that I have no doubt often been distressed by the dirty and unhygienic condition of my telephone. Do not like to say that I have never thought about it, so permit him to come in, shake his head at the telephone, and say Look at that, now, and embark on long and alarming monologue about Germs. By the time he has finished, realise that I am lucky to be alive at all in midst of numerous and insidious perils, and agree to telephone's being officially disinfected at stated intervals. Form, as usual, has to be filled up, Man then delivers parting speech to the effect that he is very glad I've decided to do this—there's so many ladies don't realise, and if they knew what they was exposing themselves to, they'd be the first to shudder at it—which sounds like White Slave Traffic, but is, I think, still Germs. I say Well, good morning, and he replies rebukefully—and correctly—Good afternoon, which I feel bound to accept by repeating it after him and he goes downstairs.

I return to Modern Freedom in Marriage and get ready to deal with it by sharpening a pencil and breaking the lead three times. Extremely violent knock at flat door causes me to drop it altogether—(fourth and absolutely final break)—and admit very powerful-looking window-cleaner with pair of steps, mop, bucket and other appliances, all of which he hurls into the room with great *abandon*. I say Will he begin with the bedroom, and he replies that it's all one to him, and is temporarily lost to sight in next room, but can be heard singing: *I Don't Know Why I Love You Like I Do.* (Remaining lines of this idyll evidently unknown to him as he repeats this one over and over again, but must in justice add that he sings rather well.)

Settle down in earnest to Modern Freedom in Marriage. Draw a windmill on blotting-paper. Tell myself that a really striking opening sentence is important.

Nothing else matters. Really striking sentence is certainly hovering somewhere about, although at the moment elusive. (*Query*: Something about double standard of morality? Or is this unoriginal? Thread temporarily lost, owing to absorption in shading really admirable little sketch of Cottage Loaf drawn from Memory. . . .)

Frightful crash from bedroom, and abrupt cessation of not Knowing Why He Loves Me Like He Does, recalls window-cleaner with great suddenness to my mind, and I open door that separates us and perceive that he has put very stalwart arm clean through window pane and is bleeding vigorously, although, with great good feeling, entirely avoiding carpet or furniture.

Look at him in some dismay, and enquire—not intelligently—if he is hurt, and he answers No, the cords were wore clean through, it happens sometimes with them old-fashioned sashes. Rather singular duet follows, in which I urge him to come and wash his arm in the kitchen, and he completely ignores the suggestion and continues to repeat that the cords were wore clean through. After a good deal of this, I yield temporarily, look at the cords and agree that they do seem to be wore clean through, and finally hypnotise window-cleaner—still talking about cords—into following me to the sink, where he holds his arm under cold water and informs me that the liability of his company is strictly limited, so far as the householder is concerned, and in my case the trouble was due to them cords being practically wore right through.

I enquire if his arm hurts him—at which he looks blankly astonished—inspect the cut, produce iodine and apply it, and finally return to Modern Freedom in Marriage, distinctly shattered, whilst window-cleaner resumes work, but this time without song.

Literary inspiration more and more evasive every moment, and can think of nothing whatever about Modern Freedom except that it doesn't exist in the provinces. Ideas as to Marriage not lacking, but these would certainly not be printed by any newspaper on earth, and should myself be deeply averse from recording them in any way.

Telephone rings and I instantly decide that: (*a*) Robert has died suddenly. (*b*) Literary Agent has effected a sale of my film-rights, recent publication, for sum running into five figures, pounds not dollars. (*c*) Robin has met with serious accident at school. (*d*) Pamela Pringle wishes me once more to cover her tracks whilst engaged in pursuing illicit amour of one kind or another.

(*Note*: Swiftness of human (female) imagination surpasses that of comet's trail across the heavens quite easily. Could not this idea be embodied in short poem? Am convinced, at the moment, that some such form of expression would prove infinitely easier than projected article about Modern Freedom, etc.)

I say Yes? into the telephone—entire flight of fancy has taken place between two rings—and unknown contralto voice says that I shan't remember her—which is true—but that she is Helen de Liman de la Pelouse and we met at Pamela Pringle's at lunch one day last October.

Will I forgive last-minute invitation and come and dine to-night and meet one or two people, all interested in Books, and H. de la P.'s cousin, noted literary critic whom I may like to know? Disturbing implication here that literary critics allow their judgement be influenced by considerations other than æsthetic and academic ones—but cannot unravel at the moment, and merely accept with pleasure and say What time and Where? Address in large and expensive Square is offered me, time quarter to nine if that isn't too late? (*Query*: What would happen if I said Yes, it is too late? Would entire scheme be reorganised?)

Am recalled from this rather idle speculation by window-cleaner—whose very existence I have completely forgotten—taking his departure noisily, but with quite unresentful salutation, and warning—evidently kindly intended—that them cords are wore through and need seeing to. I make a note on the blotting-paper to this effect, and am again confronted with perfectly blank sheet of paper waiting to receive masterpiece of prose concerning Modern Freedom in Marriage. Decide that this is definitely not the moment to deal with it, and concentrate instead on urgent and personal questions concerned with to-night's festivity. Have practically no alternative as to frock—recently acquired silver brocade—and hair has fortunately been shampoo'd and set within the last three days so still looks its best. More serious consideration is that of taxi-fare, absolutely necessitated by situation of large and expensive Square, widely removed from bus or tube routes.

Have recourse, not for the first time, to perhaps rather infantile, but by no means unsuccessful, stratagem of unearthing small hoards of coin distributed by myself, in more affluent moments, amongst all the handbags I possess in the world.

Two sixpences, some halfpence, one florin and a half-crown are thus brought to light, and will see me handsomely through the evening, and breakfast at Lyons' next morning into the bargain.

Am unreasonably elated by this and go so far as to tell myself that very likely I shall collect some ideas for Modern Freedom article in general conversation to-night and needn't bother about it just now.

Go through customary far-sighted procedure of turning down bed, drawing curtains and filling kettle for hot-water bottle, before grappling with geyser, of which I am still mortally terrified, and getting ready for party. During these operations I several times encounter sheet of paper destined to record my views about Modern Freedom in Marriage, but do nothing whatever about it, except decide again how I shall spend the money.

Am firmly resolved against arriving too early, and do not telephone for taxi until half-past eight, then find number engaged, and operator—in case of difficulty dial O—entirely deaf to any appeal. Accordingly rush out into the street—arrangement of hair suffers rather severely—find that I have forgotten keys and have to go back again—make a second attack on telephone, this time with success, rearrange coiffure and observe with horror that three short minutes in the open air are enough to remove every trace of powder from me, repair this, and depart at last.

After all this, am, as usual, first person to arrive. Highly finished product of modern civilisation, in white satin with no back and very little front, greets me, and I perceive her to be extremely beautiful, and possessed of superb diamonds and pearls. Evidently Helen de Liman de la Pelouse. This conjecture confirmed when she tells me, in really very effective drawl, that we sat opposite to one another at Pamela Pringle's luncheon party, and may she introduce her husband? Husband is apparently Jewish—why de Liman de la Pelouse?—and looks at me in a rather lifeless and exhausted way and then gives me a glass of sherry, evidently in the hope of keeping me quiet. H. de L. de la P. talks about the weather—May very wet, June very hot, English climate very uncertain—and husband presently joins in and says all the same things in slightly different words. We then all three look at one another in despair, until I am suddenly inspired to remark that I have just paid a most interesting visit to the studio of a rather interesting young man whose work I find interesting, called Hipps. (Should be hard put to it to say whether construction of this sentence or implication that it conveys is the more entirely alien to my better principles.) Experiment proves immediately successful, host and hostess become animated, and H. de L. de la P. says that Hipps is quite the most mordant of the younger set of young present-day satirists, don't I think, and that last thing of his definitely had *patine*. I recklessly agree, but am saved from further perjury by arrival of more guests. All are unknown to me, and fill me with terror.

Find myself at dinner between elderly man with quantities of hair, and much younger man who looks nice and smiles at me. Make frantic endeavours, without success, to read names on little cards in front of them, and wish violently that I ever had sufficient presence of mind to listen to people's names when introduced—which I never do.

Try the elderly man with Hipps. He does not respond. Switch over to thinking he knows a friend of mine, Mrs. Pringle? No, he doesn't think so. Silence follows, and I feel it is his turn to say something, but as he doesn't, and as my other neighbour is talking hard to pretty woman in black, I launch into Trade Depression and Slump in America. Elderly neighbour still remains torpid except for rather caustic observation concerning Mr. Hoover. Do not feel competent to defend Mr. Hoover, otherwise should certainly do so, as by this time am filled with desire to contradict everything elderly neighbour may ever say. He gives me, however, very little opportunity for doing so, as he utters hardly at all and absorbs himself in perfectly admirable lobster *Thermidor*. Final effort on my part is to tell him the incident of the window-cleaner, which I embroider very considerably in rather unsuccessful endeavour to make it amusing, and this at last unseals his lips and he talks quite long and eloquently about Employers' Liability, which he views as an outrage. Consume lobster silently, in my turn, and disagree with him root and branch, but feel that it would be waste of time to say so and accordingly confine myself to invaluable phrase: I See What He Means.

We abandon mutual entertainment with great relief shortly afterwards, and my other neighbour talks to me about books, says that he has read mine and proves it by a quotation, and I decide that he must be distinguished critic spoken of by H. de L. de la P. Tell him the story of window-cleaner, introducing several quite new variations, and he is most encouraging, laughs heartily, and makes me feel that I am a witty and successful *raconteuse*—which in saner moments I know very well that I am not.

(*Query*: Has this anything to do with the champagne? *Answer*, almost certainly, Yes, everything.)

Amusing neighbour and myself continue to address one another exclusively, and am sorry when obliged to ascend to drawing-room for customary withdrawal.

H. de L. de la P. refers to Pamela—everybody in the room evidently an intimate friend of Pamela's, and general galvanisation ensues. *Isn't* she adorable? says very smart black-and-white woman, and Doesn't that new platinum hair suit her too divinely? asks somebody else, and we all cry Yes, quite hysterically, to both. H. de L. de la P. then points me out and proclaims—having evidently found a *raison d'être* for me at last—that I have known Pamela for years and years—longer than any of them. I instantly become focus of attention, and everyone questions me excitedly.

Conversation closes, as men are heard upon the stairs, with H. de L. de la P. assuring us all that Pamela is one of her very dearest friends, and she simply adores her—which is supported by assurances of similar devotion from everyone else. Remain for some time afterwards in rather stunned condition, thinking about Friendship.

July 1st.—Once more prepare to leave London, and am haunted by words of out-of-date song once popular: *How're you Going to Keep 'em Down on the Farm,*

Now that they've seen Paree? Answer comes there none.

Suit-case is reluctant to close, I struggle for some time, and get very hot, success at last, and am then confronted by neatly folded dressing-gown which I have omitted to put in.

Telephone rings and turns out to be Emma Hay, who is very, very excited about satire which she says she has just written and which will set the whole of London talking. If I care to come round at once, says Emma, she is reading it aloud to a few Really Important People, and inviting free discussion and criticism afterwards.

I express necessary regrets, and explain that I am returning to the country in a few hours' time.

July 4th.—Return home has much to recommend it, country looks lovely, everything more or less in bloom, except strawberries, which have unaccountably failed, Robert gives me interesting information regarding recent sale of heifer, and suspected case of sclerosis of the liver amongst neighbouring poultry, and Helen Wills claws at me demonstratively under the table as I sit down to dinner. Even slight *faux pas* on my own part, when I exclaim joyfully that the children will be home in a very short time now, fails to create really serious disturbance of harmonious domestic atmosphere.

Shall certainly not, in view of all this, permit spirits to be daunted by rather large pile of letters almost all concerned with Accounts Rendered, that I find on my writing-table. Could have dispensed, however, with the Milk-book, the Baker's Bill, and the Grocer's Total for the Month, all of them handed to me by Cook with rider to the effect that There was twelve-and-sixpence had to be given to the sweep, and twopence to pay on a letter last Monday week, and she hopes she did right in taking it in.

Robert enquires very amiably what I have been writing lately, and I say lightly, Oh, an article on Modern Freedom in Marriage, and then remember that I haven't done a word of it, and ask Robert to give me some ideas. He does so, and they are mostly to the effect that People talk a great deal of Rubbish nowadays, and that Divorce may be All Very Well in America, and the Trouble with most women is that they haven't got nearly Enough to Do. At this I thank Robert very much and say that will do splendidly —which is true in the spirit, though not the letter— but he appears to be completely wound up and unable to stop, and goes on for quite a long time, telling me to Look at Russia, and wishing to know How I should like to see the children whisked off to Siberia—which I think forceful but irrelevant.

Become surprisingly sleepy at ten o'clock—although this never happened to me in London—and go up to bed.

Extraordinary and wholly undesirable tendency displays itself to sit upon window-seat and think about Myself—but am well aware that this kind of thing never a real success, and that it will be part of wisdom to get up briskly instead and look for shoe-trees to insert in evening-shoes—which I accordingly do; and shortly afterwards find myself in bed and ready to go to sleep.

July 8th. — Just before lunch Our Vicar's Wife calls, and says that It's too bad to disturb me, and she only just popped in for one moment and has to nip off to the school at once, but she did so want to talk to me about the concert, and hear all about London. Rather tedious and unnecessary argument follows as to whether she will or will not stay to lunch, and ends — as I always knew it would — in my ringing bell and saying Please lay an extra place for lunch, at the same time trying to send silent telepathic message to Cook that meat-pie alone will now not be enough, and she must do something with eggs or cheese as first course.

(Cook's interpretation of this subsequently turns out to be sardines, faintly grilled, lying on toast, which I think a mistake, but shall probably not say so, as intentions good.)

Our Vicar's Wife and I then plunge into the concert, now only separated from us by twenty-four hours. What, says Our Vicar's Wife hopefully, am I giving them? Well — how would it be if I gave them "John Gilpin"? (Know it already and shall not have to learn anything new.) Splendid, perfectly splendid, Our Vicar's Wife asserts in rather unconvinced accents. The only thing is, Didn't I give it to them at Christmas, and two years ago at the Church Organ Fête, and unless she is mistaken, the winter before that again when we got up that entertainment for St. Dunstan's?

Conversation temporarily checked, and I feel discouraged, and am relieved when gong rings. This, however, produces sudden spate of protests from Our Vicar's Wife, who says she really must be off, she couldn't dream of staying to lunch, and what can she have been thinking of all this time?

Entrance of Robert—whose impassive expression on being unexpectedly confronted with a guest I admire—gives fresh turn to entire situation, and we all find ourselves in dining-room quite automatically.

Conversation circles round the concert, recent arrivals at neighbouring bungalow, on whom we all say that we must call, and distressing affair in the village which has unhappily ended by Mrs. A. of Jubilee Cottages being summoned for assault by her neighbour Mrs. H. Am whole-heartedly thrilled by this, and pump Our Vicar's Wife for details, which she gives spasmodically, but has to switch off into French, or remarks about the weather, whenever parlour-maid is in the room.

Cook omits to provide coffee—in spite of definite instructions always to do so when we have a guest—and have to do the best I can with cigarettes, although perfectly well aware that Our Vicar's Wife does not smoke, and never has smoked.

Concert appears on the *tapis* once more, and Robert is induced to promise that he will announce the items. Our Vicar's Wife, rather nicely, says that everyone would love it if dear little Vicky could dance for us, and I reply that she will still be away at school, and Our Vicar's Wife replies that she knows *that*, she only meant how nice it would be if she *hadn't* been away at school, and could have danced for us. Am ungrateful enough to reflect that this is as singularly pointless an observation as ever I heard.

What, asks Our Vicar's Wife, am I doing this afternoon? Why not come with her and call on the new people at the bungalow and get it over? In this cordial frame of mind we accordingly set out, and I drive Standard car, Our Vicar's Wife observing—rather unnecessarily—that it really is *wonderful* how that car goes on and on and on.

Conversation continues, covering much ground that has been traversed before, and only diversified by hopes from me that the bungalow inhabitants may all be out, and modification from Our Vicar's Wife to the effect that she is hoping to get them to take tickets for the concert.

Aspirations as to absence of new arrivals dashed on the instant of drawing up at their gate, as girl in cretonne overall, older woman—probably mother—with spectacles, and man in tweeds, are all gardening like mad at the top of the steps. They all raise themselves from stooping postures, and all wipe their hands on their clothes—freakish resemblance here to not very well co-ordinated revue chorus—and make polite pretence of being delighted to see us. Talk passionately about rock-gardens for some time, then are invited to come indoors, which we do, but cretonne overall and man in tweeds—turns out to be visiting uncle—sensibly remain behind and pursue their gardening activities.

We talk about the concert—two one-and-sixpenny tickets disposed of successfully—hostess reveals that she thinks sparrows have been building in one of the water-pipes, and I say Yes, they do do that, and Our Vicar's Wife backs me up, and shortly afterwards we take our leave.

On passing through village, Our Vicar's Wife says

that we may just as well look in on Miss Pankerton, as she wants to speak to her about the concert. I protest, but to no avail, and we walk up Miss P.'s garden-path and hear her practising the violin indoors, and presently she puts her head out of ground-floor window and shrieks—still practising—that we are to walk straight in, which we do, upon which she throws violin rather recklessly on to the sofa—which is already piled with books, music, newspapers, appliances for raffia-work, garden-hat, hammer, chisel, sample tin of biscuits, and several baskets—and shakes us by both hands. She also tells me that she sees I have taken her advice, and released a good many of my inhibitions in that book of mine. Should like to deny violently having ever taken any advice of Miss P.'s at all, or even noticed that she'd given it, but she goes on to say that I ought to pay more attention to Style—and I diverge into wondering inwardly whether she means prose, or clothes.

(If the latter, this is incredible audacity, as Miss P.'s own costume—on broiling summer's day—consists of brick-red cloth dress, peppered with glass knobs, and surmounted by abominable little brick-red three-tiered cape, closely fastened under her chin.)

Our Vicar's Wife again launches out into the concert—has Miss P. an *encore* ready? Yes, she has. Two, if necessary.

She supposes genially that I am giving a reading of some little thing of my own—I reply curtly that I am not, and shouldn't dream of such a thing—and Our Vicar's Wife, definitely tactful, interrupts by saying that She Hears Miss P. is off to London directly the concert is over. If this is really so, and it isn't giving her any trouble, could she and would she just look in at Harrods, where they are having a sale, and find out what about tinned apricots? Any reduction on a quantity, and how about carriage? And while she's in that neighbourhood—but not if it puts her out in any way—could she just look in at that little shop in the Fulham Road—the name has escaped Our Vicar's Wife for the moment—but it's really quite unmistakable—where they sell bicycle-parts? Our Vicar has lost a nut, quite a small nut, but rather vital, and it simply can't be replaced. Fulham Road the last hope.

Miss P.—I think courageously—undertakes it all, and writes down her London address, and Our Vicar's Wife writes down everything she can remember about Our Vicar's quite small nut, and adds on the same piece of paper the word "haddock".

But this, she adds, is only if Miss P. really *has* got time, and doesn't mind bringing it down with her, as otherwise it won't be fresh, only it does make a change and is so very difficult to get down here unless one is a regular customer.

At this point I intervene, and firmly suggest driving Our Vicar's Wife home, as feel certain that, if I don't, she will ask Miss P. to bring her a live crocodile from the Zoo, or something equally difficult of achievement.

We separate, with light-hearted anticipations of meeting again at the concert.

July 10th.—Concert permeates the entire day, and I spend at least an hour looking through *A Thousand and One Gems* and *The Drawing-room Reciter* in order to discover something that I once knew and can recapture without too much difficulty. Finally decide on narrative poem about Dick Turpin, unearthed in *Drawing-room Reciter*, and popular in far-away schooldays. Walk about the house with book in my hand most of the morning, and ask Robert to Hear Me after lunch, which he does, and only has to prompt three times. He handsomely offers to Hear Me again after tea, and to prompt if necessary during performance, and I feel that difficulty has been overcome.

Everything subject to interruption: small children arrive to ask if I can possibly lend them Anything Chinese, and am able to produce two fans—obviously made in Birmingham—one cotton kimono—eight-and-eleven at Messrs. Frippy and Coleman's—and large nautilus shell, always said to have been picked up by remote naval ancestor on the shore at Hawaii.

They express themselves perfectly satisfied, I offer them toffee, which they accept, and they depart with newspaper parcel. Later on message comes from the Rectory to say that my contribution to Refreshments has not arrived, am covered with shame, and sacrifice new ginger-cake just made for to-day's tea.

Concert, in common with every other social activity in the village, starts at 7.30, and as Robert has promised to Take the Door and I am required to help with arranging the platform, we forgo dinner altogether, and eat fried fish at tea, and Robert drinks a whisky-and-soda.

Rumour has spread that Our Member and his wife are to appear at concert, but on my hoping this is true, since both are agreeable people, Robert shakes his head and says there's nothing in it. Everyone else, he admits, will be there, but *not* Our Member and his wife. Robert is put at the very end of front row of chairs, in order that he may get off and on platform frequently, and I am next him and have Our Vicar's Wife on my other side.

I ask for Our Vicar, and am told that his hay-fever has come on worse than ever, and he has been persuaded to stay at home. Regretful reference is made to this by Robert from the platform, and concert begins, as customary, with piano duet between Miss F. from the shop and Miss W. of the smithy.

Have stipulated that Dick Turpin is to come on very early, so as to get it over, and am asked by Our Vicar's Wife if I am nervous. I say Yes, I am, and she is sympathetic, and tells me that the audience will be indulgent. They are, and Dick Turpin is safely accomplished with only one prompt from Robert—unfortunately delivered rather loudly just as I am purposely making what I hope is pregnant and dramatic pause—and I sit down again and prepare to enjoy myself.

Miss Pankerton follows me, is accompanied by pale young man who loses his place twice, and finally drops his music on the ground, picks it up again and readjusts it, while Miss P. glares at him and goes on vigorously with *Une Fête à Trianon* and leaves him to find his own way home as best he can. This he never quite succeeds in doing until final chord is reached, when he joins in again with an air of great triumph, and we all applaud heartily.

Miss P. bows, and at once launches into *encore*—which means that everybody else will have to be asked for an *encore* too, otherwise there will be Feelings—

and eventually sits down again and we go on to Sketch by the school-children, in which paper fans and cotton kimonos are in evidence.

The children look nice, and are delighted with themselves, and everybody else is delighted too, and Sketch brings down the house, at which Miss Pankerton looks superior and begins to tell me about Classical Mime by children that she once organised in large hall—seats two thousand people—near Birmingham, but I remain unresponsive, and only observe in reply that Jimmie H. of the mill is a duck, isn't he?

At this Miss P.'s eyebrows disappear into her hair, and she tells me about children she has seen in Italy who are pure Murillo types—but Our Butcher's Son here mounts the platform, in comic checks, bowler and walking-stick, and all is lost in storms of applause.

Presently Robert announces an Interval, and we all turn round in our seats and scan the room and talk to the people behind us, and someone brings forward a rumour that they've taken Close on Three Pounds at the Door, and we all agree that, considering the hot weather, it's wonderful.

Shortly afterwards Robert again ascends platform and concert is resumed. Imported talent graces last half of the programme, in the shape of tall young gentleman who is said to be a friend of the Post Office, and who sings a doubtful comic song which is greeted with shrieks of appreciation. Our Vicar's Wife and I look at one another, and she shakes her head with a resigned expression, and whispers that it can't be helped, and she hopes the *encore* won't be any worse. It *is* worse, but not very much, and achieves enormous popular success.

By eleven o'clock all is over, someone has started *God Save the King* much too high, and we have all loyally endeavoured to make ourselves heard on notes that we just can't reach—Miss Pankerton has boldly attempted something that is evidently meant to be seconds, but results not happy—and we walk out into the night.

Robert drives me home. I say Weren't the children sweet? and really, it was rather fun, wasn't it? and Robert changes gear, but makes no specific reply. Turn into our own lane, and I experience customary wonder whether house has been burnt to the ground in our absence, followed by customary reflection that anyway the children are away at school—and then get severe shock as I see the house blazing with light from top to bottom.

Robert ejaculates, and puts his foot on the accelerator, and we dash in at gate, and nearly run into enormous blue car drawn up at front door.

I rush into the hall, and at the same moment Pamela Pringle rushes out of the drawing-room, wearing evening dress and grey fur coat with enormous collar, and throws herself on my neck. Am enabled, by mysterious process quite inexplicable to myself, to see through the back of my head that Robert has recoiled on threshold and retired with car to the garage.

Pamela P. explains that she is staying the night at well-known hotel, about forty miles away, and that when she found how near I was, she simply had to look me up, and she had simply no idea that I ever went out at night. I say that I never do, and urge her into the drawing-room, and there undergo second severe shock as I perceive it to be apparently perfectly filled with strange men. Pamela does not introduce any of them, beyond saying that it was Johnnie's car they came in, and Plum drove it. Waddell is not included in the party, nor anybody else that I ever saw in my life, and all seem to be well under thirty, except very tall man with bald head who is referred to as Alphonse Daudet, and elderly-looking one with moustache, who I think looks Retired, probably India.

I say weakly that they must have something to drink, and look at the bell—perfectly well aware that maids have gone to bed long ago—but Robert, to my great relief, materialises and performs minor miracle by producing entirely adequate quantities of whisky-and-soda, and sherry and biscuits for Pamela and myself. After this we all seem to know one another very well indeed, and Plum goes to the piano and plays waltz tunes popular in Edwardian days. (Pamela asks at intervals What that one was called? although to my certain knowledge she must remember them just as well as I do myself.)

Just as it seems probable that *séance* is to continue for the rest of the night, Alphonse Daudet rises without any warning at all, says to Robert that, for his part, he's not much good at late nights, and walks out of the room. We all drift after him, Pamela announces that she is going to drive, and everybody simultaneously exclaims No, No, and Robert says that there is a leak in the radiator, and fetches water from the bathroom.

(Should have preferred him to bring it in comparatively new green enamel jug, instead of incredibly ancient and battered brass can.)

Pamela throws herself into my arms, and murmurs something of which I hear nothing at all except Remember!—like Bishop Juxon—and then gets into the car, and is obliterated by Plum on one side and elderly Indian on the other.

Just as they start, Helen Wills dashes out of adjacent bushes, and is nearly run over, but this tragedy averted, and car departs.

Echoes reach us for quite twenty minutes, of lively conversation, outbreaks of song and peals of laughter, as car flies down the lane and out of sight. Robert says that they've turned the wrong way, but does not seem to be in the least distressed about it, and predicts coldly that they will all end up in local police station.

I go upstairs, all desire for sleep having completely left me, and find several drawers in dressing-table wide open, powder all over the place like snow on Mount Blanc, unknown little pad of rouge on pillow, and face-towel handsomely streaked with lipstick.

Bathroom is likewise in great disorder, and when Robert eventually appears he brings with him small, silver-mounted comb which he alleges that he found, quite incomprehensibly, on lowest step of remote flight of stairs leading to attic. I say satirically that I hope they all felt quite at home, Robert snorts in reply, and conversation closes.

July 13th.—Life resumes its ordinary course, and next excitement will doubtless be return of Robin and Vicky from school. Am already deeply immersed in preparations for this, and Cook says that extra help will be required. I reply that I think we shall be away at the sea for at least a month—(which is not perfectly true, as much depends on financial state)—and she listens to me in silence, and repeats that help will be wanted anyway, as children make such a difference. As usual, Cook gets the last word, and I prepare to enter upon familiar and exhausting campaign in search of Extra Help.

This takes up terrific amount of time and energy, and find it wisest to resign all pretensions to literature at the moment, and adopt role of pure domesticity.

the lady vanishes

Ethel Lina White

savages

Shirley Conran

gone with the wind

Margaret Mitchell

the provincial lady

E. M. Delafield

jaws

Peter Benchley

the pan book
of horror stories

Selected by Herbert van Thal

not a penny more,
not a penny less

Jeffrey Archer

ten stories

Rudyard Kipling

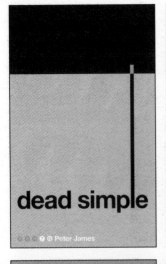

dead simple

last bus to woodstock

eye of
the
needle

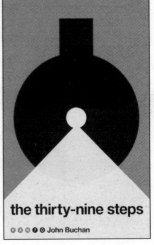

the thirty-nine steps

the
hitchhiker's
guide to the
galaxy

Douglas Adams

the lost world

Sir Arthur Conan Doyle

childhood's end

Arthur C. Clarke

the
time
machine

H.G. Wells

the dam busters

⊙⊙⊙⊙⊙ Paul Brickhill

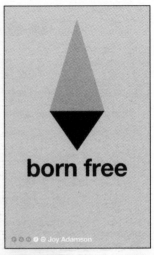

born free

⊙⊙⊙⊙⊙ Joy Adamson

england,
their
england

℗⊙⊙⊙⊙ A.G. Macdonell

it
shouldn't
happen
to a vet

⊙⊙⊙⊙⊙ James Herriot

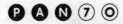

The Hitchhiker's Guide to the Galaxy – Douglas Adams

Born Free – Joy Adamson

Not a Penny More, Not a Penny Less – Jeffrey Archer

Jaws – Peter Benchley

The Dam Busters – Paul Brickhill

The Thirty-Nine Steps – John Buchan

Childhood's End – Arthur C. Clarke

Savages – Shirley Conran

The Provincial Lady – E. M. Delafield

Last Bus to Woodstock – Colin Dexter

The Lost World – Sir Arthur Conan Doyle

Eye of the Needle – Ken Follett

It Shouldn't Happen to a Vet – James Herriot

Dead Simple – Peter James

Ten Stories – Rudyard Kipling

England, Their England – A. G. Macdonell

Gone with the Wind – Margaret Mitchell

The Time Machine – H. G. Wells

The Lady Vanishes – Ethel Lina White

The Pan Book of Horror Stories